S0-BIM-690

The Organ Grinder

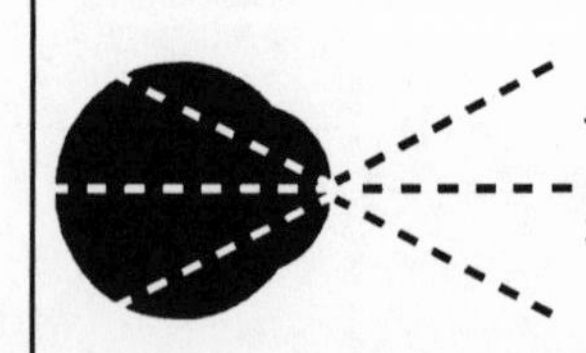

This Large Print Book carries the Seal of Approval of N.A.V.H.

A DUTCHMAN HISTORICAL MYSTERY

THE ORGAN GRINDER

MAAN MEYERS

THORNDIKE PRESS
A part of Gale, Cengage Learning

Detroit • New York • San Francisco • New Haven, Conn • Waterville, Maine • London

This novel is a work of fiction. Names, characters, places, and incidents are either the product of the author's imagination, or, if real, used fictitiously.

Thorndike Press® Large Print Historical Fiction.
The text of this Large Print edition is unabridged.
Other aspects of the book may vary from the original edition.
Set in 16 pt. Plantin.
Printed on permanent paper.

LIBRARY OF CONGRESS CATALOGING-IN-PUBLICATION DATA

Meyers, Maan.
The organ grinder : a Dutchman historical mystery / by Maan Meyers.
p. cm. — (Thorndike Press large print historical fiction)
ISBN-13: 978-1-4104-1270-6 (alk. paper)
ISBN-10: 1-4104-1270-9 (alk. paper)
1. Police—New York (State)—New York—Fiction. 2. New York (N.Y.)—History—1898–1951—Fiction. 3. Large type books. I. Title.
PS3563.E889O74 2009
813'.54—dc22 2008043722

Published in 2009 by arrangement with Tekno Books and Ed Gorman.

Printed in the United States of America
1 2 3 4 5 6 7 13 12 11 10 09

For Bonnie Claeson and
Joe Guglielmelli,
who with their Black Orchid Bookshop,
always gave us total support and
encouragement.

PROLOGUE

Wednesday, June 7, 1899. Evening.

That they were gentlemen of means, all of them, was immediately revealed in their elegant evening clothes, their crisp white shirts and black ties, their cigars, the snifters of brandy in their hands.

Their faces would not be recognized by the ordinary New York working man who was intent on keeping a roof over his family's head and food in his children's mouths. Yet these gentlemen represented a core element in the past, present, and in particular, the future of the City.

At the sixteen-storied German Renaissance–styled Waldorf-Astoria, the largest, most resplendent hotel in New York, where they met this evening in one of the thirteen hundred private rooms, they did not stand out. Men in evening dress frequented the forty public rooms, the dining rooms, the private rooms, that were part of the hotel's attraction. The women they sometimes brought with them were not their wives.

No women attended this meeting.

Large black ceiling fans and small standing ones in corners of the room did little but nudge the oppressive air. In spite of the extraordinary heat, which had broken existing records for this date, these men were here for this meeting, rather than strolling with wives or sweethearts or taking a cooling carriage ride through Central Park.

They were gathered around a great table, some sitting, some standing. Oswald Cook, the portrait photographer, sat among his peers quite comfortably. To his right sat financier Harrison Stokes, the husband of Cook's second cousin Louisa. To his left, James Hays, a cotton broker.

Among those present were Louisa's younger brothers, John Neldine Burgoyne III, known as J.N., and Lawrence, known as Baby, recent graduates of Yale College.

Whitney Lyon, a robust figure of a man, rose and called the meeting to order. "We need to organize, for we feel that as a class, we are downtrodden and need protection badly."

Oz hid his amusement behind his tilted glass. Downtrodden indeed.

"We need protection from the Park Department," Lyon continued.

F. S. Stevens, who'd been president of the last Open Air Horse Show, offered, "We also need protection from that being known as the bike cop, who tries to stop our automobiles by grabbing us by the collar and telling us to travel so many miles an hour."

"Outrageous." This last was bellowed by General George Moore Smith.

"Gentlemen," Lyon said, "we need a stable or a station for our machines. I have been to many stables in the City to find shelter for my machine, but keepers would not take it at any price. They consider it an enemy of the horse."

"The future of our City lies in transportation and expansion," Baby said, beaming at Stokes.

Voices were raised all around. "Hear, hear."

Stokes glared at his brother-in-law. Baby couldn't understand what he'd done wrong.

Lyon continued, "I propose we form a club, a common center where owners of self-propelled pleasure vehicles may exchange views and create a depot for the proper storage and care of vehicles."

"Hear, hear."

Quickly, a committee was formed to draft resolutions and by-laws to be presented at the next meeting. Whitney Lyon was chosen chairman pro tem, James Hays, secretary, and Harrison Stokes, treasurer.

"What shall we call ourselves?" Stokes asked. "We must have a respectable name."

"The Automobile Club of New York," Hays offered.

"We must think of the future," J. N. Burgoyne said. "Rather, the Automobile Club of America."

They didn't all leave at once. The grand hotel was a comfortable place for gentlemen to enjoy one another's company. Thus several, including Oz Cook and his young Burgoyne cousins, J.N. and Lawrence, James Hays, and Harrison Stokes and William Grimes, Stokes's business partner, who had joined the group late, lingered over their brandies, their cigars, talking politics, the formation of the Rapid Transit Commission and the fierce land speculation along the theorized route the subway system would take. It was coming on toward midnight when our gentlemen stirred into movement.

"Delmonico's?" J.N. suggested, as they made their way through the crowds in the opulent lobby. Tall and well built, J.N. had dark brown hair, but, like Oz, the piercing blue eyes of the Neldines.

The young man, who had entered the family banking business after the war, had a taste for attractive women and they for him. And an evening about town was filled with beautiful women in beautiful gowns of the latest French fashion, none of whom his mother would have approved.

Both J.N. and his brother had played football at Yale and fought in Cuba with the First U.S. Volunteer Cavalry, better known as Teddy Roosevelt's Rough Riders. They'd been the only volunteer cavalry to see action in the little war. A little war that had corrected J.N.'s previous too-pretty looks by adding a scar to his left temple. The ladies thought it dramatic.

His younger brother Baby kept up with J.N. in spite of his bad leg. Baby more than belied the appellation, he made a mockery of it. Though six feet two inches in height and well over two hundred pounds, the younger Burgoyne was of a serious and somewhat naive bent. His hair was the same black as his brother's. He kept it close shorn because it reminded him of the glory days of the war.

Baby's climb up San Juan Hill had left him with a sometimes-gamey left leg, which he hoped would do him good in a courtroom some day. He was studying the law at

Columbia as well as working for his brother-in-law at Stokes and Grimes.

The group headed for the main entrance, which took them through Peacock Alley, so called because ladies wearing the latest fashions from Paris passed through this corridor, and the locals lined up on either side to watch the dress parade.

"Does anyone need transportation?" Oz looked past the waiting carriages for his automobile. Although the Waldorf-Astoria was situated on Fifth Avenue, from Thirty-third Street to Thirty-fourth Street, the main entrance was on Thirty-fourth Street.

The air was thick with moisture, sponging up and retaining the smells of horse manure.

"All this putrefaction," James Hays said, waving his hand at the line of horses and carriages, "will be eliminated when the automobile achieves its proper recognition."

The few automobiles belonging to visitors to the Waldorf-Astoria were consigned to a side street, and so moving slowly in the heat, our group ventured a short way from the hotel.

With the afterglow of the electric lights of the gracious hotel just behind them, an ominous pairing of sounds — the crack of a whip, followed by a woman's cry of pain — stopped them short. The crack again.

"Thieving whore!"

"No, please, God help me."

A small dark figure with a long pigtail leaped from one of the automobiles. In seconds, the huge man in the black silk hat, who had been standing over a woman cowering on the ground, was on his back, his whip in the pigtailed man's hand.

"Wong." Oz's voice was low and even. The Chinaman nodded with a short jerk of his head, but did not release his hold. Moving quickly, the gentlemen surrounded the three.

From his place on the ground the man snarled. "She's a lying, thieving whore. She has my wallet."

"I don't," the woman cried, sobs breaking her voice. "He must have left it in the cab. You may search me if you like."

Baby laughed.

"Release him, Wong."

Wong obeyed.

"Whoremasters." The huge man spat, then pushed them aside. Reclaiming his whip, he tucked it under his arm and hastened away.

Wong returned to the black automobile and used its battery head lamps to light the street. The men bent over the woman on the street. Hands were offered.

"Thank you kindly, gentlemen." She

reached up to take one, giving her saviors a half-smile, then blanched, snatching her hand back with a frightened gasp. Cowering, she scuttled away like a crab.

J.N. pursued. "Please. Let me help you."

The girl gathered her skirts, scrambled to her feet, and ran off into the darkness, leaving J.N. shaking his head. The woman's haste was such that she did not notice the fat billfold lying on the ground.

"Astonishing," Grimes said.

"Indeed," Harrison Stokes agreed.

"But what a beauty," J.N. observed.

Oz nodded. The girl was no stranger to him. He'd seen her before, at Sophie's. And something seemed to have frightened her a good deal more than the whipping.

Part I

Chapter 1

Wednesday, June 21. Midmorning.

The barrel organ had two wheels and handled like a pushcart. Every part of it gleamed in the bright sunshine. Even the country scene painted on its side seemed to glow with its own light.

The man known as Antonio Cerasani rolled the mobile contraption over the broken cobble to the corner where Broome met Jefferson Street. Two other organ grinders played farther down Broome, but Cerasani calculated there was still money to be made.

He settled the cart as close to the curb as possible and in the least of the refuse that layered the streets in this section of the City. With the cart in place, he began to crank the organ. Music poured from the barrel with a sweet abundance, almost blocking out the sounds about him of babes howling, the crushing, scraping, thick shoes on the walk, metal-clad hooves and wheels clamoring on the cobblestones, passersby in screaming conversations. The noise of everyday life. But here the very intensity of it was an abomination.

Indifferent to the heat of the day, Tony wore heavy trousers, a vest, and a long brown coat. His shabby, dark brown hat sat atop his black hair. An enormous mustache hid his mouth. Only the wisp of smoke from the stub of the twisted black Italian cigar gave any indication of where it was. Contradicting his station of life was a gold ring with a cluster of diamond chips on his left index finger.

The bitter tang of the cigar almost wiped away the stench of horse shit. Almost. The Grinder hated the smell, from when he was a boy in Palermo and had to sleep in the stable of his father's padrone. New York was a giant stable full of horse dung, particularly in this neighborhood, where the White Wings, the street-sweeping brigade, seldom ventured.

It would be a miracle indeed if they came to clean the cobble road, let alone the asphalt pavement. Here, the roads were ankle high in dung and garbage, and the air, only barely perfumed by the salty smell of seaweed from the East River, was putrid with the rot of humanity.

"La donna è mobile" rolled from Tony's machine. To help make himself heard above the other grinders, he sang in a sweet tenor voice. "Women are fickle, like a feather in the wind."

"Women may be fickle but men are fools."

Recognizing the voice, he turned and nodded to the Neopolitan female he knew as Pancetta. She had a pig face and snout, and was always in black like the rest of the crones who populated Little Italy and the Lower East Side.

He did not stop grinding his tune as he said, "The men you're talking about are fools because they think with what's between their legs."

She touched his coat and recoiled in mock horror. "How can you wear that horse blanket in this heat? With your money, you should have better clothes."

"And are you some woman of fashion from the Ladies Mile that I should take your advice? You dress like the grave."

The woman waved her heavy arm, including him and the street in her gesture. "Why do you do this? Nonna pays you enough so you can sit in a saloon and drink grappa and smoke your stinker in comfort."

"And spend my money so I have nothing

left for my old age. Who will take care of me then, huh? You?"

She smiled, showing two gold incisors, with two very pointy canines flanking them. "Would you like that? I could feed you, make you very fat."

"Basta."

"Is it done?"

"Done as a doornail. You have something for me?"

The woman reached into her overflowing oilcloth bag. "You have something for me?"

"No. She wore no jewelry."

"What?" Expelling raspy air, the fat one began to choke.

Tony eyed Pancetta dispassionately. "She didn't have it."

The woman now had control of her breathing. Her sallow complexion had changed to blood red. "Then I have nothing for you."

"Whore." The organ grinder pulled his hand back as if to strike.

Slanting her bag, the woman thrust it toward the man so he could see her hand holding the very large revolver. "Call me that again and I'll kill you. By the Madonna, I swear."

"It wasn't on the girl. But I did the job, I deserve to get paid."

"You did half the job. And you already got half the pay. You get the rest when you bring us what we want." She shifted her hand from the gun and brought out a length of sausage wrapped in paper. "You want pepperoni?"

"No." He could barely hide his disgust.

"Good. More for me." The woman unwrapped the pepperoni and gnawed at the sausage with her rat teeth.

CHAPTER 2

Wednesday, June 21. Midmorning.

Burning rage filled Tony's throat, but with a force of will he contained the anger until it cooled. Finally he turned away, spitting in the gutter. When he looked again, the pig woman was halfway down the block.

Once more the strains of "La donna è mobile" rolled from Tony's machine; he sang in his rich, full voice, "Women are fickle, like a feather in the wind."

The children on the street laughed as they danced haphazardly to the organ grinder's music. He was in no mood for them. What did it matter if pennies wrapped in paper dropped from those windows and fell at his feet? His luck was bad today. The way things were going it would be shit wrapped in the paper.

He searched the tenement windows, where once-white sheets, now grim dinge, stirred languidly in the tepid breeze. Several pennies landed at his feet.

The organ grinder tipped his brown hat to his benefactors, collected the coins, and dropped them in his coat pockets, continuing to grind out his music.

One lone coin lay just beyond Tony's stretch, but he did not want to interrupt the flow of music for the moment it would take to claim it, lest he lose further pennies. Tony cranked and Verdi gushed, but no more coins rained down on him.

The clamor broke through all other sound. Shouting, blaspheming. Pounding feet. Racing toward the organ grinder were four boys, their arms slender as the sticks they carried, their clothes ragged and dirty.

Tony knew these boys; they lived on the street. They would steal the nails from the Savior's cross. Immediately he stopped playing. The noise of the streets held sway again. He bent to retrieve the last coin, his coin. Suddenly, with a cruel twitch of his ass, the largest of the boys bumped Tony, knocking the grinder into his hand organ, setting it trembling, akilter. Grabbing at the cart for balance, Tony misjudged and sank to his knees in the gutter filth.

Screeching with laughter, Butch Kelly leaned over, scooping up Tony's errant penny. The runt of the lot, Patsy Hearn, stuck his tongue through his scabby lips and gave the grinder a razzberry tart.

Tony's hands began separate lives. His right felt for the coin, no longer there, his left worked at steadying the cart. He clambered to his feet and brushed what offal he could from his trousers.

Again rage surged, all but suffocating him. First Pancetta, now this. He shook his fist at the departing youths and damned them, their forms and faces indelible in his mind.

The fist relaxed, and his hand went back to his pocket, where it rested on the slender knife in the cloth sheath that was strapped to his thigh under his trousers. He loved his stiletto so much he had named her. Marie. But Marie was no virgin; she had tasted blood many times.

The organ grinder knew that just as he could not deal with Pancetta today, he could not pursue these filthy little devils. If he did, one would surely circle back and steal his organ. He was not so green a horn to let that happen to him. No. He clamped his jaw tighter on the twisted cigar.

Pancetta had insulted him. The boys had insulted him. All showed disrespect. Antonio Cerasani from Ciminna, a village on a hill in north-central Sicily, never forgot an insult. He knew where Pancetta lived. As for these four, he would meet them again.

Anyone watching the rude boys would have seen them running along Jefferson Street down to South Street. Here the East River and the docks stopped their straightaway rush. Nine or ten blocks farther south was the bridge to Brooklyn. It was their playground, all of it.

The four, all dressed alike, in raggy knickerbockers and vests and broken shoes wrapped with cloth and cord, ducked past horsecarts and drays, shouting to each other, snatching food from pushcarts, brandishing their broomsticks, sometimes jabbing at each other, sometimes threatening to jab passersby. Frequently they used their sticks to knock a hat or two from a head. They ran along the narrow, cobbled streets almost down to the East River.

South Street and the streets leading to it and the harbor were overlaid with a kind of sludge different from elsewhere in the City. This filth bore elements of tar and seawater, for the East River like its sister the Hudson over to the west, is not truly a river but rather a tidal estuary.

The East River is a saltwater strait that links Long Island Sound to New York Harbor. The river is fed by both the sound and the harbor. Tidal movements route ocean water from the harbor north into the river twice daily, while more saltwater from the sound flows from above.

At South Street, the pavement was broken, creating a channel that cut through the sidewalk and ran into an empty, filth-ridden lot on Jefferson.

Ships dotted the harbor. The boys could hear the water lapping at the docks, the noise and bustle of the sawmills at the lumber yards. Sawdust smelled sweet amidst the fetid, the salt and the tar. Stevedores unloading a ship shouted at each other and cursed the heat.

Butch threw a rock at a seagull, resting on a piling, and missed. The gull gave a raucous caw, flapped its wings, and flew away. "Shit. Seagulls make good eating."

"They're tough as an old woman's ass," Colin said, gnawing on the remnant of a potato he'd filched on the way.

"Yeah," Butch shot back, "your mother's."

It was Colin who finally broke the stare between them, saying, "Let's see if we can get some work on the docks."

Butch Kelly swung his stick. "Too hot to work." He pointed the stick into the lot. "Run out, Patsy."

Patsy made an ugly face.

"Run out."

Patsy Hearn shielded his eyes from the sun as he ran toward the heap of refuse near the back of the lot. Beyond it was some skimpy brush and, amid more garbage, a dying black walnut tree, its trunk slashed by lightning.

"Fecking Butch Kelly with his fecking games," Patsy muttered. Forever making Patsy the goat. When they played pitch and toss, Butch always cheated, stealing his fecking penny. Just like now with the dago's coin. Butch would pocket the money and never share. And when they played tag or hide-and-go-seek, Patsy was always It. Now this catstick game. Here Patsy was in the hot sun sweating buckets, while Butch was swinging his stick, mostly hitting the air, sometimes hitting the pussy, and Tom Reilly and Colin Slattery was up close and catching it. And dumb shit-ass Patsy was out here in the stinking wilderness being cooked by the sun.

Butch hit the pussy and it flew high, way over Tom's and Colin's heads.

"Open your eyes, Patsy." Butch's laugh was nasty.

Patsy ran like a greyhound. If he caught the fecking thing, maybe they could stop and get something to wet their throats. Nail some bloke toting the growler. Beer would taste good just about now. That's what he was thinking on when his wiry body slipped in the slimy runoff from the rotting waste. He took a header smack into the disintegrating trunk of the tree. Still, he reached up, and damned if the fecking pussy didn't drop right into his hand, like it was meant to.

"Hey, boyos," Patsy yelled, out of breath, brushing splinters from his hair. "I got it."

He leaned against the scarred trunk sucking in short gasps of air full of soot and ashes. His eyes wandered to the pile of refuse the other side of the tree, then focused on something among the rubbish that caught the sunlight. Something shiny.

A silver dollar maybe!

Or maybe just a tin can.

He moved closer, then stepped back.

"Holy Mary." The boy crossed himself, but he was not afraid. He was barely ten, and not even a year off the boat from Cork. Still, it was not the first dead body he'd ever seen.

CHAPTER 3

Wednesday, June 21. Midmorning.

But it was the first *naked* dead woman he had ever seen. Curled up on her side she was, the ground a rusty black crust. Her clothes lay in rags all around her.

"Jeeeze," Colin said, peering over Patsy's shoulder as Patsy kicked the refuse away.

They milled around uneasily, unable to pull their eyes from the sight, until the toe of Tom's shoe accidentally touched her. With the touch, she slid over on her back, totally exposed. Her eyes stared blankly at them.

The motion surprised the boys, and they jumped back.

After a moment, Patsy said, "Don't she stink something awful?"

The four edged toward the body again.

"She's worm meat," Butch said. He gave Patsy a powerful push aside and reached down and grabbed the shiny object that had caught Patsy's attention in the first place.

"Hey, give me that," Patsy shouted. "I found it." He tackled Butch. Tom and Colin jumped in, and they were all trading punches, yelling and raising a huge volume of dust and dirt.

Colin head-butted Butch, knocking the wind out of him, making him drop the treasure. Both boys dove for it, as did Patsy and Tom.

A whistle shrieked. "All right, all right, what's going on here?" A tall, rawboned copper in blue came toward them swinging his stick.

The boys broke and ran.

Patrolman Mulroony grinned as the dust cleared. He made no move to go after the hooligans. Hooking the strap of his stick on his badge, he lifted his hat and dried the sweat from his head with the heavy sleeve of his uniform. Too hot. Besides, they was just boys who, with school out and no work, had too much vinegar. Boys like that fought over nothing.

He sniffed the hot, stagnant air. With August weather in June, the City was a stinking, rotting hell.

Mulroony gave the lot a cursory look. Garbage everywhere. Them sheenies think nothing of just throwing their refuse right out the window. He shaded his eyes from the sun. What was that odd little flutter of white in all that refuse? He poked his stick into the pile, raising a most godawful stink.

"Mother of God," he muttered.

The girl, naked except for a blue hat with a sunflower, lay on her back, arms at her side, her long black hair tangled in the garbage. Her eyes were open, glassy. The hat, which made the forsaken soul look comical, was askew, magnifying the comedy.

Mulroony reckoned the rags on the bloody ground about and under her were what was left of a blue dress and a white shift. The white was what had caught his eye. Poor lass, exposed for all the world to see.

She'd been murdered horribly. Stabbed in the belly and then ripped up to the breast bone. The blood was dried black and the maggots was having their feast. Mulroony reached down, plucked the largest patch of blue cloth and covered the girl's parts. Before he put his whistle to his lips, he straightened her hat, too, so she wouldn't go to Jesus looking like a clown.

Chapter 4

Thursday, June 22. Late morning.

Eyes closed, sighing, Sophie Mandel lay submerged in her lukewarm milk bath, a green silk turban covering her white blond hair. Her head rested on a hemp mat on the rim of the porcelain tub, as she tried to relax. But Sophie was unable to relax. She prided herself on her relationship with her girls. They came to her with their problems. Never before had one of her girls gone missing for over thirty-six hours. Sophie paid her tariff to the coppers when it was due, so she was fairly certain that Delia Swann had not been arrested. If she had, surely Sophie would have heard by this time.

"Daisy." She spoke to the tiny colored maid who sat beside the tub fanning her with two large rice paper fans.

"Yes, ma'am."

"See if Delia came back."

"I checked a while ago."

"Check again."

Setting the fans on the clothes hamper, Daisy left the room. The tub of milk sloshed as Sophie, secure in the knowledge that she was still beautiful, ran her hands over her exquisite limbs.

"Not there, ma'am." Daisy resumed fanning.

Sophie sat up and motioned for Daisy to fetch her towels. She'd waited long enough. "Telephone Mulberry Street. Ask Captain Clancy to call on me."

When Bernard J. York became police commissioner of the Metropolitan Police Department of the City of New York in 1898, the year he came home from his service as a major in the Spanish-American War, one of the first things he did was establish the Commissioner's Squad to deal with special cases.

A special case could be anything from murder to certain indiscretions that needed special attention lest embarrassment or worse fall on the police department and the City.

During the little war with Spain, York had been served very well by two men who in peacetime were policemen. When he came home and was appointed commissioner,

York made Police Lieutenant Fingal "Bo" Clancy an inspector and put him in charge of the Commissioner's Squad. The squad, which answered directly to the commissioner, had only one other permanent member, John "Dutch" Tonneman, newly promoted from sergeant to captain.

What exactly does a two-man squad do? Anything the commissioner sees fit for it to do.

And in order to help the squad deal with its varied assignments, it had the power of the commissioner's office to requisition men from any other part of the force.

The shiny black Oldsmobile stopped at the bottom of Twenty-sixth Street in front of an imposing gray stone building. Bellevue gave Sophie the shudders, though not because of the morgue that shared the building with the hospital. Morgues were easy. You were dead. Hospitals were another thing. They were uncertain. You could go in with a small complaint. Then suddenly you were dead.

The wooden Olds runabout was an open two-seater. Sophie and Leo Stern, her protector, her chauffeur and sometime lover, sat atop the engine. Leo stepped down, raising his driving goggles. He brushed the fine layer of grit from his white duster and hat, then saw to Sophie.

For riding in her automobile, Sophie wore an extravagant mauve hat; a veil of fine mauve netting covered her face. She handed off her parasol to Leo, accepted his helping hand, and set her feet in their white kid boots firmly on the ground. Her traveling costume was a smock of mauve that concealed her from head to slim-booted ankle.

Two men stood waiting outside the hideous building. They were a study in contrasts. The first, a big, dark-haired Irishman, sported a substantial mustache. At thirty-four, he was the elder of the two, but not by much. This was Bo Clancy. The second man was of equal height. His ruddy complexion and thick yellow hair were a legacy from his Dutch ancestor, the first sheriff of New York. This was Bo Clancy's thirty-two-year-old cousin, John Tonneman, known as "Dutch."

"Anyone would think she was a lady," Bo muttered.

"Wait here," Sophie told Leo. Removing her veil and traveling cloak slowly, she patted her hair and adjusted her hat with its huge ostrich feathers securely with its pin.

She was only delaying the inevitable. For a moment she pondered life's, or was it death's, irony. Now it was the morgue that was uncertain. So long as Sophie stayed outside, Delia was alive. But once she went in and looked at the dead body Bo Clancy wanted to show her . . .

Impatient with her hesitation, Bo came forward. "Better to get it done," he told her. In gilt, over the door he held open, were the words "MORGUE. WELCOME TO THE DEAD HOUSE."

"Good day to you, Sophie," Dutch Tonneman said.

"I'm not so sure, Mr. Tonneman."

The curved heels of Sophie's boots made soft clacks over the brick tiles. Bo tucked her gloved hand into the crook of his arm and led her to a room about twenty feet square, whose walls were jagged stone. The smell of disinfectant was overpowering. This anteroom seemed smaller with each passing minute. She heard the murmur of voices as Tonneman spoke to one of the attendants.

The room ended abruptly at a steel and glass screen. On the other side of the screen was another similar room. Sophie saw five stone tables on iron frames. Misty shafts of sunlight fell from slits of windows above, illuminating the horror of what lay on each table: sheet-covered lumps. Dead people.

Clothing hung on numbered hooks on the wall behind the tables. The blue hat with the drooping sunflower on hook number two looked terrifyingly familiar.

A hose tied into a loop and hanging from a hook in the ceiling projected flowing water onto the bodies.

"The cold water's to keep the rot-stink down," Bo said.

Sophie probed her purse for her scent. "Not doing a very good job, is it?" She held the lavender sachet to her nostrils. "Can we get this over with, please?"

Dutch joined them, gave Bo a nod.

"Uncover number two," Bo ordered.

A young man with hair almost the color of Sophie's suddenly materialized from the other side of the screen. Protecting his long gray coat and gray trousers was a white apron. A stiff straw hat, which would be as appropriate on a butcher, completed his uniform.

Carrying a heavy bolster, the young man crossed to table two, pulled back the sheet, and placed the bolster beneath the corpse's head. Propped up so, the head was now visible.

Sophie swayed, mumbled the Hebrew prayer for the dead.

"Do you need to get closer?" Bo asked.

"I need to get out of here." She stopped. "Was there a locket?"

"No. Is it her?" He rolled his eyes at Dutch. They knew very well the body was that of Delia Swann.

"Yes, damn you, it's Delia. Now get me the hell out of here." Sophie'd hardly taken a step when she slumped over Bo's arm. Bo ended up carrying her to the medical examiner's office.

The smelling salts Dutch moved back and forth under Sophie's nose brought her around, made her cough, then sneeze. She was lying on a hard horsehair couch.

"How did it happen?" Sophie asked. "Was she hit by a carriage?"

"Nothing so friendly," Dutch said. "A knife did this job."

Sitting up abruptly, Sophie looked from one copper to the other. "What do you mean?"

"She was murdered, Sophie," Bo said.

"Who was the last customer she was with?" Dutch asked.

"You know how long I'd stay in business if I blabbed the names on my client list?"

Bo's manner was unrelenting. "We got to know who her gentlemen were."

Silent for a moment, Sophie shifted her attention to Tonneman. "Ask your lady friend, Dutch Tonneman."

Dutch stared at her. "My lady friend?"

"Miss Esther, the photographer. The very same."

"What does Esther have to do with Delia Swann?" Dutch said uneasily. He felt Bo's eyes on him.

Sophie shrugged. "The last time I saw Delia she was off to Gramercy Park to keep an appointment with Miss Esther Breslau."

Chapter 5

Thursday, June 22. Midday.

The Oldsmobile made noises like a dying bull and pulled away. Bo stormed out on the street making similar sounds. Waving his arms at a passing hackney, he yelled, "Follow that damned machine."

The driver, an elderly fellow with stringy brown hair to his shoulders, moved a big lump of tobacco from one cheek to the other, and snorted. "Not on your tintype. If I get within three feet of that contraption my nag Bessie will have us in the Bronx."

"Take us to number five Gramercy Park West," Dutch said.

"Well, now we're talking," the hackney driver said. "We're practically there."

Bo settled back, disgruntled. "You're so goddam sure that's where she's going?"

In contrast to his cousin, who was Irish through and through, Dutch was Irish only on his mother's side. They'd grown up, first fighting each other, then anyone who was fool enough to take on the two of them.

Since Bo'd been made inspector of the commissioner's fool unit, it seemed to Dutch he'd been wilder than ever, jumping into things, doing them the complicated way. He'd been like that when they were growing up, always getting Dutch into trouble. And like that in Mr. Hearst's War, nearly getting them killed a dozen times. But also, getting them out of it, Dutch had to admit. That's why the colonel had gotten Bo that medal.

The partners each thought his own thoughts as the driver manipulated his way through the tangle of carriages and wagons and carts. Time was passing, and they'd only gone two blocks.

"We should have walked," Bo groused.

"You're right," Dutch admitted.

Bo fell silent, then raised his eyebrow.

"The locket," Dutch said.

"Right."

"I'm surprised you didn't jump on her about it."

"Are you ragging me? Yes, you are. I know when to hold back."

"Yes, you do."

"Yes, you do, Inspector," Bo ordered.

"Yes, you do, Inspector," Dutch complied.

Then he twisted his cousin's ear. They started tussling like two kids, until the driver shouted, "Cut it out back there, or I'll have the law on you."

"We are the law," Bo shouted back.

"As if I didn't know," the driver retorted. "You'd think they'd get you boys nicer hats."

"We buy our own," Dutch informed him.

"The more shame for it. The Rough Rider hats would look a darned sight better."

"I have a Rough Rider hat," Bo shouted. "And rightfully so."

The driver spat tobacco juice into the street. "I hear tell you boys do all right what with so many people thanking you kindly for your good deeds."

"Some of us do, and some of us don't. It's a different story since the colonel purified us."

They all laughed. Theodore Roosevelt was now the governor of the state, but in 1895, he and his three fellow commissioners had started the cleanup of the force.

Bo took out a cigar and lit it. "I figured the dead girl to be Sophie's all along, kind of remember seeing her at Sophie's house. I just wanted it by the book. And I didn't want Sophie to get her guard up."

"You think she's involved?"

"Until I know different. I don't trust her

or that crazy Leo Stern."

"The locket's important."

Bo puffed at his cigar. "When there's murder everything is important. We'd better sound Mulroony out. I wouldn't put it past that bog-trotter to lift a bauble from a corpse."

"There they are." Dutch leaned forward. "Pull up right behind that automobile."

"I'll stop here, lads, if you don't mind. I don't want to be dragged to the Bronx."

The men jumped down. Bo gave the driver two bits.

The old man pocketed the twenty-five-cent coin. "I did better before the purification."

"So did we," Bo said dryly.

Chapter 6

Thursday, June 22. Midday.

"You haven't told me what you think," Esther Breslau said, somewhat impatiently, as Wong cleared the remains of their midday meal from the table. She had shown her almost-complete portfolio of photographs for her current enterprise to her mentor just prior to their dining.

Oz could not tell Esther what he was thinking. His thoughts only had room for her, her piquant face, her stunning jet-black hair. He prided himself on his attention to detail, but if asked later he could not have described her costume or anything else but her sweet face.

On occasion it was difficult for Oswald Cook to believe that this sophisticated young woman had been a greenhorn from Poland, only a few short years before.

After he hired her, mainly because she spoke Yiddish and could help him in his photographic work among the immigrants on the Lower East Side, Esther came to be more than the wealthy photographer's interpreter and assistant.

She had an eye, Esther did. It wasn't long before the photographic apprentice became a fellow artist.

Oswald Cook, a slight, graying man in his late forties, had clear blue eyes except when he was felled by what he referred to as his lone remaining vice: the passion for drink. Then the whites of his eyes became webbed with streaks of blood.

Until he met Esther his world was his work. He had no room for women in his life. Now, Esther was his world.

The ash on Oz's cigarette had grown well beyond safety. He took a deep inhalation. It didn't dare stir. Finally, his thin long fingers tapped the ash free.

"Well?"

Esther's impatience made Oz smile fondly at her. "Some will say these studies are pornography," he responded, lighting another cigarette from the glowing butt of the first.

"No one whose opinion matters to me."

He gave his protégé a small fond smile. "Well, then —"

"Do you think my work is pornography, Oz?"

"According to Mr. Webster, that's what the word means, writings about harlots. *Porne* means 'harlot.' "

"Noah Webster has been dead for over fifty years. Moreover, I don't use words, I use pictures."

Wong made no sound as he set the coffee urn on the table, but his thin lips twitched. He poured coffee into the fine china cups that had been in Oz Cook's family for generations.

"Your choice of subject, as Monsieur Lautrec's, will be condemned by . . . some . . ."

"I don't care about 'some,' I care about your professional opinion."

"Well then," Oz said, "my professional opinion is that your work is splendid, that you will surpass your teacher, and that you will make a great deal of money if we publish your photographs of New York's demimondes in a book."

"Oh, no," Esther despaired. "The wrong people will buy it."

The inspiration for her daring project had come out of the tragedy of her friend Robert Roman's death in '95. At the time, she had met the beautiful Madame Sophie, whose face was rich with character. She had seen the faces of the girls who worked in Sophie's brothel and had wanted to record them. Their sense of themselves, while wholly different from Esther's, fascinated her. So she had begun. Now, after two years, she was almost finished.

And although roll film, thanks to the Kodak company, was being used by photographers around the world, she, and Oz, continued to work with glass plates for their clarity of line and richness of shading.

A bowl of tiny, wild strawberries and another with clotted cream was set before them. Clearing used dishes to his tray, Wong left it to Esther to spoon a portion of the fruit for herself and one for Oz.

Oz shook his head to the dessert. "You treat me as a child," he complained mildly. He loved the fuss she made over him. Now and again he missed the man he'd been when she came to work as his assistant four years earlier. During that time Oz had been on a downward spiral, devoted to alcohol and opium.

This glowing young woman, occupying the top floor of his house on Gramercy Park, with her *joie de vivre* and curious mind, had made him want to live again.

Although he had little use for women, he had offered her marriage when he saw he might lose her to that clod of a policeman, John Tonneman. But she had refused Oz's name and money. To Oz's glee, she had refused Tonneman's marriage proposal as well.

Oz realized that as long as he lived, with his reliance on her, she would not leave him. So he had devoted himself to Esther and enjoyed an extraordinary lust for real life, with an entirely forgivable relapse into his old ways now and again.

Together, they had completed his master work on photographing the immigrants, many of them her people, who lived in the tenements on the Lower East Side of Manhattan. And it had been acclaimed for what it was: A fitting companion to the books and photographs of Jacob Riis.

"We encountered one of your subjects, one of Sophie's girls, near the Waldorf the other night," Oz said. "Most likely saved her from a brutal beating."

"How awful. But Sophie doesn't let her girls walk the streets. It's too dangerous. Which one was it?"

"I believe her name is Delia —"

They were interrupted by a strange sound, not unlike a dozen of those rachety rattles hauled out to celebrate the arrival of a new year. This symphony of discord destroyed the relative peace of Gramercy Park, but its one-cylinder familiarity made Oz smile.

Birds took flight and white-clad nannies quickly darted protectively in front of their young charges. Everyone stopped and stared at the open Oldsmobile that made its way into the square and halted with a burst of flatulence, perfuming the front of Oswald Cook's house with the piquant odor of gasoline.

The self-propelled vehicle had been a token of gratitude to its new owner from a very grateful political gentleman from Albany, Judge James Van Norden.

When Leo removed his goggles, one of the nannies giggled. Marked with the dust of the road he looked like a colored minstrel singer.

Still, even with his dusty face and the knife scar on his right cheek, Leo was a well-presented man. Now, as always, aware of this, he removed his hat and smoothed hair that glistened with pomade.

Sophie closed her parasol and peeled away her veil and traveling hat. The small crowd gasped; Sophie Mandel was a beautiful woman. Acknowledging their admiration like one to the manor born, she took Leo's hand and stepped out of her carriage and onto Gramercy Park West.

Leo's mustache was perfectly waxed to points, and even under the automobile duster, he wore an expensive black suit and tie with a white silk shirt. He withdrew a cigar from his inside coat pocket, lit it, and gripping it between his gold teeth, puffed, the tobacco fortifying what might prove to be a long wait.

Sophie stood poised for a moment. Her mauve costume absorbed the sun as if it were part of the sun's own light. She took in the luxuriant aspect of the gated park, its full-leaved trees swaying in the silky breeze, the flower beds giving off their sensual perfume. It seemed that all the birds in the world, recovered from their automobile-induced shock, were chirping from the trees.

Sophie breathed it in deeply. Anything to forget how Delia looked on that slab. Or the notion that she might be next. Leo opened the parasol and handed it to her.

Oh, how she would love to own one of the golden keys and be one of the chosen allowed to open the iron gates of this private reserve.

Imagine, Sophie Mandel in Gramercy Park, the exclusive, tranquil retreat of the Gramercy residents, who dwelt in the red-brick and brownstone town houses ringing the park. Perhaps she should buy a house on Gramercy Park.

The thought floated away as reality returned and she considered Oswald Cook's and Esther Breslau's home. Although they lived in the same house, Sophie knew Oz Cook well enough to understand that women were not his vice. So they were not lovers.

Still, his resentment of the good-looking copper, Dutch Tonneman, was something Oz didn't bother to hide. It amused Sophie to see how Esther Breslau, who hadn't even been born in this country and spoke with a Polish accent, kept her two rather interesting suitors at arm's length.

No. 5 Gramercy Park West was a fine town house that boasted a tiny plot of garden brimming with velvety petunias to the left, protected from errant dogs and little boys by a black wrought iron fence. Ivy climbed the redbrick walls. Flower boxes rested in all but a few of the windows. Yes, a house such as this would please her immensely. But it was an unlikely daydream, for she knew the residents would never allow her to buy into their enclave.

No matter how much she offered, she was not one of them and never would be. Though, soon she'd have enough money to retire. She was almost respectable, even now.

Sophie motioned to Leo. Just as Leo raised the brass knocker, a brougham drawn by a cautious chestnut approached Sophie's Oldsmobile. Leo hesitated.

"Go on," Sophie snapped, annoyed with herself. In her dismay, she had mentioned Esther Breslau to the two coppers and had asked about the damned locket. Now with them hanging on her every word, she wouldn't be able to speak freely.

Leo lowered the knocker with a smart rat-tat-tat on the heavy, carved oak front portal.

The door opened immediately, almost as if the manservant had been waiting patiently on the other side for her arrival. She knew the Chinaman as well as anyone could know one of those slanty-eyed devils. Wong had been to her establishment many times, not for himself but for his master, Oswald Cook.

"Miss Sophie." Wong wore his usual costume of shiny black smock over baggy black trousers. A black skullcap covered the top of his head and a pigtail hung to his waist.

"I'm calling on Miss Breslau, Wong. Please ask her if she'll see me in private." Sophie spoke deliberately, with a slight tilt of her right shoulder. She knew Wong could see Detectives Clancy and Tonneman coming up behind her. He made room for her to enter.

When the door closed, Leo turned back to the street. With tremendous respect, the crowd, all except for the two detectives, parted for him. He returned to his contraption, which was now surrounded by oglers. Even Gramercy Park had its oglers.

Bo muttered an oath while Dutch used the knocker. There was no response.

As Sophie waited in the vestibule, she could hear the coppers working on the door. The knocker clapped again. Damn those coppers.

Wong reappeared. "Busy day," Wong said. "Please go to the studio, Miss Sophie. Two flights up, door to the right of the landing." Like many, Sophie was always amazed at the Chinaman's perfect toff English.

He waited until she was out of sight, then opened the door. "Ah, the gentlemen of the law."

"We're with Sophie," Bo grunted.

"She didn't mention you, gentlemen."

"Forget it, Wong," Tonneman said. "We want to see Miss Esther."

"Miss Esther is otherwise occupied. Perhaps you could return later. Or you may wait." He nodded to the parlor.

Bo was furious. "That whore knows something she ain't telling us."

"Never mind, it'll all come out fast enough."

As if declaring his right to stay, Dutch hooked his derby on one of the hall stand's knobs. The stand also contained a large mirror and a marble table, its top bare, except for the telephone. To the right of the mirror was an umbrella stand. Dutch took Bo's derby and secured it on the knob below his. To Wong he said, "We'll wait. Please tell Miss Esther and Mr. Oz we're here."

Sophie had listened to the exchange from a place on the second floor landing where she couldn't be seen. She was satisfied. Now, to the business at hand. Esther Breslau had to have been the last person to see Delia Swann alive. Delia had been terrified, hadn't wanted to leave the house on Clinton Street. Sophie had sent her here in the Olds with Leo.

She had to be certain that Delia, in her terror, had not told Esther what she had revealed to Sophie. For if she had, then both Sophie and Esther were in great danger.

CHAPTER 7

Thursday, June 22. Afternoon.

Esther stepped back and examined the photograph mounted on the easel in front of her. She had the same reaction each time, the surge of excitement that quite took her breath away. It was her first attempt at such a big print. The photograph was as large as some of the Rembrandt portraits she'd seen in the Metropolitan Museum of Art.

She stepped close again. The face was true enough, the wide sensuous mouth, the melancholy eyes, with their disturbing tinge of fear.

The details, aside from the face, had lost too much definition. Perhaps she had enlarged the photograph a bit too much. Or perhaps the details were less than important. Could she get the clarity and the size at the same time? She resolved to work on it and on the one still drying in the darkroom, the second study she'd taken of the same subject.

All of Esther's portraits of the demimondes of the City were hypnotically luminous, the contrast of light and dark exquisite. The women posed naturally, a few more proud than others, some in fine dresses, ball gowns, several conservatively in day dresses, others even more informally, in dressing gowns, heads to one side, hair up or down around bare shoulders as the light played over the lush tones of their skin.

Lips curved into half-smiles, or pursed voluptuously, carried a sullen invitation. But with few exceptions, it was the eyes of the girls in the photographs that drew one in. Esther had cleared away the lies of daily existence and captured their deep sadness with her camera.

Everywhere in their shared studio were photographic studies in process, Oz's and Esther's. Some were matted and bedded in fine folios; others in wood frames hung on the walls. And the most recent, on the easel. No photograph in the studio of these two perfectionists was ever completed. There was always work in progress.

A peremptory knock, then the door opened revealing Sophie in full sail, like the figurehead of a ship. Wong touched her elbow, and Sophie started; she hadn't heard him on the stairs.

"Miss Sophie to see you, Miss Esther."

"Thank you, Wong. Tea, please."

"I need something stronger than tea," Sophie said, plunging into the modest room. Her presence was so considerable that she made the room even smaller.

"Tea, Irish whiskey, and almond cookies, Miss Esther." He was gone as suddenly as he'd appeared.

Esther smiled. Wong's words and tone were not judgmental. The perfect servant.

"It's good to see you again, Sophie. Won't you sit down?"

"No time for lardy-dardy manners, Esther. There are two cops in your parlor right now who are breathing down my neck. I don't like it. I have to know . . ." Sophie saw the huge photograph on the easel; in spite of her airs, her mouth open wide, she fell into a chair. Beads of sweat appeared on her upper lip. "Oh, my God." As Sophie gaped at the oversized photograph, she put her hand to her heart. "It's Delia, bigger than life. Alive and dead at the same time."

Sophie surprised herself and Esther by reverting to an old-country custom. Holding the first two fingers of her right hand close to her mouth, she spit between them.

The ritual made Esther think of the old country; she resented it. "What do you mean?"

"Delia never came back after sitting here for you, and now she's in the morgue, dead."

"Dead?" Esther stared at Sophie, then at the photograph of the girl, Delia Swann. The girl with fear in her eyes.

"Dead. Murdered." Sophie blotted the perspiration from her face with a lace handkerchief. She slumped in the chair, the handkerchief concealing her eyes, and sat, silent, except for her uneven gasping breaths.

Esther was shocked. Not only by Delia's death, but by Sophie's behavior. Sophie was a very strong woman. One of her talents was keeping her emotions in check at all times.

Several minutes passed with Esther waiting for Sophie to come back to herself. Finally Sophie lifted her head and said, "You must tell me what she told you."

At this moment, Wong arrived with a tray on which were tea fixings, a plate of cookies, and a crystal decanter full of the deep honey gold Jack Daniel's sour mash whiskey from Tennessee. He looked a question at Esther.

"We'll serve ourselves, thank you, Wong."

He bowed and left.

When Esther poised the pot over Sophie's cup, Sophie waved it away and gave herself a hefty measure of whiskey instead. She offered the bottle to Esther, who shook her head.

Sophie took a good swallow, set the cup down. "How long was she here?"

"She came at two." Esther poured tea for herself and twisted a wedge of lemon into it. "We had tea when we finished, so it must have been after five when she left. What happened to her?" Esther felt an enormous melancholy. She knew that prostitutes' lives were dangerous, even if it were not for the diseases transmitted from their liaisons. She had learned from the girls that a client could make hideous physical demands of them, including torture and beatings.

"Someone stuck a knife in her and dumped her in an empty lot like she was garbage." Sophie wiped a tear from her eye. She was very fond of her girls. As with most of the women who ran houses of prostitution in New York, she felt a responsibility to the girls who worked for her. She saw that they had regular medical care and that they came to no harm from any client while they were under her roof. A client who displayed brutal tendencies was banished from Sophie's domain. "Not one of my clients," Sophie added, watching Esther's face.

"Who then would want to do such a thing? Was she robbed?"

Sophie's eyes bore into Esther. "Of what?"

"Why of her purse. Jewelry. What else?"

"The damn coppers told me they found no purse or jewelry . . . no locket. You must know she always wore the locket." Sophie nodded to the photograph, then her eyes widened. "She's not wearing the locket."

Esther studied Delia's photograph. "No, she's not. Of what significance is the locket?"

"I'm not sure." Taking another swallow of her whiskey, Sophie sighed. "It was all she had of her mother, she always said. Delia was a sweet-natured girl, nothing bothered her. About a week ago she became very fearful. It had something to do with the locket. She became afraid to leave the house. I thought she was being foolish, so I persuaded her to come pose for you. I thought the outing would be good for her."

"Her death is not your fault," Esther said.

"Oh, I know that." Sophie brushed Esther's sympathy aside. She had no patience for it. Nor did she have a conscience. "Delia told me the locket was her birthright. She put it in my hands to hold for her —"

"Then you have it safely put away."

"No. She changed her mind and was wearing it when she went off to see you. If she was wearing the locket when she was killed, whoever killed her took the locket."

Esther frowned. "How do you know that?"

"Whoever killed her, tore away her clothing . . ." Sophie looked meaningfully at Esther. "To her bare skin. If he did not find the locket, he will come looking for it. To me. To you."

Sophie was quite pale, and her nervous gestures disturbed Esther. "I'm sure you have little reason for concern," Esther said. "What could there be in a locket that would make someone murder Delia?"

"She said nothing to you about it?"

"We talked about many things. She had plans for her future. She seemed to have some prospects . . ."

"There, you see. Prospects. My girls talk and talk about marrying a wealthy client. Some of them do. Delia didn't have clients like that. Recently she hinted at other expectations. They had something to do with that locket." Sophie rose. "Be careful. I have learned to trust my instincts in situations like this." She poured another half cup of whiskey from the decanter, swallowing it quickly. "What will you tell your coppers?"

"Just what I told you," Esther said. "I have no reason to do otherwise."

After showing Sophie to the stairs, Esther went back to the studio and closed the door. She stood and stared at Delia Swann, who stared back at her. Moving slowly, Esther opened the door to the darkroom, entered, and closed it behind her. She turned on the red light. The other photograph she had taken of Delia Swann was hanging from the wire by clothespins, drying.

This Delia stood one hip forward, one bare shoulder toward the camera. She wore a white lace camisole, exposing as much breast as grand ladies exposed in ball gowns, and short silk drawers. White stockings clung to her gartered thighs. Wrapped about her one shoulder and her tiny waist, concealing little, was a long fringed shawl.

Around her throat was a black velvet ribbon from which hung a tiny gold locket.

CHAPTER 8

Thursday, June 22. Late afternoon.

If she kept her gaze high and ignored the clutter of poles and wires for the telegraph and the electric, she could admire the sun hanging in the sky like the fat succulent yolk of a fried egg.

A cooling breeze came off the East River. That was why she liked it up here. Far from the rest of the City with its swarms of people. This was her very own village, smaller than her birthplace, Marcianise, near Naples, but the entire block on upper Park Avenue between 108th Street and 109th Street was hers alone. On the West Side, for the past ten years there had been an explosion of building — brownstone houses and apartment houses — thanks to the Elevated taking trains up Eighth Avenue, but here, for the time being, she was saved from that.

"Ey, Nonna." Benito Scarpa tipped his hat

to the deceivingly frail-looking woman as she came into view, trying not to look directly into her bulging eyes. She was a devil woman, but there was nothing he could do about it. Without her, he and his family would not eat or have a roof over their heads. Ey, wasn't she the one who got the City to bring electricity up here?

Nonna's hair burned like a flame under her black hat. Benito's father called red-heads *malpelo,* evil hair. Benito would cross himself when he was out of her sight, then thank the Madonna for his good fortune.

Benito could always tell it was noon exactly when Nonna Pasquarella came out of her house with her Pekingese dog to take one of her "constitutions," before eating her midday meal. Nonna liked to walk her *regno.* Discreetly behind her were some of the men in black, of various sizes and shapes: Her bodyguards. There were ten total. All relatives. She was never without two or three of them.

The street in front of Nonna's stable was filled all day and night with the activity of coachmen, grooms, and horseshoers who worked for Nonna.

On her second walk, in the late afternoon, there were children, and for the children, Nonna Pasquarella had special treats hidden away in the deep pockets of her black dress. Her biscotti were made with hazelnuts imported from the old country. For her workers she allowed no hard liquor, only beer from the breweries perhaps a mile south. Nonna's own drink was the green aromatic *assenzio,* better known as absinthe, with its bitter licorice flavor.

A hansom cab drove up and stopped opposite the stable. The driver jumped to the road and helped the heavyset woman in black down. "Wait here," she told him, then she crossed the street.

When Nonna held out her hand, the snout-nosed woman bent forward and kissed it. "God be with you, Nonna." Sweat poured down the fat one's face and stained the underarms and back of her dress. Pancetta was a faithful soul, but she was a pig. Today her porcine odor was mixed with fear.

Nonna folded her hands across her waist. "It is done?"

"It is done." Pancetta kept her eyes on the ground, her hands behind her back.

"Give me the locket."

"The locket was not found."

The slap would have resounded like the report of a firecracker, were it not for the hammering of the blacksmith. Only those watching would have seen Pancetta draw back and hold her hand to her face.

Nonna said, "Do not tell me what I do not want to hear."

"He said she wore no jewelry."

"So the organ grinder goes into business for himself."

Pancetta cleared her throat. Her sausage fingers fumbled at the neck of her dress. "I don't think —"

"I don't pay you to think." The words were cold steel. "And I don't pay you to fail me." Nonna's eyes fixed on her servant. "You didn't give him the money?"

"No," Pancetta croaked.

"At least that you did right. Tell the organ grinder he will not see his money until he produces the locket. Give him to understand that Nonna does not take kindly to those who go into business for themselves on her back. Now get out of my sight."

The fat woman felt she was strangling in her dress. She pawed at the collar as she rushed across the street to the waiting hansom and scrambled into it like a blind one. The cab rolled off.

Nonna did not like problems. Now she had one. Attended by three of her men in black, she crossed the dirt road to her farmhouse deep in thought.

Her home was beautifully furnished. She

settled into her favorite chair in her parlor, her feet on a footstool, to consider what to do. Her vital glass of absinthe appeared immediately, delivered by Mario. She nodded at Mario, a distant relation, now her butler. He smiled and withdrew.

"Gieulietta," Nonna shouted. "Play for me." Gieulietta, a plain girl in a blue muslin dress, played soothing songs on the piano. It helped the digestion. It helped clear the mind.

They would be meeting tonight for him to make his final payment. His terms had been generous. He had said the woman never parted with the locket. The locket was an essential ingredient, and now Nonna did not have the locket. When he asked and she said no, Nonna would seem a fool. This angered her. Somebody would pay for her shame.

As Gieulietta played, a thought presented itself to Nonna Pasquarella. What if the organ grinder was not lying?

Chapter 9

Thursday, June 22. Late afternoon.

The organ grinder lived in a room on the top floor of a tenement on Prince Street, around the corner from St. Patrick's Church. Not the big fancy church they built for the rich on Fifth Avenue, but the old St. Patrick's, from 1809, on the corner of Prince and Mott.

St. Patrick was an Irish saint, and this was an Irish church. They hated Italians here, making them go to the basement for a separate mass.

But church was for the old ladies in black anyway, not for Tony Cerasani. He hadn't been to confession since he was twelve. He was thirty now. A man can collect a great many sins on his soul in eighteen years.

His room was small, which was good. He could see everything he owned: the hand organ propped against the wall, his good suit hanging over his coat on the back of the door. At this moment, his hat shared the table with his shaving gear.

Tony opened the straight razor. It had been the only thing left to him by his father. He slid the small standing mirror to him; the face he saw was his father's. He trimmed around his magnificent mustache without benefit of lather. He had no use for King Gillette's safety razor or fancy soaps.

Madonna, he had no use for anything in this terrible country. Once he saved enough money he'd go home a wealthy man and do nothing but drink and eat, have plenty of women and bask in Ciminna's nurturing sun.

Satisfied, he honed his razor on the stone and strap till it was back to its perfect edge. His dinner was crusty Parmesan and bread. He ate, chewing methodically, and washed his meal down with a lifeless Chianti. Even Italian victuals tasted terrible in America.

He plucked a straw from the wine bottle's woven covering and picked his teeth. Feeling a sharp twinge of pain, he opened his mouth wide and held up the mirror. Jesus, he'd lost one of his gold teeth. The one in the back on the left.

Anger burned in him. He had been paid only half his contract because of the missing locket. He had to produce it before he could collect the rest. Pancetta had treated him without respect.

Now this. Tony didn't like spending money, but once spent he wanted to keep the value. Now he'd have to spend money to replace the lost tooth.

He needed something stronger than wine to ease the pain and warm his bones. Winter, summer, what did it matter here? He was always cold in this country.

Grappa was comfort to Tony's belly; it calmed his pain, restrained his anger. He sat in a dark corner of Giuseppe's saloon for hours chewing his cigar, but only on the right. Drinking, thinking.

It was very late when he started home. In front of St. Patrick's on Mott Street, he paused. The rectory door opened. A Sister of Mercy spied Tony, crossed herself, and retreated inside. Tony spat at the door and the Irish bitch behind it. How long he stood there, he didn't know. At the end he went into the church.

In the rear, to the left of the last row of benches, were the four doors of two confessionals. No parishioners waited on the benches.

He ran his fingers over the latticework screen of the nearest priest door, his nails making a clicking noise.

He was startled when someone, clearly a mick, and obviously awakened from sleep, said, "Yes? Do you wish to make your confession?"

"No." The organ grinder did not even try to keep the sneer from his voice. "Go back to your dreams of plump little boys."

On his walk home he saw himself as a boy at confession, a wrathful crucifix poised above him.

"May the Lord be in your heart and in your mind that you may properly confess your sins," the priest said. "In the name of the Father and the Son and the Holy Spirit."

The young Tony crossed himself. "Bless me, Father, for I have sinned. It has been one week since my last confession."

The organ grinder shook his head and the memory disappeared. He had stopped drinking too soon.

But the priest from his memory wouldn't go away. "Visit the Sixth Station of the Cross, say three Hail Marys, three Our Fathers, and perform an act of charity before the week is out."

"Thank you, Father. I feel much —"

The priest from his memory, because it was a busy day, interrupted. "Go in peace, my son." The panel slid closed.

Tony thought, oh, if it could only be that easy. But the sins on his soul were too great to be absolved by a such simple penance.

"Oh, my God, I am heartily sorry for having offended thee and I detest all my —" He stopped when he saw that instead of going home he'd returned to Giuseppe's.

The church was a jail. Worse, a rope around his neck. Damn the church. He had work to complete, the rest of his contract to fulfill. There was money to be made. Religion was for the rich. Or the old and the helpless. He was none of these. He pushed open the door to Giuseppe's and went in.

Chapter 10

Thursday, June 22. Night.

It was a delicate mission of utmost secrecy. Consequently, Baby had not driven his new Benz or even hired a hack for the full journey. To ensure ultimate circumspection, nothing would serve but the Elevated, which fortunately offered all-night service. Of course, after the new subway was built, anonymity would be there for the asking.

The new subway was much on his mind. The enterprise would provide money — *for the asking,* to a select few. A select few who had had the foresight to buy up the right property at the right price.

He'd stayed late in the office reviewing clients' portfolios, writing recommendations as to the timing of buying and selling. He was a very good analyst of economic and market trends. Still, nobody would credit his recommendations, because both Harrison Stokes, Baby's brother-in-law, and his partner, William Grimes, were very proprietary about their clients. They would digest his analysis and if they found something useful, they would make it their own. But that was the way Wall Street worked, and Baby accepted it.

It was after eight, though still quite light outside. The rain that had punished his game leg was over. Baby put the files away and dropped his recommendations on Grimes's pristine desk. He set his boater on his head, grabbed his mahogany stick, and left the office building at 45 Beaver Street, somewhat enviously checking the activity at Delmonico's across the street.

Glad to be swinging his cane, rather than leaning on it, Baby walked to the Morris Street Station of the Sixth Avenue elevated line terminal at the bottom of Beaver Street. An adventure, Baby thought.

He rarely used the El. Still, the Sixth Avenue line was deemed the City's finest. He, however, preferred riding on the ground. In carriages and hacks. And now at last, in his own Benz self-propelled vehicle.

He climbed to the top of the stairs, thinking of Cuba, and the *great day of his life.* These stairs certainly weren't San Juan Hill, but nothing was. Or ever would be.

The platform was crowded. People of all

classes, including his own, stood expectantly, peering down the tracks to their right. At the top of the stairs he bought his ticket. As he strolled out onto the platform, a whistle, then a rumble accompanied by a billow of steam, announced the incoming South Ferry to Central Park train.

The car was well lit and, though the air coming through the open windows was sooty, redolent with coal and wood, the breeze made the ride quite comfortable.

Baby had forgotten how noisy the Elevated could be. A howling monster. It was a quick way to get around town, but a better day was coming.

Frowning at the gummy sensation under his feet, he sat on the cushioned seat beside a stout man smoking a fragrant Havana. Apparently some riders did not appreciate the braided mat on the car's floor and had baptized it with tobacco juice. Baby decided a cigar was a capital idea and lit one of his own.

With the crowded train traveling at a speed of twelve miles an hour, the thirty-minute ride was faster than his beloved Benz could manage. The abrupt curve before the station prompted the more experienced passengers to stand and queue up at the doors, anticipating the stop at

Fifty-fourth Street where the Sixth Avenue line connected with the Ninth Avenue line.

The Ninth Avenue El traveled north through the tenements and brownstones of the West Fifties and then into the West End, the sparsely populated region of the West Sixties and Seventies. The area on the West Side beyond Sixtieth Street was just starting to show improvement. Building of brownstones and hotel residences was active, anticipating the arrival of underground rapid transit: the subway.

Darkness was beginning to fall over the City. The train he'd arrived on began its journey back from whence it had come as Baby descended to the street.

Wondrous quiet. All the noise and corruption of the business of New York came to a halt in the presence of the splendid Central Park that was the City's pride.

As he approached the Merchants Gate, the vehicle and pedestrian entrance to the Central Park at Columbus Circle, Baby saw, illuminated by a street lamp, an old immigrant woman in black sitting on a bench to the left of the gate. A scarf tied under her chin all but hid her red hair. She appeared to be lost in her own thoughts and did not look at him.

A short distance from the woman, Baby

was confronted by a swarthy, thickset young man who materialized from out of the darkness.

His grasp secure on his stout mahogany, Baby bowed politely. "Sir? Perhaps can you help me. I have a packet to deliver."

"Give it here."

Startled, Baby saw the words had come from the thin lips of the old woman on the bench. Pivoting in her direction, he felt her protruding eyes on him. "Ma'am, I would be a fool if I did not put my delivery into the right hands."

The man in black growled and stepped closer to him.

"Patience, Giorgio, he's doing his job." To Baby, she said, "My grandson is very eager. You have something to give me, *for a real reason.*"

That was the correct answer. *For a real reason.* "Is the deed done?"

"Yes."

"And I am to receive something — a token."

"Alas," the woman said. "That will take a little longer."

"And alack," he countered mockingly. "It is not my understanding of the arrangement."

"You will have your token."

"When?"

"When it is recovered." She held out her hand. "In the meantime, you will pay what I am owed."

Baby realized at once that the woman took him for a fool. "The first payment has already been made. The final payment is based on the . . . token. You will communicate as you usually do when you have recovered the token." Baby spoke firmly. When it came to paying out money, one had to be resolute.

The woman nodded. It was what she had expected. But Giorgio came charging at Baby like a mad bull. Baby stepped aside, struck the young man on the back of the head with his mahogany, and watched as his attacker sank to the ground.

The old woman raised a queen's hand and shook her head. Another thickset young man, whom Baby had not noticed, halted in his tracks. "My apologies, sir. You are quite correct. Be assured that the unfinished business is being attended to as we speak. What was promised will be done. It is a matter of honor. My apologies are sincere. Giorgio is an impetuous boy with very little thinking substance."

"Ma'am, honor is what moves the world. After commerce, that is."

A strange sound, a chuckle, came from her unmoving lips. "I like you. With *testicoli* like yours you could be Italian. But no matter what I think, when Giorgio wakes he will vow vengeance. I will keep him in leash. But one day he will seek you out and kill you."

Baby bowed. "Ma'am, I thank you for your warning, but if I wasn't concerned about the Spanish killing me, I will not be concerned about an Italian attempting the same."

Yet Baby moved quickly from Central Park. He was a romantic soul and had enjoyed the intrigue, pitting himself against adversaries. But this adversary was an old woman, and there was something particularly menacing about the old woman and her minions.

He was returning empty handed. Well, not exactly empty handed. He still had the packet of money.

Chapter 11

Thursday, June 22. Midafternoon.

Esther heard the soft footsteps in the studio. She opened the darkroom door and stepped out. With a quizzical look, Oz moved around her and into the darkroom.

Inspecting the photograph of Delia Swann, he said, "What did Sophie want?"

"That poor girl, Delia. She's been murdered."

"Our Delia here? This one?" When Esther nodded, he said, "The man I told you about. The one that was beating her, of course. Delia had separated him from his wallet."

"She was terribly frightened when she was here to pose. I could hardly get her to remain still." Esther sighed. "That poor girl."

The faintest of murmurs alerted them to Wong's presence. "Miss Esther, Mr. Tonneman and Mr. Clancy are in the parlor waiting to speak to you."

"Aha! This doesn't sound like a personal visit, arriving as they did right on Sophie's lovely heels." Oz took Esther's arm. "We'd quite forgotten about the minions of the law, Wong." The corners of his lips twitched. "Well, let's face them together, shall we, my dear?"

"Esther doesn't know anything about this," Dutch said. He had quite worn a path across the India carpet.

Seated in the largest chair, a rose damask Belter, set in front of the cold fireplace, Bo crossed right leg over left and studied his cousin, with a jaundiced eye. "You'd better let me do the talking. She's got you wrapped around her little finger."

"I'm going to marry her."

"Have you discussed this with her lately?"

"None of your business."

"Keeps saying no, does she? Smart girl."

Wong opened the double doors, then stepped back for Oz and Esther to enter. Sunlight from the parlor window threw dappling light on everything and everyone. Dutch stopped pacing, Bo stood. "Miss Breslau. Mr. Cook," Bo said, his brash charm much in evidence. "Sorry to break into your afternoon, but there are some questions that need asking."

"Police business," Dutch added. "A situation involving the murder of someone you may know."

"Mr. Clancy, Mr. Tonneman, good afternoon. Won't you be seated? A murder, you say?" Oz pointed Bo back to the Belter chair. He settled Esther in the smaller lady's chair that had been his mother's favorite. Standing behind Esther, his hand on the rosewood back of her chair, his fingers touched her shoulders every so often, as if by accident.

He acts like he owns her, Dutch thought, steaming, adrift in the middle of the room. "It's the murder of Delia Swann we are here about. Sophie told us —"

"Wouldn't you be more comfortable seated, John?"

First words she says to him, and she sounds like Ma. Wouldn't both love that. "Thank you, Esther." He crossed in front of the fireplace and sat opposite his partner. Was Bo smiling? He'd kick his damn ass. "Sophie told us Delia was here posing for you and never came back to the house afterward."

Bo set his cigar in the plate on the smoking stand next to his chair. "Miss Breslau, you may have been the last person to see her alive. Except for the murderer."

"Who probably followed her here and waited for her to come out," Dutch added.

"Oh, no." Esther paled. She looked up at Oz.

Bo said, "We need to know what she said to you."

"Nothing unusual. I could see she was frightened about something, but she didn't confide in me."

Dutch noticed fondly that when Esther was upset her Polish accent, usually faint, became more pronounced.

"What is it you think Miss Swann may have told Miss Breslau, gentlemen?"

Rolling his eyes at Dutch, Bo said, "We don't know. That's why we're here."

"Perhaps you aren't aware that two weeks ago, outside the Waldorf-Astoria, several gentlemen and I were able to save Miss Swann from a severe beating. It seems she helped herself to her escort's billfold."

"Well, now we're talking," Dutch said. "Who was her escort?"

"I don't know. He left in rather a hurry. As a matter of fact, so did she. We found his billfold, with his money intact I might add, on the sidewalk after she ran away. One of us picked it up and said he'd return it."

"Who?" Dutch brought out a pad from

his pocket.

"Damned if I can remember."

"Would you be kind enough, Mr. Cook, to give us the names of the gentlemen you were with that evening."

"I think it might be better if I were to contact them," Oz said.

"This is a police investigation," Bo responded. "You'd best let us handle it."

"Esther, what was Delia Swann wearing when she was here?" Dutch asked.

"Why do you ask?"

"It's important."

"She wore a dark blue poplin dress with a small collar. Would you like to see how she looked when she was here? The photograph is finished. It's in the studio."

"We would," Bo said. "And maybe while you show it to us, Mr. Cook can come up with that list."

Bo and Dutch followed Esther up the stairs. At the door to the studio, Esther asked, "How was she killed?"

"A knife in the gut," Bo said, enjoying Esther's flinch.

Dutch elbowed his cousin, and Bo gave him a mighty wink.

Standing aside, Esther pointed to the photograph of Delia Swann, the same photograph that Sophie had seen. "Looks a lot different," Bo said.

"She's alive here, Mr. Clancy. She would look different."

"No, ma'am, I mean . . ." Floundering, he looked at Dutch. Dutch had to smile. Bo had walked right into that, brazen as you please, and got tripped up.

"Whoever killed her, tore her clothes off, Esther," Dutch said gently, and even so, saw tears spring to her eyes. He took her hand.

"He was looking for something, we think." Bo peered at the photograph. "I don't see no jewelry."

"Jewelry?"

"Sophie said she was wearing jewelry." Satisfied, Bo pointed to the door. "Let's go, Cuz."

Esther found she was reluctant to release John Tonneman's hand.

"May I call on you later?" Dutch said, pleased.

"You may join us for supper, at eight o'clock." The shine in her eyes gave him hope. Or was it the tears? Nevertheless, it gave him the same sort of dumb hope he'd had ever since she'd first refused his offer of marriage in 1895.

Wong was waiting when they came downstairs. He offered their hats and a linen envelope easily identified as Oz's personal stationery, which Bo took without a word and slipped into his inside pocket.

"Wong, Mr. Tonneman will be joining us for supper . . ."

Wong opened the front door to let the detectives out. A frisson of a melody came as if in response. Notes full of nostalgia, rich with feeling, floated around them. It was a strange sound for Gramercy Park. Children and nursemaids, who had been attracted earlier by Sophie's automobile, were drawn by the magic of the music and the swarthy man who sang in accompaniment.

Esther knew the music. "La donna è mobile." From the Italian opera *Rigoletto.* She stood outside and listened. The organ grinder's black eyes settled on her as if she were his sole audience.

Chapter 12

Monday, June 26. Morning.

Although respectable people still lived on Grand Street, between Sheriff and Willet, it was now less than its name proclaimed. Once, this thoroughfare had truly been grand.

Descendants of its earlier residents had quit this part of the City long ago. People wanted to spread out beyond the snarl of lower Manhattan, and the Els on Second, Third, Sixth, and Ninth Avenues made that possible. They could now have both convenient and fast transport to and from their work place and distance from the clamor of the elevated trains at the same time.

John "Dutch" Tonneman and his mother lived in one of a group of identical four-storied brick and mortar genteelly shabby houses on Grand Street. These houses had been built in 1830 and were all that remained of a once-flourishing middle-class residential district.

Only shutters and stoops were unique to each house; all else was identical. The Tonneman house had been Old Peter's, Dutch's great grandfather. The surrounding homes had been owned at their outset by various members of the Jacob Hays family.

Newly wed, Dutch's father and mother had started their family in this house in 1866, only months after Old Peter's wife, Charity, had died. To Meg Clancy, Dutch's mother, the house had been a palace, with parquet floors covered in carpets, mahogany banisters, plaster patterned ceilings, attractive fabrics on the walls and furniture. Imagine, Meg Clancy with a Persian on the floor.

Not much had been altered since '66, although now the house did have running water and electricity. Flower boxes sat on the outside sills of the first-floor front windows. A wrought iron railing flanked the six steps leading to the front door.

Light shone through lace curtains. The house smelled of cabbage but also of sugar, cinnamon, and apples. The parlor was immaculate, albeit packed with furniture: a sofa, chairs, side tables, everything covered with embroidered doilies. Footstools of various heights were in place in front of chairs and the sofa. A glass-enclosed bookcase and a "square piano" took up what little floor space was left. In a corner near the entrance to the dining room, an old grandfather's clock ticked its way toward eight.

A large arched doorway led to a dining room and the formal table set with linen and crystal, where Dutch now sat. On the sideboard was a silver box polished to a dull gleam.

The crucifix was in its place on the wall. Meg had hung it there herself when she arrived as a bride. Close by the crucifix in a niche was a statue of the Virgin Mary. On the wall opposite the sideboard, a Sacred Heart.

Irish on his mother's side, Dutch on his father's, but mostly Irish and definitely Catholic by upbringing, John Tonneman had grown up taking for granted the Catholic Church and all its accoutrements.

Tonneman considered himself Catholic, that was certain. But since he'd met the Jewish girl, Esther Breslau, four years earlier and discovered that his own father's people were Hebrews going all the way back, he viewed Meg's religious ways and views with less certainty.

He was staring at the fiery, blood-dripping image of the Sacred Heart when Meg said,

"You didn't eat what I left out for you last night." She refilled her son's cup with coffee. A tiny, round woman with fair skin and a stubby nose, Meg wore her white hair in a tight bun.

Tonneman looked up from his newspaper. "What, Ma?"

Meg repeated what she'd said. She smoothed the linen apron across her ample bosom and fussed with the sleeves of her black dress.

"I told you I was having supper out."

Meg sighed dramatically. "That heathen girl makes you forget all about your poor Ma, John Tonneman."

Setting the *Herald* aside, Dutch said, "Ma, I'm going to marry Esther, and she's a Hebrew, not a heathen. You might as well say I'm a heathen, being that I'm half Hebrew myself." He grinned at her, trying to make light of his curious circumstance. "Come to think of it, you're the only one in the family that's pure Irish."

"See now she's got you blaspheming." Meg crossed herself twice, mumbling a Hail Mary. And a third time, to get her to the end. "Annie's found a real nice Irish Catholic girl for you. Susan Callahan —"

"Ma, now stop. Annie's not one to interfere, so I don't know what you've been telling her."

"It's time you gave me grandchildren."

"I have five sisters, Ma, and Annie included, they've given you more than enough grandchildren."

At this point Meg Tonneman, nee Clancy, burst into tears.

It was always the same finish to the same argument. When Bo arrived, Dutch was apologizing and Meg was drying her eyes.

"You be careful, boys," Meg called after them. "And John, I almost forgot, Father Duff says you're to come by the rectory."

"What's that all about?" Bo asked as they set out.

They were heading for the Seventh Precinct on Clinton Street, off Delancey, to talk to Officer Mulroony.

"Ma must have talked to old Duff about Esther and me."

Laughing, Bo said, putting on the brogue, "Sure an' you're gonna listen to everyt'ing the old fart tells you."

"In me own sweet time, Cuz, in me own sweet time."

Ten minutes later they walked through the door of the Seven. "Top of the morning, brother," Bo told his brother Ned, who served as desk sergeant. Just off the entranceway, several docile drunks slept on a bench in a corner, while two working girls on the opposite end of the bench were chattering mouth to ear.

Six feet tall, Ned was the smallest fry of the clan Clancy. He was well known for his truculence, an attribute that led readily to being a desk sergeant.

Ned half stood in his chair behind the high bench, leaned forward, and thrust his broad jowls into Bo's. "What the hell do you want?" The perfect desk sergeant.

Before Bo could speak, the door he and Dutch had just come through opened again. Flora Cooper, a New York *Herald* reporter, and a girl Bo thought of as a hum-humdinger, stepped in.

Typically, the point of a yellow pencil jutted out from Flora's roll of dark golden hair under her lopsided hat. And typically she struck a lucifer against the wall and lit a Cycle. "As I live and breathe. Inspector Bo and Captain Dutch. Big as life. What are the commissioner's fair-haired lads doing in this low-life part of town?"

Flushing red, Bo said, "Get outta here, Flora."

"Wait just a damned minute," Ned shouted. "You don't go telling anyone to get outta my station house."

"What you going to do, tell Ma?"

"This is my house, my rules."

Bo bowed to his brother. "Yes, darling sergeant. My apologies."

"That's settled, then?"

"Yes," Bo said.

"Good." He turned to the newspaper woman. "Get outta here, Miss Cooper."

Flora rolled her eyes. "God save me from Clancys." But she didn't budge.

"Out," said Ned. "Or I'll have you thrown out."

"I dare you."

Dutch liked Flora. She was a tough one. She stood there arms akimbo, pugnacious as Ned himself. Dutch glanced from Ned to Bo. Truth to tell, Bo liked Flora a lot. They'd met back in '95 when Flora had given them a key piece of information in the Robert Roman murder case. Since then Dutch reckoned Bo felt about Flora the way Dutch felt about Esther.

"You're testing my patience," Ned said. "Begone or I'll bounce you out myself."

"You wouldn't."

Dutch nodded his head vigorously. "Yes, he would, Flora."

"All right, I know when I'm beaten. But what can you tell me about the girl, Delia Swann, who was found stabbed to death in an empty lot on South Street last Wednesday morning?"

"Get out, Flora," Bo, Ned, and Dutch said.

She made a face, ground the butt of her cigarette into the station floor with her boot, and left.

"Now," Ned said to Bo, "I have a lot of work to do, and no time to be wasting it on you."

"I can see that, my darling brother. We would like to speak to Patrolman James Mulroony."

"So would I. The spalpeen didn't make roll call this morning."

"Was he off yesterday?" Dutch asked.

"Yeah. He's been on the job ten years and rates Sunday. But he didn't come in today neither."

Bo narrowed his eyes. "What do you say, Dutch and I go wake him up? Where's he live?"

"On Suffolk. Will McNulty is his roundsman. I already sent him over."

"What number Suffolk?" Bo was halfway to the door.

Dutch held back while Ned ran his thumb down the morning report. "Let's see, let's see. Number ninety-seven." Ned looked up, suspicious. "What the hell is going on here? I want you two to keep your noses outta my business."

"It already is our business, Ned." Dutch tossed his words at the desk sergeant as he hurried out. He caught up to Bo on the far side of Delancey. "Number ninety-seven is at the corner of Rivington," Dutch told Bo. "It was part of my first beat."

"And didn't I walk the same?" Bo asked his partner.

Rivington was only one block past Delancey. As they approached it they spotted a chunky, pink-faced policeman, easily recognized as Will McNulty. As usual every one of the brass buttons on Will's blue uniform threatened to pop any moment.

"Hey, Will, you wake up Mulroony?" Dutch called.

"He ain't there. What he do? Kill the mayor?"

"No, the pope," Bo said.

"You shouldn't joke about those things, Bo Clancy. You'll burn in hell."

Bo sneered at the roundsman. "How did you ever get any rank?"

"Hard work." Then with a twinkle, Will added, "More than I can say for you detectives."

"What's your next step?" Dutch asked, tiring of these two ragging each other.

"When he's really soused, Mulroony likes

to do the Russian baths down the block here on Rivington."

"They call it the *shvitz,*" Dutch said.

"And sure, you'd know that, wouldn't you?" Bo said.

McNulty was already rushing along Rivington as Dutch replied, "Sure and I would. It means sweat in Jew talk."

They entered a four-story building permeated with the smell of lye and pickled herring. The roundsman marched to the end of the hall, leading his comrades downstairs to the basement. He opened a door to a steamy box of a chamber that had wooden benches climbing up the rough wall in three steps. On the lowest bench rested an oak leaf brush and a wooden bucket that was used to splash cold water on the patrons.

McNulty looked around the steam room and tentatively touched the metal door on the right-hand wall. By his reaction it was hot. "Ready for business," he mumbled. "That's the coal furnace which makes this hellish Jewish heat," he informed the two other cops.

"Hello, my friend William." A humpedback man appeared behind them; he was the size of a leprechaun and spoke English with a thick Russian accent. "It's only Monday. Did I make mistake by the count?"

McNulty glowered at the Jewish leprechaun. "Can that, Mendy. We're looking for Jim Mulroony."

The Russian fingered his wispy gray beard and, through heavy-lidded eyes, examined Dutch and Bo. "He came last night. Soused. He's upstairs, room five, sleeping it off."

Mendy's shout brought another leprechaun, this one younger, with a straight back and no beard. Mendy Junior, no doubt, Dutch thought. Quick words in Yiddish were exchanged, then the bearded Mendy led them up the narrow stairs to cubicle five. All the cubicles seemed oddly silent. No snores, no heavy sleep breathing.

"It's quiet up here," Dutch said.

Bo grunted. "Not much traffic last night?"

"Only him overnight." Mendy drew aside the large sheet that served as a curtain.

The room was just big enough to hold a plain narrow wooden table and a one-suit whorehouse closet. On the table, Mulroony lay wrapped in another large sheet, his long legs hanging off one end and his head almost off the other.

He seemed asleep, but he wasn't. A large red splotch stained the sheet where it covered his chest, and a great puddle of blood had pooled under the table.

CHAPTER 13

Monday, June 26. Early afternoon.

"Miss Flora Cooper to see you. Are you in?"

Sophie looked up from her account books, surprised. The only time she had a visit from the press was for business. Hers and theirs. She bought ads, they bought pleasure. But they were always men.

Removing her eyeglasses, Sophie placed them in their embossed silver case, the case in a drawer. Her account books followed. It always paid to be nice to the press. "Show Miss Cooper in, Daisy. And bring us some tea."

"Miss Mandel?" The girl who came into the parlor was tall, though not as tall as Sophie, and wore a very proper suit and hat. Except the hat was tilted, half on, half off, barely covering thick honey-blond hair, with a pencil sticking out of it. "Thank you for seeing me."

"I was curious," Sophie said. "You are

younger than I thought you'd be."

"Age doesn't matter. It's determination that counts." Flora looked around the gaudy parlor room appreciatively. It was as she'd heard. Mirrors everywhere. She pulled over a chair and sat down facing Sophie. "You are also younger than I'd imagined." She located a crushed box of Cycle cigarettes in her bag, but it turned out to be empty. She dropped it into her bag and brought out a fresh box. "Smoke?"

Sophie smiled a secret smile and shook her head. The smile concerned the pretty girl whose picture was on the Cycle box. She looked like a girl who had worked for Sophie in '95.

"Mind if I do?"

"Not at all." Sophie pushed the glass ashtray toward Flora.

"What can I do for you, Miss Cooper? Ah, here's Daisy." Conversation stopped as Daisy set out the tea.

Flora sat back in her chair watching Sophie and blowing perfect smoke rings, which rose wraith-like, held a moment, then dissolved. When Daisy left, Flora said, "I've come to ask you about Delia Swann."

The question caused Sophie's hand pouring the tea to tremble ever so slightly, but enough for Flora to take notice.

"Tragic," Sophie murmured. She retrieved a lace handkerchief from her sleeve and dabbed at her eyes.

"Yes," Flora agreed, taking out a small notepad from her voluminous bag, pulling her pencil from her hair.

"You can put those away. All I need is for you to write a story about Delia and this house. Commissioner York sees that, I'm closed down, boarded up, and fishmongers are selling their stinking wares outside my door."

A particle of cigarette paper had adhered to Flora's lip. She chewed it away. "I'm going to write it whether you talk to me or not. This way I write it friendly."

"Are you threatening me?"

"I wouldn't dare, Miss Mandel. Merely stating the facts. I'll call this a rooming house for young ladies. Everyone will know the truth, but that should keep Commissioner York serene and out of your hair."

Sighing, Sophie said, "My ladies do see clients outside, although I urge them not to. Here I can protect them, you see. Outside, well . . ." Her shrug spoke volumes.

"Oh," Flora said, pencil poised. "Has something like this happened before?"

"There are some men who feel the need to cause pain, and when they reveal them-

selves, they are not made welcome here."
Sophie sipped her tea and watched Flora. "Once in a while one of my girls will get hurt, but murder? Never."

"Who was Delia Swann? How did she come to you?"

"She arrived here two years ago with one of my regular girls. Celeste found her begging near the Grand Central Depot and brought her to me. She was filthy and ragged, like a small animal that has been beaten into submission. Not a pretty sight, I can tell you. It took her a long time to heal."

Flora's pencil was flying. "She became one of your girls."

"She had already been with a man before she came here," Sophie said.

"I wasn't making any judgments, Miss Mandel."

"Just keeping the record clear."

"Her real name was Delia Swann?"

"That's the moniker she gave me."

"You believed her?"

"My dear Miss Cooper —"

"Flora."

Sophie nodded. "Flora. It's not my place to believe or disbelieve. Some of my girls use the name they were born with, others don't. I leave the choice to them. I'm not really interested in who they were in another life."

From somewhere nearby came the ring-ring of a telephone. It clamored for attention three times and then stopped.

"How old was Delia when she came here?"

"Who knows?" The shade of a smile crossed Sophie's lips but didn't show in her eyes. "Now, if you'll excuse me. I have to prepare the evening's social schedule for my ladies."

"So you are unable to tell me anything more about her?"

"Why, may I ask, is there so much interest in a murdered whore?"

"So much interest?"

"The police. Now you."

"I'd thought to write a special piece about the short, unhappy life of a girl. But now something else has come up."

"And what is that?"

"Sophie!" Leo burst into the room. He was in his shirtsleeves, a skullcap on his crown. "Oh!" The shock of seeing a real lady in Sophie's parlor brought him up short. As did the look on Sophie's face. "I didn't know you had company."

"This is Miss Flora Cooper. She was just leaving." Sophie thought, What was the something else that had come up?

Flora stood reluctantly. "Mr. . . . Leo?" She offered him her hand.

"Charming." Leo lifted her hand to his lips. "I am Leo Stern, Miss Mandel's business manager."

"Leo! Miss Cooper is a journalist."

"You're the Flora Cooper who wrote about poor Delia's death?"

"Yes, Mr. Stern."

"And you are paying a condolence call. How very kind. Isn't Miss Cooper kind, Sophie dear?"

Simmering, Sophie wanted to brain him. She hated Leo when he pulled his gent act.

"I'll see you out, Miss Cooper." Leo took Flora's elbow and ushered her into the hallway. "Daisy," he shouted, sounding more like his real self. Irritated at Daisy's absence, he all but dragged Flora to the front door and out. Dusting his hands, he marched back to the parlor.

Had he delayed another minute he would have seen the front door open and Flora looking woefully at her hat, now crushed to a fare-thee-well. She had used it to prevent the door from closing completely. Flora tiptoed to just outside the parlor.

"You never know when to stop." Annoyance from Sophie.

"She's a pretty one."

"She was about to tell me something important when you burst in on us," Sophie said angrily.

"*I* have something important to tell you right now. I had a call from my snitch at the precinct."

"So?"

"Mulroony, the copper who found Delia?"

"Yes?" Sophie pushed the tea tray aside, pulled her account books out of the drawer, and restored her glasses to her nose.

"They found him in a Russian *shvitz* on Rivington. Somebody gut stabbed him just like they did Delia."

There was utter silence for a brief moment, then, "God save me," came Sophie's small cry. "I'm next."

Chapter 14

Monday, June 26. Early afternoon.

Well, Flora Cooper mused, stepping off the single, white marble step that led to No. 79 Clinton Street. What was Sophie hiding? Reporter's instinct had told Flora that Delia Swann's murder was more than the death of a common prostitute. Now it looked as if her instinct was right.

Flora had followed Bo Clancy and Dutch Tonneman to Rivington Street that morning and learned only a few minutes after they did that Mulroony had been murdered.

Who killed Mulroony was the obvious question.

More interesting was: Why kill Mulroony?

Maybe because he'd discovered Delia Swann's body?

What else had he discovered?

Why was Sophie now afraid for her own life?

Flora nibbled on her pencil. What was she

missing here? Perhaps she should wander over to the Seven and see what was happening. Mulroony's murder would have them all running around like chickens with their heads chopped off. Well, not Bo Clancy, that was for sure. He talked crazy sometimes, but he was a sharp one and so was his cousin Dutch.

She started walking. Delia. No purse or jewelry, her clothes torn to shreds, her undergarments missing. Mulroony, who'd found her, also dead, naked in a sheet. Sophie, with whom Delia had lived, thinking she's next.

Was someone looking for something? Something Delia had. Was Delia a blackmailer? Flora did love puzzles. She had three pieces to play with so far.

A hackney coach came down the street toward her. Now here was luck. She raised her hand to catch the driver's eye. As he went right by her, she muttered a curse under her breath. But when he pulled over to the curb down the street in front of Sophie Mandel's house, she saw he had a passenger.

Flora held her crushed hat to her head and rushed back to Sophie's to try to grab the cab. Breathless, she stepped back and waited for the passenger, a woman, to alight.

The driver scrambled down from his place and opened the door for his passenger. It was Dutch Tonneman's lady friend, Esther Breslau. A leather case hung by a strap from her shoulder.

Flora admired Esther Breslau's smart attire. The practical business suit, white shirtwaist with a large black and white striped taffeta bow at the throat, the wide-brimmed straw hat decorated with a big bunch of artificial roses looked just swell. Flora would have loved to look like that, but she knew that on her, after a few hours, the outfit would be wrinkled and ash dusted and ink stained.

Flora stepped forward, first saying, "Driver." Then adding, "Miss Breslau! What a surprise to meet you here."

Dismayed, Esther felt a rush of crimson coloring her face. How inconvenient to run into Flora Cooper at this moment, and — the Almighty help her — in front of Sophie Mandel's house of prostitution. She recovered her composure as she paid the driver his fare. Then, drawing a box camera from its leather case, she made a photograph of Sophie's building.

When she was done she advanced the roll film and returned the camera to its case. "And what a surprise to meet you here,

Miss Cooper."

They were not unacquainted. Bo Clancy and Dutch Tonneman had brought them together for picnics and promenades. But they were cautious with one another, as they were with the two detectives who courted them.

"Well, I'm just doing my job," said Flora. "I came to see Sophie about Delia Swann." Her eyes settled on Esther's camera case. "Say, didn't I hear you were making photographic studies of these girls?" Now she remembered where she'd heard it. Bo Clancy had made a joke about it. "Did you do one of Delia Swann?"

"So what do you say, lady?" the driver interrupted. "You want to go somewhere or not?"

"I don't want to keep you, Miss Cooper." Esther assumed what she hoped was a most ingenuous smile. Flora Cooper was very sharp. In other circumstances they might be friends.

"The cop that found Delia was murdered last night," Flora said abruptly.

"Oh!" Esther's head snapped back as if Flora had slapped her.

Ah, Flora thought, what have we here? Could this possibly be the fourth piece in my puzzle? "And Sophie is frightened she'll be next."

Through tensed lips, Esther said, "Maybe it's merely a coincidence."

The hackney driver ahemed. "Ladies . . ." Snorting, the chestnut mare pawed the cobblestones.

"Just a moment, driver. You did make a picture of Delia Swann, didn't you, Miss Breslau?"

Esther nodded. What a fool she was. She had been playing a game with her life, all because she treasured her independence. "I made several photographs of Delia."

"When?"

"Not long ago."

Flora slipped her arm in Esther's. "I believe you are in danger, then, Miss Breslau. We may be able to help each other." She didn't wait for Esther to respond. "Driver, take us to Gramercy Park."

CHAPTER 15

Monday, June 26. Afternoon.

Uncharacteristically silent, Flora's eyes darted every which way. She was not prepared for the Chinese manservant who opened the door for them, or the pure elegance of the house on Gramercy Park where Esther lived.

Esther understood. When as a young immigrant with high hopes Esther had first come here four years earlier to be Oz Cook's assistant, she too had been overwhelmed.

Now, the minute Esther set foot in this house, she felt relief. She was safe here.

Wong presented Esther with a card. "Mr. Lawrence Burgoyne called." A hint of a smile found its way through Wong's usual impassive expression. "He charged me to tell you he was devastated at not finding you at home."

"Thank you, Wong," Esther said. "This is

Miss Flora Cooper."

"The journalist," Wong said.

"You read the *Herald*?" Flora said, surprised.

"We have it delivered," Esther said.

"Will you take tea, Miss Esther?"

Esther looked at Flora, who nodded. "Yes. In the studio."

"Mr. Oz is making a photograph."

"In my sitting room, then."

With Esther leading the way, they climbed the stairs to her rooms on the fifth floor.

"You and the Baby Burgoyne?" Flora actually tittered. "I don't believe it."

Esther smiled. "He wants to marry me and take me away from all this."

"And he actually thinks you will? That I believe even less." Flora shook her head. "Men."

The whole of the fifth floor had been servants' quarters when Oz was a boy. After the death of his parents, Oz had found Wong, who ran the household efficiently and preferred to dwell on the ground floor near the kitchen. The fifth floor had been a storage area until Esther came to work for Oz.

At the time, Oz was making photographic studies of tenement life, much as Jacob Riis had done. He prowled the Lower East Side at night with Esther at his side translating for him. Esther also held the container after Oz ignited the cartridges of magnesium flash powder necessary for making photographs at night. All the while Wong sat in the carriage, ever their vigilant protector.

Because it was often night work and because Esther lived as a boarder in a tiny airless room on the Lower East Side, Oz had insisted she move into the unoccupied top floor of his house.

He had constructed a flat for her. A sitting room, a bedroom, and a private bath. The rooms were bright, filled with color and the scent of fresh flowers. The furniture was tasteful and spare, put together from what had been stored there. Through the open windows came the hushed sounds of the street below.

Esther explained this all to Flora as they removed their hats and sat down in her tiny parlor.

"Will you have a smoke?" Flora asked. She took a battered tin of Cycles from her bag, opened it and offered one to Esther.

"No, thank you."

"All us girls are doing it."

"I know."

"On the sly of course."

Esther had observed Flora puffing away

on the street, not so much on the sly.

"Okay," Flora said, lighting up. "It's nice here."

"Yes, isn't it?"

"A little unconventional, don't you think, living with an unmarried man?"

"You're not someone anyone would call conventional yourself, Miss Cooper."

"Why don't you just call me Flora and I'll call you Esther?"

"Okay. Flora."

"Okay. Esther." She shoved her cigarette into the corner of her mouth and rummaged around in her bag, finally pulling out a small notepad. Taking the yellow pencil from its usual resting place, she said, "So what do you know about Delia Swann?"

A discreet knock brought Wong into the room with a tea tray. He set it up for them on the low table in front of the sofa and left without a word.

"Don't you get the feeling that he was standing and listening right outside the door?" Flora asked.

"No doubt. Wong feels part of his job is to watch over us. And he does it well. Cream and sugar, Flora?"

"Yes. So what do you know about Delia Swann?"

Esther prepared the tea and handed a cup

to Flora. "As you said, I have been doing studies of the demimondes of New York. Delia posed for me."

Flora made a show of examining the Spode china cup she was holding.

Unnerved by the silence, Esther said, "For the Creator's sake if you have something to say, out with it."

Setting down her cup, Flora said, "Sophie's afraid. And when I told you about Mulroony, I saw you were, too. What are you afraid of?"

"I don't know. And if I knew, I certainly wouldn't tell you. I shouldn't want to see it in the *Herald.*" Esther moved the plate of tea cakes closer to Flora.

"You can trust me." Flora ate a tea cake in two quick bites.

"Really?" Esther's tone was filled with irony.

"Okay." Returning the pencil to her hair, Flora folded her notepad and put it back in her bag. "Off the record. Talk to me. I know I can help. I won't print anything unless you give me permission. Just talk to me." She raised her teacup to her lips and sipped. "I feel there's something going on here that's more than a whore's murder. Two people are dead." Flora was so intent, she hardly noticed her feet running on the floor though she sat in place with her teacup rattling against the saucer in her hand.

Should she trust Flora? Esther wasn't sure. The girl was independent and clever. She knew John Tonneman liked her. He'd told her he believed she might marry Bo some day.

"Delia was here posing for me on the day she disappeared."

"How do you know it was the same day?"

"She never returned to Sophie's. No one saw her alive after she left here, late last Tuesday afternoon."

"Then you may very well be the last person to have seen her alive."

"Except for the murderer."

"Except for the murderer," Flora repeated studying Esther's visibly distressed face. "What did Delia say to you? She must have been here for a while."

"She was."

"What time did she leave?"

"Five, perhaps. No later than five-thirty. She seemed frightened. I asked her if there was something I could do for her. She told me she was working it out."

"Working what out?"

"What belonged to her, she said. She would at long last get what was rightfully hers by law."

Flora took another cake; she tapped it on her cup. "The question then is who was Delia before she was a whore. Who she was before she became Delia Swann." The cake fell into the tea. Unabashed, Flora drank the contents of the cup down. "If we could find out who she was, maybe we would know why she was murdered."

"How would you do that? I mean, find out who she was."

"I'm a journalist. If there's a way, I'll find it."

"But what about the patrolman? Why was he killed?"

"She was dead when he found her. What else, do you suppose, he found?" Flora stood. "Sophie knows more than she's saying. She most likely knows Delia Swann's real name." Pinning her crushed hat back on her head, Flora was suddenly anxious to leave. "Thank you for talking to me. If you think of anything else, please telephone me at the *Herald.*" She produced a card and wrote another number under that of the *Herald.* "This is where I have a room. If you leave a message for me, I'll get it." Handing Esther the card, she said, "And Esther, I wouldn't go out alone until the murderer is found."

"I won't be frightened into being a prisoner in my own house."

"I understand." Flora smiled. "I wouldn't either." She offered Esther her hand like a man, and Esther took it. They had reached an understanding.

CHAPTER 16

Monday, June 26. Midafternoon.

It had been five days since Patsy had found the naked dead lady and snagged the treasure. He had it safe, wrapped in a cloth and pinned on the inside of his threadbare trousers. His so-called friends, Butch, Tom, and Colin, never let Patsy out of their sight.

A mean one, Butch was, him of the orange hair and the big hands that swelled up when he hit people. Patsy, the runt of the gang, small and wiry, had fought for what was his.

Butch had snatched Patsy by the hair and smashed him in the face for his stubbornness, but Patsy got away, less some hair and with a black eye and a bloody nose. But with the treasure.

They walked along Delancey, looking for castoff smokes in the gutter, trying to figure a way to steal money for food.

Butch picked up a cigar butt and lit it. Through the smoke he said, "If we sold the fecking treasure Patsy's hoarding, we'd be eating high off the hog right now."

From the looks that passed between Colin and Tom, Patsy was sure Butch was boiling up for another go for the treasure. To keep Butch at bay, Patsy offered and the rest agreed: they would divvy up whatever they got. But Patsy would keep it in his possession until they did.

They walked and ran and bounced along with Butch nagging at Patsy, punching and pinching him like he was playing. But Patsy knew Butch wasn't playing — he was dead serious.

At Ninth Street, a large painted sign on the side of a three-story brick building announced that Morris Siegel bought and sold gold and jewelry.

"What about there?" Tom asked.

"No kikes," Butch yelled.

They continued walking.

"We ought to sell it uptown so the bulls can't trace it back to us," Colin said.

"Koch," Butch said. "A German, married my cousin. His da's a faker on Tenth and Second."

"How come you never mentioned him before?" Colin demanded.

Colin was a dark one, in complexion and temperament, what they called the Black

Irish, inky hair and a strong nose. He was almost as big as Butch and on some days thought he was as tough.

Butch glared at Colin.

Colin glared back. Not today, he thought. "Koch, it is."

At Tenth Street, Patsy grew nervous. Butch had all the cards. These were Butch's relatives and friends they were going to. "No."

"What?" Butch roared.

"I changed my mind."

Ever Butch's toady, Tom cried, "But you said —"

"Patsy found it," Colin yelled over the rest. "He decides." The four stood in the middle of the street arguing. Around them rolled carts and wagons dragged by tired old horses.

A carter yelled, "Get outta the gutter."

"You're holding up the parade," an ice wagon driver hollered.

"Quit your yapping," Butch howled. Much the way he had attacked Patsy, he grabbed the ice nag's mane and kicked the creature. The driver swatted Butch across the side of the head with his stick, sending Butch flying into horse dung.

The other boys burst out laughing seeing Butch sitting in the pile of shit. They held their noses, crying, "Stinky, stepped in shit. Stinky. Phew."

When they stopped laughing, Patsy said, "What about the sheeny's place we passed on Ninth Street? If he tries anything we could make easy work of him."

So, choosing to do business with the Jew because a Jew was safe, and to thwart Butch, Patsy ran back to Ninth Street. The others followed.

Patsy had thought the Jew's shop was in a three-story brick building. But instead it was in a cramped lean-to built against the building.

"Look at this," Butch shouted, coming up behind them, stinking of dung. "He's so fecking poor he'll offer us less than any other Yid."

Colin had to agree. "And that's nothing."

"Let's ask him anyways," Patsy insisted. "Just to get a price."

But when they went in, and Patsy started to unpin the rag wrapping from inside his trousers, the skull-capped, barrel-chested young man behind the makeshift counter shook his head. "I can't help you, boyos. Ain't you heard? The cops is mad as hell and coming down on everybody because one of theirs got hisself killed." Still, as he spoke, he leaned toward Patsy. "You want to show me what you got there?"

"Let's go," Butch said, shoving Patsy aside. "We don't want to do business with you anyways."

Siegel was not at all unhappy to hear this. He'd spent two weeks in the Tombs last time the cops got annoyed at him.

Back in the street, Butch spat at the shack. "Did you hear that son of a bitch? 'Boyos' he called us. Like he had a right. I'm going to smash his hut and then him."

"Think you can?" Tom asked. "He ain't so small."

Butch backhanded Tom, sending the runty boy sprawling. Although a mite bigger than Patsy, Tom was obviously not as hard as his friends. Tears welled in his eyes, but he forced them back. Running his grubby fingers through his fair hair, he got to his feet and waited for whatever was going to happen next.

"Forget about it," said Colin. "It's not like the Jew did us any wrong."

"He killed our Lord," Butch snarled. "That's enough for me. I'm smashing his shack."

At that moment Morris Siegel appeared in his doorway, a shiny Cavalry sword in his right hand.

"Fecking kike bastard," Butch said. "We're

going back to Tenth Street."

"No, we ain't," Patsy replied, hackles up at the menace in Butch's eye.

Suddenly Butch's meaty hands shot out. He tore Patsy's pants and seized the rag-wrapped package. "Now, we'll do things my way." The three took off and left Patsy holding up his pants, screaming.

Morris Siegel, who'd seen the larceny, shook his head at all gentiles and retreated into his shack.

Looking about wildly, Patsy spotted a length of rope hanging from the back of a wagon. He yearned to noose it round Butch's neck. Instead, he tied his pants up with it and followed the others.

But when they got to the shop on Tenth Street, Koch, the faker, told them the same thing the Jew had. "I don't even want to look at it. If I'm tempted I might end up with a club on my head. The coppers is rousting everyone."

On the street Patsy got his nerve up. "Give it back."

"Or what?" Butch raised his fists.

"Nothing," Patsy mumbled.

The four, broke and hungry, trudged back to their crib on Broome Street behind Dinty's Saloon. Rushing growlers all night gained them enough change for one bowl of stew, and a taste of beer, but they went to sleep with rumbling stomachs.

Patsy's stomach hurt so much it woke him. Butch was snoring to beat the band, in his hand the rag holding the treasure. Patsy seethed. Using an empty beer bucket, Patsy clobbered the bastard's dome, stole back his treasure, and bolted.

CHAPTER 17

Monday, June 26. Afternoon. To Tuesday, June 27. Morning.

His feet were bleeding. Butch had taken his shoes, so Patsy had been forced to run off without them. But still he ran, bloody feet or not, clutching the treasure in his hand. Panting, Patsy slipped into an alley. He rested his head against a water barrel taller than he was and caught his breath.

With no pin to be had, Patsy placed the rag-wrapped prize into the one pocket that Butch hadn't torn away. On tiptoes, he lifted the cover of the barrel, reached in, cupped his hand and quenched his thirst.

He should hide here for a while in case they were out looking for him. Patsy settled himself on the ground behind the water barrel. He'd have to be watchful. Eventually, they would tire of the chase.

In the end, he had little patience for waiting. He came out the heel end of the alley and circled round till he was in front of Morris Siegel's lean-to against the brick building on Ninth Street.

But no one was there.

Exhausted, the boy tried the door to the building but it, too, was locked. He tottered round to the back, huddled himself into a ball, and collapsed into fitful sleep.

In the morning when the sun glared him awake, he thought to wait for the faker, Morris Siegel, but thirst and hunger changed his mind. He wasn't going back downtown where Butch was. Uptown it was.

At Fourteenth Street, he drank and washed at a horse trough.

Sitting on the curb he watched pigeons stealing oats from an old bay's feed bucket. He edged over and, gripping his cap, tried to capture a bird. Several more attempts brought only laughs from two carters starting their day gnawing on crusts of bread.

"Give me a piece of bread. I ain't eaten since yesterday."

"Go away. I ain't got enough for myself."

"How about a penny, then?"

"Scat, you little bastard." The carter brought his fist up.

Patsy turned away. He didn't know what to do. On his home ground at least he knew where he could cadge some food.

The best he could think of was to work on a pigeon, which he could do anywhere. But he needed to set a trap. A box and a stick would do it. He'd seen such in the lot back of where Morris Siegel's shop was. All he needed was bait.

Using his cap as a glove again, he scooped up a handful of oats and ran, heading downtown. The two carters didn't even give him the respect of shouting, let alone chasing after him.

At Ninth, he tried Siegel again. Still not there. He found the box and stick just where he thought they'd be, among the rubble in the lot behind the brick building. He sprinkled oats on the ground, tied his pants rope to the stick and used it to prop the box over the bait. Then he waited for a pigeon to walk under the box.

The sun was noon high and still no Siegel. Worse, no pigeon. And Patsy had eaten more than half his bait.

Finally, a sparrow came nibbling at the oats.

Patsy pulled the stick. The sparrow was trapped.

Now what? There was not much meat on a sparrow.

Wearing the cap as a glove again, Patsy lifted the box and felt for the sparrow. The small bird squirmed in his hand. Patsy tore the box away. Next, he had to find a fire to cook his breakfast. All he had to do was squeeze and the bird would be ready for the fire.

"What you doing down there, boy?" The shout came from an old woman, her head and shoulders halfway out a second-floor window of the redbrick building. "Jacob, go see what that boy is doing out back."

Patsy knew he had to get out of there. He ran toward the lean-to. And smack into Colin.

"I got him, I got him," Colin screamed, grabbing Patsy's arm.

The sparrow fluttered out of Patsy's hand, as Patsy set his foot behind Colin and pushed, tripping Colin up. "No, you ain't." Patsy broke into a staggered run, holding up his falling down knickers, dodging past carts and horses, crossing the street. He could hear the others yelling to each other as they followed him and locals comments.

"Ahoy, boy. I think your pants is too loose," someone shouted.

"Here, you kids," another called.

A horse reared, upsetting its cart. Milk spilled on the cobblestones. Behind Patsy, they were slipping and sliding all over the place. He burst out laughing, but didn't slow down.

"Where's the coppers when you want them?" a hackney driver demanded.

But the boys were still behind him, even gaining on him, as Patsy ran farther and farther east. If he wasn't careful he'd end up in the river. If he hadn't stopped to trap the bird . . .

"There he is!" Tom screamed. "I got him."

They came thundering down the street at him, toppling pushcarts, with people jumping out of the way, everyone screaming.

A shrill whistle cut the air. "Shit," Patsy said, "now the cops is in it." Out of the corner of his eye, he saw the blue uniforms, two of them. And behind him he heard the pounding feet of his friends, getting closer and closer. He kept running, head turning, feet pumping, smelling the river now. Maybe he could lose them in the water. That was crazy. He couldn't swim.

"Get him!" Butch's voice had murder in it.

Patsy could almost feel their breath on him.

Another whistle slashed the air.

Tom's hand caught Patsy's shirt. Patsy's legs spun in the air. The shirt tore when Patsy jumped. Water closed around him.

Chapter 18

Tuesday, June 27. Morning to twilight.

"Father? It's me, Dutch." No response to his knock. The rectory was silent. Dutch opened the door and called again, "Father? You there?" Nothing. So that was that. He had done as Ma had asked. It wasn't his fault Father Duff wasn't where he was supposed to be. The old priest was probably only going to preach to him about Esther, anyway.

He circled St. Agnes, thinking about Mulroony. The poor bastard had been killed the same way as Delia Swann. Coincidence? Doubtful. Mulroony had seen or figured out something. And the killer either wanted to know what it was, or didn't want anyone else to know what it was. That was why Mulroony had to die.

Or Mulroony could even have been trying a little blackmail on the side.

Dutch stood in front of the church. The

four steps leading inside were grooved by generations of worshipers. The flower garden in front was dried out. Pigeons picked at the parched earth, coming away with nothing. The Madonna to the left and her companion St. Agnes, to the right, no longer pristine white, defaced by the scars and nicks of time, looked like they'd been in a fight and both had lost. The past few years St. Agnes Church had been going down a steep hill.

A flash of sunlight bounced off one of the stained windows and forced Dutch to close his eyes. He wasn't superstitious but he was Irish, and he was Meg Clancy's son. Suddenly he felt like the worst of sinners.

He hurried into the church, genuflected, blessed himself with holy water. Here and there, old women, their covered heads bowed, were like black dots on the worn pews. The scent of incense was strong, hanging like a divine cloud from the vaulted ceiling. He inhaled the fragrance and stared at the cross above the altar with Catholic eyes. No denying, it was wonderful to be a Catholic. And terrible.

It was true Dutch Tonneman wasn't with the Seven. It was also true he and Bo had worked very different jobs before Commissioner York chose them for his special squad, which made them not like the rest of the force.

But that was before Mulroony. The patrolman's death had changed everything. Every cop in New York, including the special squad and the fat-assed desk sergeants, along with the rank and file, had one mission now: find the villain who'd dared to kill a member of the force. And put him down.

And if they caught Delia Swann's killer in the process, good enough.

Bo chose to follow the saloons and blind pigs. Dutch's route took him to the whorehouses, of which there were plenty. If he back-tracked the trail from Mulroony's finding the body of Delia Swann, he might find the answer. With his suspicions of Sophie Mandel and Leo Stern very much on Dutch's mind, he made Sophie's nest his first stop.

Just over the door of No. 79 Clinton the red globe of an electric light glowed faintly in the twilight. Off to the left hung a red-tasseled pull. Dutch gave it a yank.

The bell inside played seven notes. Esther had told him they were from "Mendelssohn's Wedding March" from *A Midsummer's Night Dream.*

He'd suggested to Esther in that case, when she married him, they could have the service performed right outside Sophie's. She had responded to his joke with one of her stern looks. Well, perhaps it wasn't the joke that she didn't like. Perhaps it was that he'd said *when* she married him, not *if* she would marry him.

He gave the red tassel another yank.

"Some gentleman's real anxious to be coming —" Daisy, Sophie's tiny African maid, was already talking as she opened the door. The girl, immaculate in her white lacy apron over her black silk dress, curtsied, and more demurely said in her deep honeyed tones, "Sorry, Detective Tonneman, thought you was a customer."

"Miss Sophie around, Daisy?" He knew damn well Sophie was there. Now, at twilight, was when the real action at the house began. He set his foot inside the door.

"Miss Sophie's not available now, Detective. Maybe you'll come back tomorrow?"

"Maybe not." Firmly forcing entry, Tonneman would have walked through the little maid had she not stepped quickly aside. "Tell her I want to see her."

Daisy, recovering, said, "Will you have a drink?"

"No." On the wall, to the left of the entranceway, was a line of scrolled wooden clothing hooks. Glancing at the mirror below, Dutch tossed his derby onto one of the hooks. "Tell Leo I'll talk to him."

"Mr. Leo is otherwise eng—"

Dutch turned and stared at Daisy.

"I'll fetch him right away, Captain, sir."

When Leo arrived, he was dressed for work except — Dutch had never before seen Leo wearing a skullcap. Leo's black suit, Dutch reckoned, would cost a week of Dutch's hard-earned wages. His white silk shirt and fancy red tie would probably cut deep into another week.

"What can I do for you, Captain?" Leo spoke through the cigar gripped between his gold teeth. His fingers shaped his well-waxed mustache into fine points. The tinkling of piano music came from the parlor.

"When did you get religion, Leo?"

Leo patted the yarmulke on his pomaded hair. "That's none of your business."

A ring of a bell, and Daisy rushed to answer the mother of pearl telephone that stood on the hall table. Both Dutch and Leo watched the colored girl unhook the ear piece and place it close to her ear.

"Good evening, Miss Sophie's residence," she said, breathing honey into the candlestick receiver.

"Hmph," Dutch muttered.

"Let's go." Leo indicated the lush parlor room, where Piano Man was loosening his fingers for the evening.

If the lanky Negro had another name, only Sophie knew it. He was a stylish man, his snappy straw skimmer banded in red, vest the same color. No tie adorned his throat. The crisp blue polka dot shirt was secured with a glistening ruby collar button. Red garters held his pulled back sleeves. A cigarette was suspended from his heavy lips, hiding pearly teeth. From the pungent odor the man was smoking cannabis, not tobacco.

Near the entrance, Leo pulled another chair over to the flat table where he usually sat when he was keeping watch over the establishment. "Captain?"

"All right." Dutch sat down. "You know a cop named Mulroony?"

"The one who died? Sure. The Seventh is our precinct."

Daisy's dulcet voice could be heard from the vestibule. "We look forward to seeing you at eight."

"Was Mulroony on your payroll?"

"No."

"I'll find out, you know."

Leo's hands traveled from his cigar to his yarmulke to his mustache. "Clinton Street wasn't his beat, but I always gave him a few bucks at Christmas. We have faith in the fine members of our police force."

A bell let off a high-pitched tone. Tonneman heard Daisy turn the crank at the bottom of the telephone, telling Central she'd finished speaking.

"What was Delia Swann to Mulroony?"

"I have no idea. Except, he knew our girls by sight." Leo gave Dutch an exaggerated wink. "Of course, sometimes he didn't just look."

"Was she one of the girls he didn't just look at?"

"No. He liked his women with more flesh on them. Is Mulroony's killing connected to Delia's?" The innocent phrasing and wide-eyed look gave the whore man away.

"You know damn well it is," Dutch said.

"Well, ain't that interesting."

"Who was Delia Swann, Leo? I think you and Sophie know. I suggest you consider Mulroony's fate and not keep any information from the police."

Leo put on a wounded look. "Why would we keep anything from you? Aren't you cops as good as our *mishpocheh* — they should only live and be well — who we also support?"

Angry, Dutch pushed back the chair and

rose. He stuck his face in Leo's. "You may be interested to know that Mulroony's uniform was sliced up much as Delia's clothing was. The murderer was looking for something. If he didn't find it, he'll come after Sophie."

They were interrupted by Piano Man shifting from tinkling into a rag. The piano's lid was up to magnify its sound.

Leo seemed to have forgotten all about Tonneman as he listened to the music.

The Negro usually stood, skipping left and right, playing all the time, ragged or sweet. Now he went from rag back to sweet, coaxing pretty tones from the Steinway, while Myrtle Mae, dressed for business in her sheer peignoir over a frilly corset, adjusted her silk stockings under her red garters, leaned back against the piano, and trilled.

Finally, Leo said, "I'll keep what you say in mind, Tonneman. And you better keep in mind that if the murderer is looking for something, he'll try your fancy lady friend, sooner than he'll try my Sophie."

Chapter 19

Tuesday, June 27. Night.

"Ey." Benito Scarpa muffled his second cry with a hand over his mouth.

"What?" Pancetta gave him the evil eye. "You're scaring the fish."

"My oar hit something."

"Well haul it out, cucumber head." She laughed as softly as she could. No sense letting the water cops know they were here.

Shipping his oars, Benito leaned over and felt around in the water. "Look at this." He pulled a sodden mass halfway into the boat. "Fish food."

"Watch it, fool," Pancetta cried. "You want to sink us?"

Benito did not look at the immense woman who sat like a queen, taking up one half of the rowboat. Nor did he give voice to his thoughts. It was only by the Grace of Jesus and Mary that they had not sunk already what with her fat ass forcing the boat deeper into the water whenever she moved.

Every night they came out and patrolled and fished, throwing out their net. And every night he feared the watery grave. With another tug, he brought the body into the boat.

"What you got?" Shielding the bull's-eye battery lamp with the tail of her shawl, Pancetta switched it on.

"A boy." Benito searched the boy's sodden clothing for coins. "Nothing."

"Too small. Throw him back." Pancetta laughed like one of the foghorns.

Benito crossed himself. Whispering a Hail Mary, he eased the boy back into the water. It was her joke, but she was right. "It's the best," Benito said, over the splash. "He's dead."

"Too bad about that kid," Pancetta said, later that night, fish blood running like wine down her jaw. The small mackerels that threatened to slip out of their net on their nightly jaunts was her favorite delicacy. She ate them raw. "Micks love mackerel. That's why they call them mackerel snappers."

"But at least they cook them."

"Ey, what do the Irish know? What the hell do you know? This is good stuff. Here, you try." She shoved a slimy offering in his face.

"Get away." Bad enough he had to work with the Pig Woman, bad enough she was always grabbing his thing and talking about them together. Now she wanted him to eat her raw fish.

"Bah, you don't know what you're missing," Pancetta said, taking the mackerel for herself.

Something bumped the boat. "Not again," Benito groaned. "Please, God."

"That dead sprat is back. This time weight him down."

Once again Benito searched about in the water. "Nothing."

"Let's get out of here," Pancetta said. "I've had my antipasto, now I'm hungry."

Benito started to tow in the net. "Give me a hand," he said. "The fish are heavy tonight."

"Men," Pancetta sneered. "You're really helpless." She gave a mighty yank and the net came into the boat.

"Basta," Benito groaned.

Caught in the net was a chunk of driftwood. And attached to the driftwood was another body.

The boat rocked like a seesaw when Pancetta stood up.

"Sit down, woman," Benito snarled. "Or we'll both end up like this one."

Bristling, Pancetta, nevertheless, sat heavily, splashing more water into the boat.

They both looked down at their haul. Another boy, dead as the one before.

Coughing, the boy rolled over on his stomach.

"Aha," Benito cried. He began to slap the boy on the back. Half the river filled the bottom of the boat.

"Shit," Pancetta spat.

Patsy heard. He blinked, sputtered. Someone was smacking him on the back. It was dark as the grave, but he was alive. He could feel the breeze of the river, smell fish. He got another smack on the back. "Hey, leave off!" he cried.

"God is good," Benito said. He stopped smacking the boy's back and helped him sit up.

Damn, Patsy thought, searching his mouth with his swollen tongue. He'd placed his treasure in his mouth for safety and now it was gone.

Part II

Chapter 20

Thursday, June 29. Evening.

With the advent of the automobile, Battling Jack West foresaw that sooner rather than later the carriage business would cease to be profitable. That was why there was a new legend on the redbrick wall of his carriage house and stable in Macdougal Alley, behind his townhouse on Washington Square North.

Right under the recessed sign for his horse and carriage service, the newer sign, painted in block letters, black on a gray shingle, said simply "CONFIDENTIAL INVESTIGATIONS. JACK WEST."

Six months earlier, Jack West bought a small advertisement with the same tasteful inscription to run weekly, in the *Herald* and the *Post.*

The client, obviously a gentleman by his dress and fine manners, had arrived at the carriage house just after dark. Jack guided the client to the second and top floor where he conducted his detective business. He noticed that the young man favored his left leg.

"Started to rain, has it?" Jack asked.

The client nodded, sat down in the chair opposite Jack's desk and got right to it. His story was that his mistress had been set upon by thieves and killed. He'd given her a heart-shaped locket and it had been stolen. The gentleman wanted to retrieve the locket because it was an heirloom belonging to his wife and in a fit of passion he had given it to his lady friend. The truth? It did not matter.

But the twenty dollar gold piece did. Jack slipped it into his vest pocket.

"That's not much to go on, heart-shaped. What else is there about the locket that will help us to identify it?"

"It's about the size of a nickel."

"Is that it?"

The client thought for a moment. "Just bring me every heart-shaped locket close to that size you find." When Jack frowned, the young man added, "In addition to your fee I'll pay you one dollar for each bogus locket and fifty dollars for the right one."

"I could go out and buy hundreds of

nickel-sized heart-shaped lockets for fifty cents."

The client measured Jack. "But you won't."

Jack West nodded. "You understand the holiday will set us back a few days, what with businesses closed." Traditionally, the City closed down for a huge celebration on the Fourth of July.

"There is some urgency," the client replied.

On leaving Jack's house the young man circled the block. Only then did he, in spite of his limp, set off apace to Thompson Street two blocks away.

What he didn't know was that Little Jack Meyers, the best hire Jack West had ever made, was right behind him. Jack West liked to know as much about his clients as possible. Their means more than their names.

With one last examination of his surroundings, the client strode to a parked Benz motor car, cranked it up, climbed in, and drove away.

Jack West proceeded by sending Little Jack round to all the fakers and uncles, starting downtown and working his way up, hot dusty day after hot rainy day. Jeweler after pawn shop.

At the end they had not one but five heart-shaped lockets, one badly dented, another with a broken hinge. Still, opined Jack Meyers, the odds were good. One of them had to be the locket the client was after.

But Little Jack was wrong.

CHAPTER 21

Wednesday, July 12. Afternoon and evening. On this particular day, the sun was high and blazing when Little Jack stopped near Madison Square and bought an ice cream sandwich from a vendor. Rotating it to keep licking up the drip, he continued uptown.

Twenty-five shops later he was at Forty-second Street, where Broadway and Seventh Avenue met. Long Acre Square. The sweat was dripping off him.

Hammerstein's new Victoria Theatre on Forty-second Street and Seventh Avenue had a show called *The Rogers Brothers in Wall Street.* Not six months before, the area had been shacks and falling-down stables. Now Hammerstein was building his Republic Theatre in the square. Recognizing a good thing, the silk hat brothels and taverns had already begun moving in, in hopes of large profits.

Well north of here was mostly undeveloped land. Although some farms remained on the west side of the Central Park, private homes and apartment buildings were going up above Sixtieth Street. Carriage factories and blacksmith shops were part of the landscape, but the automobile would put an end to that all too quickly.

Soon enough the subway would open upper Manhattan to development; land had become increasingly valuable, and the small farms were all but finished. But that was of no concern to the speculators who were determined to make their fortunes on the building of the subway.

The next shop Little Jack visited was owned by a faker whose sign said he was A. Siegel. The small place huddled under the dark and dingy Ninth Avenue El. A pale, narrow-shouldered man removed the jeweler's glass from his eye and frowned at Jack.

"You got something to sell?"

"To buy, if you got it," Jack said in Yiddish, which brightened the man a trifle. "A locket, heart shaped."

"Yeh." Siegel's Yiddish was with a Russian inflection. "One of that gang of pickpockets came in with one last week, to sell outright. They usually go straight to the dago across the street because he sends them out and buys what they bring back. Two bits, is what I offered. Wasn't worth more. He laughed in my face. I watched him take it across the street."

Salvatore Galipo's shop window was so grimy you could hardly see through. A couple of toughs were at the edge of the pavement playing toss penny. One had a sailor's pigtail, the other was dark like an Indian.

Keeping a weather eye on the pair, Little Jack peered into the shop. It was filled with old lamps, dusty furniture. In the back was a jewelry case.

The fact that Galipo was Italian made Little Jack wary. There were stories about bandittos pulling a switch on the badger game, where a mark was nailed for being found with a compromising item of property.

Well, there was nothing for it. He would go inside and see if Galipo had the locket. When Little Jack opened the door, a bell clanged overhead. The two at the curb kept tossing their coins. Jack walked in and shut the door.

Suddenly, something hairy flew by his face. He ducked, losing his nerve for a moment. The huge, hairy thing landed on the jewelry case next to an oil lamp and meowed loud enough to wake the dead. It woke the cadaverous man sleeping in the rocking chair. His squinty eyes fixed on Little Jack.

"What you want?"

"Maybe you have a nice gold locket?"

"Maybe." Yawning, the man reached up and pulled the long-haired gray cat down on his lap. "Dolce," he whispered in the cat's ear as he stroked it.

The creature meowed, opening its mouth wide, baring ferocious teeth, then purred.

"So show me," Little Jack said. He didn't like cats. They was just furry rats.

Languidly, Galipo set the cat on the floor and got to his feet. He brushed the top of the case with the sleeve of his shabby gray coat, then set a worn square of black velvet on the case. He reached inside the case, taking his time picking out what he sought.

Little Jack moved from foot to foot in an attempt to discourage the loudly purring cat, who had attached itself to him and was brushing back and forth against his legs.

Onto the black velvet Galipo placed two lockets. Both were heart shaped; one was smaller than a nickel, the other was larger. "Which one?"

Little Jack studied each. "How much?"

"Fifty. Each."

"Cents?"

"You a wise guy? I don't like wise guys. Fifty bucks. Each."

"Too much."

"For both."

Jack squelched a laugh at the ridiculous drop in price. He let it out as he headed for the door.

"Thirty for both."

Jack measured the man for a moment. "I'll get the moolah and come back."

"Make it quick," Galipo said.

When Little Jack left the shop, the two penny tossers followed. Galipo shouted Italian at them and they went back to their game.

Taking the Elevated, Little Jack was at Macdougal Alley in half an hour. Jack West listened to his report, then hitched up the old Victoria. They drove up Broadway.

"You think Galipo will be straight?" Little Jack asked.

"I doubt it."

"Do we go in together?"

"No. You alone. I'm the element of surprise."

"If we go in together," Little Jack said, "they might not try anything."

"You go in alone. Unless you're afraid."

"I'm not afraid."

Jack West grinned. "I thought that's what

you'd say."

When Little Jack came out of Galipo's shop, he made a great show of patting his fob pockets to let Battling Jack know he'd done his job.

Battling Jack twitched Sullivan's reins ever so lightly. But before Little could reach the Victoria, he was surrounded by four derby-hatted toughs with brass knuckles.

Two of the hooligans, the one with the pigtail and his partner, were near Battling Jack's size. The dark one and his mate, though smaller, still outweighed and out-sized Little Jack. And they had sticks.

Battling Jack retrieved the stick at his feet. His stick was bigger and heavier. He licked his chops as if he was settling down for dinner.

Shouting like a male banshee, Jack West leaped from the Victoria, knocking down the *schwarz.* With one pass of his stick he swept the other to the ground to join his comrade. Face to face with the third, Jack West swept the derby from the tough's hairless head, and swinging back, smacked him with the stick.

Little Jack, with the best of intentions, came running to do his part. His intentions were better than his step, which went right into horseshit. He slid to the curb and cracked his head on a lamp post.

Shakily, he got to his feet as a body flew to the left, now one to the right. The pig-tailed one attempted to crawl away. Jack West kicked him in the ass, spun around, gave the bald one a taste of the same boot in the chin, and continued his villain tossing.

Little tottered across the street, panting for breath, just as the last of the criminals was running off.

Smirking, Battling Jack pushed his hat to the back of his head. "Glad you could make it."

Across town at the Waldorf-Astoria, the Automobile Club of America gathered for its second meeting. The occasion was marked by an official group portrait photograph made by their co-charter member, Oswald Cook.

When Oz arrived with Esther, all the gentlemen rose. They had heard of her. Who had not? And not one of them quite understood the relationship between Oz Cook and his protégé. Still, they were curious, and titillated.

Oz didn't care for the muted murmur that spread around the room, where the members of the Automobile Club of America stood or sat, smoking their cigars, drinking their brandy.

If one listened carefully once could detect a certain coldness in his voice. "Gentlemen, may I present my associate, Miss Esther Breslau, who will help me make our photograph this evening."

Two bellboys followed, carrying a wooden tripod and a case of eight-by-ten-inch glass plates. Oz himself carried the Graflex, while Esther took charge of the lenses and cartridges of magnesium flash powder, which, in spite of the electric lighting, would be necessary for a sharply defined indoor portrait. At Oz's request the bellboys waited by the door.

Esther, dressed impeccably in a well-fitted suit of blue-and-white-striped silk and a dark blue hat with an ostrich feather, was immediately surrounded by the Burgoyne brothers, Baby and J.N., each vying for her attention. J.N., the more dashing to the two, brought her hand to his lips.

Impatience was added to Oz's annoyance. "Please, cousins, stand back and let us set up."

"May I be of some help?" William Grimes had found his way to Esther's side. "William Grimes," he said, putting out his hand. When Esther responded with hers, he too raised it to his lips. Esther, who viewed J.N.'s hand kiss as silly, flushed at Grimes's attention. "Charming," Grimes said, as he wondered where he could quarter a fourth mistress. "Don't you agree, Stokes?"

"Oh, indeed," Stokes said. He was quite tired of hearing about Esther Breslau from his in-laws, who considered the woman a threat to his wife's and her brothers' inheritance.

He was not captive to her charms either; he preferred his women fair, with a little more flesh on their bones. Still, she had a certain radiance about her that he found, at this moment, disconcerting. "Come, Grimes," he said. "Let them do what they have to do and have done with it."

Oz arranged the members in two rows on one side of the table, officers sitting and the rest standing. He left a place for himself farthest right, next to Grimes and behind Stokes. He focused the camera, offered a small bow to Esther, then walked to his place.

Esther gazed through the lens. "Hair is blowing."

"Turn off the fans," Oz commanded.

When fans were off, Esther said, "It looks fine." She took the glass plate, fixed it in a wooden holder and inserted it into the back of the camera.

"Very well. Gentlemen, hold your positions. There will be a flash of light, and I will press the shutter. I beg you not to move, even after the shutter is pressed."

She ignited the flash powder and, in the ensuing light, pressed the shutter. The room filled with hazy smoke.

"You can relax now," Esther said, after a wait of several minutes. "But don't move from your stations."

"Fans," Oz called.

Esther removed the glass plate and returned it to the box, inserted another plate into the holder and placed the holder into the back of the camera. By this time, thanks to the fans, the smoke had abated.

"Are you ready, gentlemen?"

"Fans," Baby called. He and J.N. smirked and elbowed each other.

The bellboys looked to Oz, who nodded.

When the fans were off, Esther said, "And again." Using another magnesium powder cartridge, she went through the same process.

Before Esther could say the photograph had been made, J.N. shouted, "Fans."

Baby echoed him. While Esther returned the plate to its case and the lens to its leather pouch, Oz collected the detritus from the used magnesium cartridges. He folded the tripod and handed it to one of the bellboys, signaling the other to take the case of glass plates.

The Burgoyne brothers, seizing an opportunity, led the advance of the members of the Automobile Club as they clustered around her. Oz was furious, even more so when he saw that J.N. was attempting to draw Esther away from the others.

"Excuse me, gentlemen, but Miss Breslau has graciously given us some of her evening. The rest belongs to her."

Esther smiled. "Thank you for being such good subjects." Her accent was exotic to the ears of these members of the Episcopal establishment.

"A delightful young woman," Whitney Lyon said, moments after Esther exited the room.

"Charming," Grimes said.

Baby and J.N. half smiled and half glared at each other.

Once the distracting presence of Esther Breslau was gone, the members of the Automobile Club were eager to get down to business, for the night was still young, and no one thought of returning home before a late supper and, perhaps, other diversions.

Copies of a draft of the by-laws were

passed around and read aloud by William Grimes. Certain corrections and additions were suggested and voted upon. After which, the by-laws were accepted.

A committee, headed by Harrison Stokes, was formed to approach the mayor regarding the mistreatment of automobile drivers by the police.

Another committee was formed to approach proprietors of large stables for storage areas for the automobiles.

Were he not occupied with the matter of the wallet, Oz Cook would have been bored. He was reminded that he had never enjoyed men's clubs. As it was, the mention of his name broke him out of his musings. His cousin-in-law Harrison Stokes gave him a nudge. Oz looked up. "I beg your pardon?"

Whitney Lyon, affirmed now as chairman, suggested to the group that with Mr. Cook's permission he would like to call for a hearty hip, hip hurray from the membership for Mr. Cook's wonderful gift to "our little club, this photograph he's made for posterity."

"Hear, hear," ran through the group, followed by the called for "Hip, hip, hurray."

Mr. Cook was gracious.

It was agreed that the next meeting would be held in September, after Labor Day.

Chairman Lyon made a motion to adjourn, and it was seconded. Some gentlemen left. The same group that had remained after the previous meeting in June stayed now, enjoying cigars and cognac and male companionship.

"Gentlemen." Oz set his empty glass down. When he had their attention, he began again. "Gentlemen, do you remember last month when we left the Waldorf, we stopped a beating?"

"The drab pickpocket," Stokes said.

Baby nodded.

"The beauty," his brother, J.N. said.

"Stokes, do you remember the billfold?" Oz asked. "Someone was going to return it to the fellow who lost it."

Stokes nodded. "Yes, the billfold."

They all agreed: they remembered the billfold.

"Good," Oz said, "now which of us was going to return it?"

His question fell on blank faces. Grimes shrugged. Baby's brow was wrinkled in sincere thought. No one, it would have appeared, had done the good deed.

Chapter 22

Wednesday, July 12. Afternoon and evening.

Bo felt like singing. Here was his beautiful Flora in her shift coming toward him, her arms outstretched.

All at once a burst of crimson appeared on Flora's rounded bosom.

No! Bo ran to her. "Flora!" he screamed.

But the girl in his arms wasn't Flora Cooper; it was Delia Swann.

Bo's head snapped up. He looked about. It appeared that no one in the Harp had noticed that he'd been sleeping. There was a trace of whiskey left in his glass. Bo poured a healthy portion from his bottle and drank, getting his mind back to why he was out this night.

Mulroony. Who killed Mulroony? And the girl, Delia. In the investigation of murders Bo found that visiting the saloons was always a good way to learn things.

The door opened and in lurched Wingy

Noonan. Just the man Bo was looking for. Bo wiggled his index finger and scraggly-bearded Wingy stumbled over.

"Good evening to you, Mr. Clancy. Good to see you again. My, the state of me right arm is pathetic today. Got hurt in the war, you know," he said, presenting the supposedly injured arm to Bo. "It's a mite thirsty I am, Mr. Clancy, sir."

Bo closed his right eye. His other eyebrow lifted and arched. "And how will you be quenching your thirst without the use of your good right arm, I'd like to know?" Wingy carried his arm all twisted, but everyone knew the arm was sound as a silver dollar.

"Why I've got an extra standing ready to help out."

Filching a soiled glass from the empty table next to him, Bo emptied its dregs on the floor and poured Wingy the measliest of tastes.

Wingy drank it up and looked at Bo with sad spaniel eyes.

"A cop by the name of Mulroony got himself killed."

"I heard it. Terrible tragic for his poor mother." Wingy crossed himself with the glass in his hand.

Bo gave Wingy another small taste.

"I don't know nothing, Mr. Clancy."

"Wingy, I'm tired. I want to go home to bed. I don't want to be pouring you dribbles of whiskey all night. If you know anything at all, tell me, and I'll pour you a proper drink."

Wingy eyed the half-filled whiskey bottle fervently.

Bo shoved it to him.

Seizing the bottle, Wingy tilted his head and had it near to his mouth before Bo yanked it back.

"Tell me."

Wingy dabbed at the spilled whiskey on his shirt with his "good" left hand and licked his fingers. "Meself, I don't know nothing, Mr. Clancy, honest, but are you acquainted with one Aloysius Rafferty?" He didn't wait for a response from Bo. "Well, he has hisself two jobs. He's a bricklayer but he also works the docks."

"Get to it or I'll crack the bottle on your head."

"Al, he saw Mulroony chasing some kids off just before he found the dead whore in the empty lot a while back."

"And where can I find this Aloysius Rafferty?"

"He likes McSorley's. That's over —"

"I know where McSorley's is." Bo slid the

bottle across the table to Wingy and made for the door. When he turned to wave goodnight to Jimmy Callahan behind the bar, Wingy had just about drained the bottle. His bad right arm seemed fine.

Outside, a carriage was letting someone off on Bleecker Street. A woman alone at this time of night. Damnation. She looked just like Flora. When he drew closer, he saw it wasn't Flora at all, and he was about to lose the moving hack. He placed two fingers in his mouth and whistled.

"I hear you," the cabbie growled, stopping.

"You were meant to." Bo climbed in.

"Where to?"

Instead of McSorley's, Bo said, "The *Herald*."

James Gordon Bennett's *Herald* newspaper made its home in a two-story building in the triangle from Thirty-fourth to Thirty-sixth Streets, where Seventh Avenue crossed Broadway. Bennett ran the newspaper from Paris, France.

In '95, while working on the Robert Roman killing, Bo and Dutch had met Bennett during one of the publisher's infrequent trips to New York.

Neither Bo nor Dutch had known the

story, but back in January of 1877, when James Gordon Bennett Jr. was thirty-five, he'd attended a party at the home of his fiancée, Caroline May, daughter of a prominent New York physician. In his cups, Bennett pissed into the grand piano while party guests bellowed and cried their shock.

The next day, Miss Caroline May informed Bennett that they were no longer engaged. Shortly thereafter, Caroline's brother beat Bennett with a cowhide whip on the steps of the Union Club.

The two men met later out of state on the field of honor. Both fired and missed. Apparently Bennett's aim didn't extend to pistols.

After that, Bennett was no longer welcome in the homes of his former friends in New York, which was why the editor of the *Herald* lived in Paris.

As Bo arrived at the southern entrance of the *Herald* building, he glanced up at the famous clock: the bronze statue of Minerva, posed over two bronze figures with sledgehammers, which they used to sound the hour on a big bell.

He shook his head. Damn, even Minerva looked like Flora. He was in bad shape. "I'd better quit drinking or marry the girl."

That stopped him. "Well, boyo, if you're thinking like that, maybe you'd better turn right around and go have another drink."

"You say something?" a passing man asked.

Bo glared.

The man realized he had an important appointment elsewhere.

Shabby newsie urchins clustered in front of the *Herald* waiting for the next edition. Bo brushed by them and ran up the stairs past the presses, which were surprisingly still.

On the second floor, picking his way between gray walls and cramped desks, he came to the back corner of the room, where Flora Cooper, the girl he thought of as a humdinger, sat.

Flora, green eyeshade on her head, pencil sticking out from her hair, was leaning back in her chair like a man, boot-clad feet on her desk. She was pitching spitballs at the metal shade of the electric lamp hanging from dangling twists of chain nearby.

By the dim light Bo could see that the sheet of paper in her typewriter was glaring white.

"I've come to take you out," Bo said, drawing a chair from the next desk up to Flora's.

"I'm busy," she said. "Is it three months, then?"

"Since when?"

"Since you last asked me." She set her feet on the floor. "You ask me out once every three months. We go out, have a great time. You ignore me for another three months. Then you show up again, and without a by-your-leave, say you've come to take me out." Her hand raked her desk looking for a lost piece of paper or a cigarette. "No more."

Bo drew an Aphrodite from his inside pocket, bit the tip, and lit up. "I'll just sit here, then, and smoke my cigar."

Flora found a loose cigarette on her desk, lit it from Bo's cigar, blew out one perfect smoke ring, and proceeded to type like a demon, her fingers little hammers pounding away on the keys.

Bo was admiring the gray ash on his cigar when she shouted, "Copy."

With the freckled-face boy on his way with her copy, Flora pinned her crushed green hat to her head and announced, "I'm ready."

Bo plucked the pencil from her hair and tossed it on her desk. "Now, you're ready."

On the street Bo asked, "Do you want to go to an Irish saloon?"

Flora's green eyes danced. "What other kind is there?" She hailed a carriage.

"Hey!" Bo was speechless at the woman's audacity.

"Forgive me," Flora said. She didn't look contrite.

The brougham took them to the bottom of the Bowery, near Seventh Street, a neighborhood full of strong smells. The perfume of the slaughterhouses, tanneries, and breweries completely overcame the milder scents of the carpenter shops and brickyards.

Flora read the sign mounted on the redbrick tenement, "Old House at Home."

Bo shrugged. "Everyone calls it for the owner: McSorley's."

"I've heard of it. It's men only."

"Fear not, you're with me." Bo stepped in and held the door gallantly for Flora.

That this was an Irish working man's saloon, there could be no doubt. With a trace of German. Irish and German alike wanted no women where they drank. Few men did.

Flora's reporter's eye caught a quick glimpse of everything all at once before the firehouse gong behind the bar went off with an almost deafening blast, making everyone freeze in place. Two gas lamps hanging over the bar shook. A rod linking the two lamps was festooned with cobweb-covered turkey wishbones. The walls themselves were covered with photographs, paintings, and tear sheets from newspapers.

The place was overrun with cats.

Again the gong sounded loud and clear. "No women, no women," the men jeered. Bill McSorley glowered at Bo.

"I'm Inspector Bo Clancy, and the lady's with me."

"Then no Clancy either," said Bill McSorley, a teetotaler. Like father, like son.

"No Clancy, no Clancy," the men taunted. The gong sounded repeatedly amidst the men's laughter.

On another occasion Bo might have fought for the right of his fair maiden to enter, but Flora Cooper was not one to condone fist-fighting, and Bo knew it. She sailed right out the door onto the street.

He compromised with McSorley on a pitcher of beer and two glasses, along with a quickly assembled plate of the free lunch of soda crackers, cheese, and raw onions. He and Flora sat out at the curb. Cheerless McSorley even sent out a chair for the lady, albeit grudgingly.

But more to the issue, after Bo had a few words with him, McSorley agreed to point out Aloysius Rafferty when he came in.

Bo and Flora drank their beers in silence

while Bo kept his eyes on the saloon.

"Why do I get the feeling you're here on business? You want to tell me what all this is about?" Flora said.

Bo spotted a young chap on the corner, dragging along the Bowery like an old man. He took up the pitcher, saying, "A minute," and stepped inside McSorley's.

When he returned he was puffing Honest Long Cut smoke out of one of the house clay pipes McSorley kept on the bar and carrying a newly filled pitcher of beer, along with three glasses.

"Expecting company?" Flora asked.

Bo pointed at the small fellow with the low-slung belly. He was covered with the reddish gray of brick dust and was bouncing along like a child going to play. "You wouldn't happen to be Aloysius Rafferty, now would you?"

The man stopped in his tracks, his belly shook.

Flora turned away before she smiled.

"And who wants to know?" the plump fellow asked.

Bo poured and held out the glass. "The man who's offering solace at the end of a weary day."

Leaning his head back, Rafferty drank the beer in noisy gulps. "I thank you, sir, whoever you are." He handed over the glass and made for the saloon door.

"So," Bo said, blocking his way, "are you Al Rafferty or not?"

"Who wants to know?"

Flora laughed.

"Inspector Bo Clancy of the New York Police Department. I want to know what you saw the day Officer James Mulroony found the dead body in the lot on South Street."

"Okay, I'm Rafferty." He edged toward the door to the saloon. "Mulroony is it? Well, I don't know if that was when he found the body, but I seen him yelling at some kids."

"What kids?"

"You know, them wharf rats that hang around on the street stealing pennies."

"Describe them."

Rafferty looked at the pitcher.

Flora poured him another glass of beer. She was enjoying herself, missing pencil or not.

"Thank you, miss," Rafferty said, taking a healthy taste. "Four. Clothes all rags." He wiped the foam from his mouth with a dusty sleeve. "Two puny ones. Nine, ten, maybe. The smallest, brown hair, the second, blond or sandy. The other two might be older. Just as raggedy but fit enough to work on the docks. The biggest had orange hair."

"Do you know them?"

"Seen them around but I can't put a name to them. They're in the neighborhood, all the time cadging. Can I go in and have me supper now?"

"Sure," said Bo. "But if you think of anything else I'm at the House on Mulberry Street. Call me on the telephone."

Rafferty let loose a disparaging laugh, sort of bowed as he presented his empty glass to Flora, and hurried into the saloon.

CHAPTER 23

Thursday, July 13. Late afternoon.

"A few cents so I may sup, kind sir." The white-haired man's voice was as frail as the old codger himself.

Dutch dropped several pennies into the unkempt fellow's outstretched hat. He walked into the saloon at Twentieth and Sixth and sat at the last table in the back. Noisy ceiling fans moved the hot air around, but the heat didn't budge. Flies hovered over the free eats, the hard-boileds and the onions on the bar.

He had met Joe Petrosino once before. Stubby, dark, marked with pox, the Italian was easy to recognize. Looking so, it was hard to credit his reputation as a man who went undetected in many disguises.

Still, Detective Petrosino had a good reputation. The Black Hand's chief adversary in New York, in all of America, worked out of the Elizabeth Street station in one of the City's toughest neighborhoods, Mulberry Bend. He'd been years trying to destroy the notorious Italian crime organization.

"Sir." The old man, dilapidated hat now plunked on his head, had followed Dutch into the saloon.

Dutch sighed. "Twice in five minutes is greedy, grandpa."

"I agree."

The vitality in the voice made Dutch look again. After several seconds of inspection, Dutch realized that the old man wasn't so old and that the rags he wore covered a rugged physique.

Dutch grinned. "All right, Petrosino, I'm impressed. But why the play acting? You don't need a disguise to talk to me."

The chief adversary of the Black Hand in America looked around. "You never know. The Black Hand is everywhere. Little Italy. Up in the woods past One Hundredth Street, on the East Side. Why not right on the Ladies Mile with the rich Episcopalians?"

"What?" the squat man behind the bar called to them.

"Two beers," Dutch replied.

"Grappa," Petrosino whispered softly to Dutch.

"One beer, one grappa," Dutch said.

"No grappa, this ain't no wop house. What I got is a jug of dago red."

Petrosino nodded, Dutch said, "Okay."

"I'm not showing off with this getup," Petrosino said. "I just came from the Hudson River docks on Twenty-third Street watching them unload a ship. The Black Hand is stealing some of those shipping companies blind. But I haven't been able to catch them at it."

"Tell me about the Black Hand."

Petrosino settled back on the bench. There was nothing he liked better than educating the Force about his personal nemesis. "It's not one organization. Many are involved. They've learned the American lesson: unity is strength. The better to keep people in a state of fear. But it's merely a seeming unity. The separate parts are always at war against each other."

The bartender banged their drinks on the bar. Dutch got up, laid a dime down, and brought the drinks back.

"Only about four years ago," Petrosino continued, "Don Giosuele, also known as Zio Mico — Uncle Mico — started the Black Hand in his First Avenue saloon, between One Hundred and Ninth and One Hundred and Tenth Streets."

"That's what you mean by up in the woods?" Dutch drank. "A lot of bad Italians in this City."

"And all the Irish are saints." Petrosino crossed himself, tasted his wine, and grimaced. "Don't judge my people too harshly. They have been abused and it has turned them to crime."

"Sure," Dutch said. "And my cousin Seamus breaks into houses because his da beat him."

The Italian cop laughed. "Maybe he's the one who stole the locket everyone is looking for."

Dutch's forehead wrinkled. "What are you talking about?"

"Haven't you got wind of that yet? From Mulberry Bend past Forty-second Street, the gonifs are all looking for a gold locket."

Inwardly, Dutch smiled. The pieces were coming together. This had to be Delia's locket, the one Sophie had asked about. To Petrosino he said, "Haven't heard about that." He drank his beer. The tasteless brew couldn't chase the ambrosia taste of this new information. He yawned, pushed the beer away. "So, what do you know about this locket?"

Petrosino tilted his head to the left. "When I pose a question like that to a suspect, it usually means I'm more interested than I want to let on."

"If you're that transparent," Tonneman said, "I would suggest you don't pose your questions like that."

"All right. You have your secrets, I have mine. But don't you find it fascinating that a chance remark should reveal a previous unknown scent of the prey?"

"I must say you Italians talk real pretty at times."

The two smiled good-naturedly at each other.

"We must have more of these talks in the future. Who knows what one might know that could facilitate the other?"

"Real pretty," said Tonneman. "Let's get back to the Black Hand."

"The strange thing is you're not looking at the Black Hand in this case. Have you ever heard of Pasquarella?"

"No. Who is he?"

"Your he is a she. Pasquarella operates a stable up on Park Avenue between One Hundred and Eighth and One Hundred and Ninth Streets, only blocks away from Zio Mico. They are sworn enemies. They've been at each other's throats since he started his very rewarding enterprise and cut into her profits."

"So we may have stumbled into the middle of a war."

"No. I have talked to my snitches, and I believe that Pasquarella is somehow involved in your case. As part of her service she provides hired assassins. For a substantial price. These killings of yours — the whore and Mulroony — they nag at my mind. Something I should recognize. One stab in the belly and then up. Nasty way to die."

"Is there a good way?"

"These two killings were done for hire. I feel it in my bones."

"You may be right. More reason for me to investigate. How do I get to Pasquarella?"

"You?" Petrosino tittered as befitting an old man. "You'll never get near her."

"Want to bet? I'll just take myself up there and arrest the evil bitch."

Petrosino forgot himself and laughed not as the frail old codger but as the robust man he was. "I'd like to see that. A tough Irish cop arresting a sweet, old grandmama surrounded by family."

Chapter 24

Thursday, July 13. Early evening.

"It's an interesting case," Dutch said, in response to Oz's question about Officer Mulroony's death.

The usual facade of polite boredom Oz Cook put on whenever John Tonneman came to dinner was absent this night. And while murders were hardly proper dinner conversation, Oz was downright curious.

The photographer slipped on his gold-framed spectacles and stared intently at Dutch. Then he removed the eyeglasses, returned them to the table, and spoke with quiet deliberation. "What could possibly connect Delia Swann to this policeman?" He signaled Wong for another bottle of the Haut Brion. The Bordeaux was the perfect accompaniment to the cold, sliced steak and russet potato salad.

"We think Delia Swann had something her murderer was desperate for because her clothing was —" Dutch stopped, flushed, and looked at Esther.

"Don't mind me. I'm not delicate."

Oz hid a smile. Tonneman persisted in treating Esther as if she were a fragile flower. Oz knew better, and it amused him to see Tonneman flounder.

The detective cleared his throat. "Some of her clothing was missing and the rest sliced up. Mulroony was first on the scene. Delia Swann was killed in a very vicious manner. There's no easy way to say this, Esther."

"Go on."

"She was stabbed. By the wound it was probably a dagger. A stiletto. In the stomach —" Dutch breathed out heavily. "Then the knife was pulled up until it was stopped by the breast bone."

Esther made no sound but her face grew pale. Oz pushed her crystal water goblet to her and she drank with urgent swallows.

Tonneman waited patiently. At Oz's nod he went on. "Mulroony died the same way in the Russian bathhouse, and his uniform was also cut to shreds." Perspiring from his efforts, he reached for his goblet.

"Flora Cooper came here asking about Delia," Esther offered casually, almost as if Dutch hadn't just described one of the most gruesome things she'd ever heard.

Tonneman's glass froze at his lips. He set it down. "What did you tell her?"

"What I told you. Flora remembered that I was making photographs of prostitutes and thought I might have made one of Delia."

"Which you had," Oz said. He pushed his plate away and lit a cigarette.

"Flora told me that Sophie is frightened she might be next."

"Well, now," Oz said, looking at his protégé with surprise. Esther was keeping her own confidence these days. This wouldn't do.

"She is certain Sophie knows Delia's real name."

"I tried to get to Sophie, but she wouldn't see me. I talked with that runt lover of hers, Leo Stern, but couldn't get much out of him, only —" Tonneman stopped. Perhaps he'd gone too far. He searched Esther's face. She seemed to have no idea she might be in danger as well.

Oz was impatient to hear the rest. "Get on with it, man."

This time Dutch chose to speak directly to Oz. "Leo said that whoever killed Delia and Mulroony would go after Esther before Sophie."

Esther blanched.

Oz grunted as if Tonneman had delivered a punch. "Esther?"

Tonneman looked from one to the other. "I keep asking myself, is Leo right? Will he attack Esther first and then Sophie?"

"But why?" Oz was shaken. His life revolved around Esther. This must not be.

"Exactly what I want to know," Dutch said. His voice was uncomfortably loud.

Esther spoke calmly, quietly. "I believe Delia's killer was waiting for her when she left here that day."

Tonneman wiped his forehead. He was sweating again. He dried his hands with the fine linen napkin on his lap. For the first time he noticed the initials embroidered on the cloth in white thread, "O N C" "Her killer may think she told you something. What did she say to you?"

"She talked about an inheritance that was rightfully hers. That's all."

Oz reflected on that piece of information. He was remembering Delia as he'd last seen her. Her expression when he and his friends came to her aid. "It wouldn't be the first time a whore came into money. Wong, you may clear away."

"Sophie made a point of asking about Delia's locket." Tonneman finished the wine in his glass.

"And?" Oz asked.

"We didn't find it."

"So the killer took the girl's locket. It was robbery, pure and simple."

"Perhaps. I'd like to take another look at that photograph you made of her, Esther."

Wong was taking his time placing dishes on his tray, Oz saw, getting himself a good listen. "Wong, we'll take coffee and brandy in the studio."

As they left the dining room, Tonneman asked, "Was she wearing a locket when she was here, Esther?"

Esther, already on the stairs, pretended not to have heard. Oz, following them, wondered again why she was keeping this particular secret.

In the studio they all three stared at the vivid portrait of Delia Swann.

"She looks like she's about to speak," Tonneman said with admiration. He put his arm around Esther and hugged her to him.

Embarrassed, Esther pulled away.

Oz denied himself a smile. "But what will she say?" he asked facetiously.

Tonneman examined the portrait. Delia's costume was high-necked, conservative, even prim. He thought out loud. "If she was wearing a gold locket, it wouldn't show in that dress."

"Why do you put so much importance into a gold locket?" Oz asked.

"No real reason," Tonneman replied. "I'm guessing. Police work is more than collecting facts and taking action. Being on the job as long as I have, you get like a gut feeling for things."

"Animal instincts, is that it?" Oz said, blandly, raising a haughty eyebrow. He pretended not to notice Esther's sharp look.

Dutch squinted at his host. Oz was fortunate Bo wasn't here. He'd seen Bo break a jaw over offenses slighter than that. He persevered. "I just learned that someone's turning the fakers and pawnshops upside down looking for a gold locket."

Wong stood in the doorway holding his tray. First moving some photographic materials aside on the work table, Esther beckoned to the servant.

"And if it were found, would it make much difference?" Esther held her hands tight against her sides.

"If it was found, it might put a stop to this killing," Tonneman said. Watching her, he could see she was upset, and he didn't blame her. He would do everything he could to protect her. If she would let him. Unfortunately for Dutch, it was very much in Esther's character not to seek help and to attempt to solve her problems by herself.

"A gold locket." Oz saw very clearly in his mind the other photograph Esther had made of Delia, half dressed, a heart-shaped gold locket hanging from a velvet ribbon round her throat. "It's all very interesting, isn't it, my dear?"

Esther lifted her chin with a touch of defiance. "Coffee, gentlemen?"

Chapter 25

Thursday, July 13. Evening.

Oz sat in the studio smoking, sipping Cognac. He'd left the door open, waiting for Esther's quiet footfall on the stairs. When it came, he unfolded himself from the Morris chair and met her in the doorway.

She was flushed, her lips swollen. Small strands of her dark hair had slipped free, giving her the look of a wanton. The boor had kissed her, that was obvious. And she'd liked it, that was also obvious.

"Come in and talk to me, my dear," Oz said. He took Esther's unresisting hand and led her back into the studio.

Esther smiled at him, a little dazed from Tonneman's kiss, somewhat apprehensive because she knew what Oz wanted to talk about. She had not told the whole truth about Delia Swann.

■ ■ ■ ■

Little Jack was leaning against the carriage house in Macdougal Alley smoking, watching the fireflies having themselves a light-flashing party. The heat absorbed the smell of horse dung and bloated all around him.

The automobile was where the world was going. He could see that. You didn't have to feed it anything but gasoline and oil. You didn't have to clean up after it. And it didn't bite you. Yes, he was going to have to make a lot of money and get himself one. Maybe one day he would even sell them.

His head was spinning with plans when who should come along but the client they'd bought the two lockets for.

"Boy, tell Mr. West I'm here."

Boy. The client was hardly older than Little Jack and he was calling Little Jack boy? Remembering Battling Jack's edict — the client is always right — Little Jack gave the client a nod and trotted to the rear door of the townhouse that faced Washington Square North and backed on the alley. He twisted the knob that rang a bell inside.

Jack West stuck his head out an upstairs window. "Who is it wants me?"

"The client's come again to see what we got."

"I'll be right there. Take him up to the office."

Even with the windows open, the office was sweltering, the sun having beaten down on the roof all day. Little Jack pulled the string, turning on the light attached to the ceiling fan over Battling Jack's desk. The client stood at the window watching the alley, waiting. The fan made a steady thumping sound as it paddled the steamy air.

Little Jack smoked and watched the client. He was real nervous. When Jack West entered the room, the client wasted no time. He didn't even bother shaking hands. "Mr. West, what do you have for me?"

Jack West sat down behind his big desk. He unlocked a drawer and took out an envelope. The client sat in front of the desk and held out his hand, but Battling Jack shook the two lockets onto the flat surface of the desk. "Have a look-see," he said.

The client reached into his coat and pulled out his wallet. From the wallet he removed a now familiar piece of paper and unfolded it on the desk.

As before, Little Jack couldn't see what was on the paper. When the young man opened one locket, then the other, holding each up to the light, Little Jack edged closer.

Finally, the client set both lockets back on the desk and folded up the paper. He took one twenty-dollar bill and two one-dollar bills from the wallet and set them down next to the lockets. "Keep searching," he said. He got up to go.

"Do you want the lockets?" Little Jack asked.

The client responded to Battling Jack, as if it were he who had spoken. "Keep them. They're not the right ones." He returned the piece of paper to his wallet and the wallet to his pocket. "I'll return in a couple of days." The young man left them. Little Jack didn't follow.

"What did you get?" Jack West asked, after they were sure the client was gone.

"Just the picture of a locket. And the initials I. B. H."

Chapter 26

Thursday, July 13. Evening.

"You may be able to fool that thick-headed minion of the law, but you can't fool me, my dear. You're hiding something. What is it?"

Esther sighed. What could she do? Oz had brought out the other photograph she had made of Delia Swann. He'd placed it over the first on the easel, so that the skimpily clothed Delia partially covered the fully dressed Delia.

Like a double exposure, Esther thought, but not really. Clothed or unclothed, Delia had never seemed the innocent. But with fewer clothes, a certain recklessness was more apparent. The shiny moist lips, the frightened, melancholy eyes.

Wong was a silent presence near the door.

"I made a promise," she said. "I was trying to keep it."

"What kind of a promise?"

"I gave my word."

"To Delia Swann?" Oz splashed Cognac into one of the empty snifters and handed it to Esther. She shook her head. "Humor me," he said. "Simply breathe in the fragrance."

Oz had been after her for years to sample his highly prized brandies. Emotionally exhausted, she chose this moment to yield, inhaling the full bouquet of the spirits through her nose. As she expected, biting. Her hand moved to set the glass down. Yet not entirely unpleasant. Rather nice. Sensuous. She wet her lips with the brandy. "Yes."

Oz watched her progress with some satisfaction. "The girl is dead. Her death releases you from your promise."

"But if one gives one's word —"

"There are different instances, with disparate situations and solutions. Revealing what she told you might bring her murderer to justice."

Esther took a real swallow. The sensation was exhilarating, but not enough to distract her from the moment. "I would like to accomplish that without breaking my word."

"It's too dangerous to work alone, my dear. We'll do this together. That's why I'm here. After all, two intelligent heads are better than one."

He'd made a joke, but she was deadly serious. "I don't seem to be approaching this properly. Perhaps what's missing is a man's point of view."

This pleased Oz so much he preened. His head lifted, his sharp features softened. He did everything but strut about the room. He looked at Wong as if to say, did you hear that? "Tell me what you know," he said.

"I went to see Sophie several days after we learned that Delia was dead. I'd been thinking about it since Sophie rushed in that day insisting on seeing me alone. I thought then and I'm positive now that she knows more than she will admit. Delia's real name, for one thing."

Oz looked grim. "All that was over three weeks ago. The trail's gone cold by now. What did Sophie admit to? Very little, I would think."

"I never even got inside the door. I met Flora Cooper in front of the building. She'd just come from interviewing Sophie. Flora agreed with me that Sophie knew more than she was telling."

"And is she your new confidant?" Oz asked, raising an eyebrow.

"Not at all." He's jealous, Esther thought. "We simply talked."

"As women are wont to do."

A glint came into Esther's eyes. "If we're going to work together —"

Oz put up his hands in surrender. "I'll be good."

"Flora remembered my project and realized that I might have made a photograph of Delia. She wanted to see it and talk with me about what Delia might have said when she was here."

"And what came out of that talk?" Oz lit a cigarette and smoked, thinking.

"As we heard this evening, it appears that everyone thinks there may be a connection between Delia's death and that of the policeman, Mulroony."

Oz looked over at Wong, whose face reflected nothing. "Everyone?"

"The police. Sophie. Flora."

"And you?" Oz's gaze was penetrating.

"Yes. Flora is going to try to discover Delia's real name. She felt that would begin unraveling the mystery. In the meantime, Sophie thinks that she and everyone else Delia saw the day she was murdered is in danger."

"And that includes you, my dear."

"Yes."

"It would have been, at the very least, good manners for you to have informed me of this, instead of letting me hear it from that cop of yours."

"And what would you have done?"

Oz considered, then said, "Worry."

She granted him the smile he hoped for, but her hands shook.

"If Sophie's fears are correct, you are a sitting target for murder."

Esther shuddered; Oz guided her brandy glass to her lips.

Esther took another sip, felt again the lovely warmth.

"Let's consider the whys and wherefores. Delia's murderer appears to be looking for something. Something he couldn't find on Delia's person, nor on the policeman's."

Esther nodded.

"I'm sure Mr. Tonneman believes the murderer is after the locket. The killer's question is, as ours must be, whom did Delia see that day? And does that mean he will call on you next?"

"John Tonneman is afraid so. Oz, he's going to ask you if he can move in here so he can intercept the murderer should he come looking for me."

An almost imperceptible twitch pulled at the corner of Wong's lips.

Oz growled. "Move in here? Not on your life. He'd be more hindrance than help. We don't need him here, do we, Wong?"

"If Miss Esther is in danger, the more protectors she has, the better it is, Mr. Oz."

"Well, we'll sleep on it." Deflated, Oz slumped in his chair.

He sat up suddenly. What was the matter with him? Esther was being cagey. She hadn't yet revealed Delia's confidence. Staring pointedly at a ribbon-tied, heart-shaped locket nestled in Delia's throat, Oz said, "All right, young lady. Have at you. Why didn't you tell Tonneman about the damned locket?"

Chapter 27

Friday, July 14. Sundown.

Esther placed the linen cloth on her head and lit the two candles. Making circles over the flames with her hands, she beckoned the flames to her, bringing her hands just shy of her face at the end of each wave. The third time, she held her hands to her face, covering her eyes, for the rest of the prayer.

"Blessed art thou, O Lord our God, King of the universe, who has sanctified us by Thy commandments and has commanded us to kindle the Sabbath-light. Amen."

"Amen."

Esther removed the napkin from her head and smiled at John Tonneman. It was always so strange to her that he knew the candle-lighting ceremony of the Sabbath, that Jewish tradition existed in his Christian family, handed down from his ancestors. Until the death of his great-grandfather he'd had no inkling that most of these ancestors had been Jewish.

So many odd and wonderful things had happened to Esther Breslau since she'd left the Lower East Side to work for Oz Cook as the photographer's assistant.

Now she was a recognized photographer in her own right. She had come a far distance from the girl her parents had planned to give to a stranger in marriage, without her consent. When she had refused, they had disowned her.

According to her parents, a woman's duty was to see to her husband's needs and to give him many children. They had never understood her, and if they could see her now, they would have been shocked at her living arrangements and her consorting with prostitutes.

Esther shook her head sadly. The Sabbath was no time to think of the bitterness of the past. She had made her peace with her parents, thanks to a cousin, and then she had come to America to build a new life.

Madame Sophie sat like a queen in the middle of her blood-red sofa. The three sofas, laden with puffed-up gold and silver pillows, formed a semicircle. The other two were for her girls. Weighty draperies in the same red hid them from the world and the world from them.

On Sophie's lap, two black velvet purses. One for the brass tokens customers bought that allowed them upstairs with one of her girls. The other purse was the night's cash.

Everyone who was anybody in New York knew about Sophie's girls. They were the pick of the crop. Every size, every shape. And each, a lady, dressed grandly. And they were free of disease.

Tonight, as usual, they sat elegantly in Sophie's parlor, to her left and to her right, posed against the gold and silver pillows. With every turn of head or body, they performed for the large gilt-framed mirrors that hung on the walls, and so, for each man in the room. They sat sipping Dr. Brown's Cel-Ray Soda, from crystal glasses, waiting to be chosen.

The potion of celery seed, sugar, and seltzer was served to the girls. When the customers ordered whiskey, the girls were given coffee-colored water.

As usual, Piano Man was at his Steinway, puffing a marijuana cigarette down to its nub, pounding ragtime, his pearly whites shining.

What was not usual: Leo was missing from his table off to Sophie's right. He was not smoking his cigar, spitting into his brass spittoon, playing solitaire, waiting for something to happen so he could take care of it. That was Leo's job, to tend to Sophie. But it was Friday night, the beginning of Shabbos. For the last two years, now, Leo hadn't tended to Sophie on Shabbos. On Shabbos, Leo tended to God.

Chapter 28

Saturday, July 15. Morning.

The house was still. As still as it could be with an even dozen girls, plus Sophie, Leo, Daisy, and Piano Man, all living under the same roof. It had been a busy Friday night. Summer weekends always were busy because families were packed off to the seashore while the gentlemen remained in town doing business.

Sophie had counted up the take, as she always did, and deposited the cash into her safe under her dressing table before going to bed. Of course, many of her long-time customers had accounts with her and paid her once a month rather than for each visit.

The creak of the floor outside her door woke her. Leo. She smiled to herself. He was weak where she was concerned.

Since he had gotten religion, Leo had stayed out of her bed on Friday night and all day Saturday, choosing instead a cot in the basement and prayers in the synagogue. Sophie considered this recent state of affairs a challenge and used all her wiles to tempt him back.

She rearranged the light coverlet decorously so that one bare breast and thigh were revealed in the soft glow of her nightlight. The door opened slowly, as if he were playing a game; she was charmed. She would play too. Licking her lips to make them glisten, she closed her eyes.

The door clicked closed. She breathed deeply to savor Leo's various scents. The smell was wrong.

It wasn't Leo.

Sophie's scream stayed in her throat, stifled by his hand, frozen by the point of a blade pressed against her breast. To her horror, the stiletto moved over her soft flesh, raising a cross of black blood all too visible in the dim light.

When the knife moved again, Sophie fainted.

The salts brought her around, but she couldn't move. The air stank of sour wine and tobacco. He'd hogtied her with her own silk stockings, damn him. The point of the dagger was now at her throat.

"The locket." A black hood hid his face.

His foreign-sounding voice was husky.

Not Russian or German, she thought. Italian. Oh, Leo, what a time for you to become godly. Hadn't she known this would happen? She had to think clearly or she'd be dead as Delia, as Mulroony.

If she told him she didn't have the locket, he would kill her at once. "Knife," she whispered, trying not to move. But her throat felt the burn of the stiletto before he moved it back to her breast. "Don't scar me," she begged.

"Where?"

"Safe." If only he would take the knife away.

"Where?" Now the blade cut a path to her stomach. Blood. How odd, it was warm. How deep had he gone? She didn't want to die like that. Like Delia. Gutted like an animal. She whimpered.

He slapped her across the face. "Quiet. Where? Or Marie will bite."

"Under my dressing table." What time was it? She was afraid to turn her head to the clock on her dressing table. Would Daisy come with her morning coffee? Sophie shivered. She'd be dead by then.

The bed squeaked as he got off, taking his stiletto with him. Uncontrolled tears dripped down her cheeks.

"Combination."

She told him the combination. He was going to kill her whether he found the locket or not. If she was dead, what did the money in the safe matter? For Leo? She thought, angrily, he should be here to save me. But he wasn't here and she had to save herself.

The assassin grunted. She heard metal scrape against wood as he pulled the safe out from under the table. She could hear him working the combination. What was taking him so long? Suddenly he was back on the bed, the stiletto pressed to her throat. "You lie. Marie doesn't like lies." The stiletto stung again, along her neck. The viscous warmth trickled down her breasts.

Sophie tried to control her terror. "Not a lie."

The stiletto moved again, this time cutting her bonds. And almost as an afterthought, her right cheek.

"Not my face."

"Do it."

Her hands moved to her cheek. The blow drove her off the bed to the floor, where she cowered, expecting more.

"Maybe Marie cut your eyes out so you can hold them. You want?"

Her hand found the button under the carpet. The foot button she used to summon Daisy. She pressed it twice with the heel of her hand. Dear God. Maybe Daisy would realize something was wrong if it was pressed twice.

He kicked her in the ribs.

She crawled to the safe. He stood over her, impatient.

"Do it," he said.

Her fingers sticky with her own blood slipped over the combination dial. She turned it and prayed. To Leo's Yaweh. To Jesus. To any God that would listen. The final click; the door to the safe opened. "There. It's all yours. Just —" She heard the sound outside her door and coughed to cover it. She moved away from the safe. "Take it."

He bent over her, the stiletto pressed against her stomach. "You give me."

Her door opened. Sophie rolled away. But not fast enough. Intense pain tore her side. She heard Daisy scream. A crash. Then a hyena like howl from the assassin. Daisy. Running footsteps, more screaming. Her own.

Sophie tried to stand. "Daisy?" She saw the small black woman crumpled in the open doorway. Blood everywhere. Her eyes filled with it. They all came running, everyone wailing at once. "I'm all right," she said, holding her side where the pain was the worst. Blood. Why was she surprised? So much blood. She was so tired.

Piano Man knelt beside her, held her in his arms. She tried to tell him she was all right, but no words came from her lips. She couldn't feel her legs, her arms. Her head began to loll.

". . . . doctor," Piano Man said, stroking her hair.

"Leo," Sophie whispered.

CHAPTER 29

Saturday, July 15. Late afternoon.

When Gouverneur Hospital opened in 1885, in a converted public market building in the middle of Gouverneur Slip, its three floors were to be used as a City emergency hospital. This quickly became obsolete; it was not equipped with an operating room, and although it was on a fairly large tract of land, market wagons regularly blocked ambulances.

The hospital was severely damaged by fire in 1895, and the City was now engaged and had been for the last two years in building a new five-story hospital in the Renaissance style with a redbrick facade facing Water Street. The wings would extend toward the East River and terminate in semicircular bays. The din of construction was unremitting.

It was here that the barely conscious Sophie Mandel was brought by ambulance.

When the extent of her injuries was discovered, there still being no working operating room at Gouverneur, some discreet phone calls were made by a frantic Leo Stern. Sophie was immediately transferred to Bellevue.

At 300 Mulberry Street, Dutch sat in the library reading through descriptions of previous murders starting with January of '98, hoping to find a match to the modus operandi of Delia Swann's and Mulroony's killer.

"Hey, Dutch!" A uniform cop stuck his head in the door. "Sophie Mandel's been knifed and her girl —"

Stunned, Dutch pushed the papers aside. "Is she dead?"

"Yeah. I mean, they took Sophie to Gouverneur. She was cut up bad, but breathing. Her nigger girl died."

"Shit! Call Bo on the telephone. If he's not home, tell him when he gets here." Tonneman shoved his pencil and notepad in his pocket and rushed out.

"From the wound," Dutch said, having conferred with the surgeon, "I'd say a dagger. Probably a stiletto. Like the others." He looked at Bo, then at his companion, Flora

Cooper. "Where you been?"

They were standing in the waiting area outside one of the private rooms at Bellevue Hospital. Sophie had been in surgery for two hours and was very sedated when she was brought up, Leo at her side. Tonneman had been unable to talk to her. The surgeon had permitted Leo inside with Sophie, but no others.

"At the *Herald,*" Bo said. "When I checked with the House, they told me you were at Gouverneur, so I went on over to Clinton Street to see the damage."

"Daisy dead?"

"Yeah. What a blood bath. Last time I saw anything this bad was when Sam Cohen cut up his wife. Come to think of it, her name was Sophie, too."

Flora pinched Bo's arm.

"It's true. Anyway, at Sophie's the girls were nuts, running around screaming and crying. Piano Man calmed them down. Jesus, If I'd known how much money could be made running a whorehouse —"

This time Flora jabbed Bo with her elbow.

"Shit. The money was spilling out of the safe. I'm not saying I would ever think of — I closed them down for a while, so we can take a good look at the premises. No one knows how he got in, but he got out the fucking roof door, left a trail of blood over three rooftops, then nothing."

"No one heard what was going on?"

"What do you think? They were dead to the world after a busy night." He moved closer to Tonneman. "They didn't hear nothing until he screamed."

"*He* screamed?"

"There was an empty pot on the floor just inside Sophie's room. The pot was warm. I'm calculating the colored girl threw hot water on him. So what they tell you? Is Sophie going make it?"

"From what the surgeon says, yes. Don't know when we can talk to her though."

The door to Sophie's room opened, and Leo peered out. "What the hell do you want here now?" Anger seemed to have robbed his eyes of pupils.

Dutch ignored the man's fury. "How's she doing?"

"What happened, Mr. Stern?" Flora asked, slipping between Dutch and Leo.

"I don't know, goddam it. She hasn't even woken up since it happened." He began wringing his hands. "I wasn't there. If I'd been there, it wouldn't have happened."

"If you'd been there, you might have gotten stuck, too," Bo said.

Dutch said, "The sawbones says Sophie's

going to be okay."

"Oh, yeah? What do they know? God knows, but he ain't talking."

"Mr. Stern, do you know that the colored maid, Daisy, is dead?" Flora asked. "Killed by the same man who stabbed Sophie."

Leo looked at her, then burst into tears. He walked off down the hall sobbing.

"Get out of here, Flora." Bo took her arm and steered her to the staircase. "It's the wrong time. We'll never get anything out of him with you around."

"I'll be downstairs, but I want an exclusive," she said. "Okay? No other reporters."

"Get going, Flora."

Once Flora was gone, Bo ducked into Sophie's room.

In the meantime, Dutch had followed Leo to the alcove that looked out over the East River.

"I understand you've gone back to the church," Dutch said.

"In a manner of speaking." Leo had pulled himself together and was smoking a cigar.

"What's it feel like to find God?" Dutch asked.

Leo shook his head. "You don't find God. He's never lost. We're the lost ones. God finds us."

"You sound like my ma and Father Duff.

Only they would say Jesus."

Leo nodded. "I follow the religion Jesus followed."

"But Jesus turned his back on Judaism."

"He did not. He wasn't against Judaism. He didn't want to end Judaism; he wanted to reform it. Jesus died a good Jew. Ask any priest."

Dutch felt his pockets for a cigar, found none.

Leo produced another Garcia Perfecto, handed it to Tonneman, then lit it for him. The two men stood silently, savoring the tobacco and the view, the sailboats dipping in the wind on the East River.

After several minutes John Tonneman resumed the conversation. "Jesus, the Jew," he prompted.

Leo peeled a bit of leaf from his tongue. "A good Jew. The turning away came from another Jew named Saul. You know him as Paul who walked the road to Damascus."

"You're kidding?"

Leo shrugged. "Who knows? Without Paul, maybe Christianity becomes a Jewish sect, like the Essenes, which is what John the Baptist was."

"My ma wouldn't like to hear that. She thinks Jews are heathens."

"I'd hate to tell you what we think Christians are . . . God is everything for the devout Jew."

"As Jesus is for us."

Leo almost exploded. "Aha!"

"What?" Dutch asked. "Oh?"

"Yes. Oh. Why do you need a middle man?"

"Jesus is not a middle man. He is the Son of God. And He is God."

"Stop with the Trinity already. It gives me a headache."

"Why don't the Jews accept Jesus as the son of God?"

"Same reason we don't accept you as the son of God."

Dutch started to cross himself, stopped. "You'll burn in Hell."

"Hell? Heaven?" Leo drew a hearty breath of cigar smoke, blew a series of white cloudy rings and admired them. "No such places."

"Then what happens when you die?"

"You die."

"I don't want to believe that."

"All right. But dying is not like going up to Saratoga for a vacation."

Dutch shook his head. "You die and that's it. It's all so clear to you. Cut and dried."

"Just the opposite. It's not clear, very blurry. I don't think we have the words, the thoughts to say what it is. The best I can tell you is that in a manner we are brought back to God as pure as we were before we were born."

"And Jesus doesn't figure anywhere in your thinking?"

"To Jews, the Messiah is yet to come. Jesus doesn't fill the bill. He's just not important to us."

"What's important to a Jew?"

"After God and Torah, we value law and knowledge."

Dutch's laugh was dark. "You, Leo Stern, value law?"

"Don't judge by me. I'm a lousy Jew. But I'm working on it." Leo cleared his throat, spotted the spittoon at the corner of the hall, walked to it, and spat. "Christianity," he said, coming back, "is a religion of charity. A Christian is supposed to have a good conscience, and follow it. Judaism is a religion of justice. You say, be moral out of the goodness of your heart. We don't count on the goodness of your heart. We say, be moral because the law tells you to be moral. We want you to be a good person. But for the sake of the poor and the needy, we don't depend on your charity. What is important is that you do what is right. On the other hand —"

"Lately I've discovered there's always

another hand with you Jews."

"How do you think we survived five thousand years? On the other hand, Hillel tells us that 'that which is hurtful to you, do not do to your neighbor.' "

"But Jesus said that. 'Do unto others.' "

"You prove my point. Jesus was a good Jew. He learned that from reading Hillel. Why . . . ?" Suddenly, the puzzled wrinkle faded from Leo's brow. "Oh, I'm beginning to see now. It's the girl, isn't it? That's what makes the goy so interested in her religion."

Tonneman flushed. He was at a loss for words, feeling he'd been caught out. He wanted to protest, to say he was half Jew himself.

Suddenly Bo's voice rang out. "Dutch, you better get in here."

Chapter 30

Saturday, July 15. Late afternoon.

Oz descended the stairs, an unlit cigarette between his lips. "Wong, I need a —" He stopped.

Huddled over the telephone in the front hall like conspirators were Esther and Wong. The receiver sat on the hook but Esther's hand still held onto the instrument. She looked at Oz, pale as death.

"What terrible tidings has Mr. Bell's contraption delivered?"

"Sophie was attacked by a man with a knife," Esther said. "Like Delia. And her girl, Daisy, is dead."

"Ghastly," Oz said. "That settles it. We're packing up and going to Newport. We've missed half the season but —"

"You may go if you wish," Esther said, "I'm staying."

Oz was not surprised. He would have been astonished if she'd agreed to leave. He countered with, "Very well, then. At least tell Mr. Tonneman what you know about the locket. And I'll get in touch with that big fellow. What's his name, Wong? The ex-pugilist — never mind, I remember. I'm going to arrange for a bodyguard for you, Esther, until this affair is over and done with and the murderer is put away."

Esther lifted her head defiantly. "I'm not a child, I don't require a nursemaid." She slipped her camera case over her shoulder and, scrutinizing herself in the mirror, pinned her bright yellow straw hat to her hair. Plucking the matching parasol from the umbrella stand, she announced, "I'm going to Bellevue to see how Sophie is. After that, I don't know . . ."

Wong, between Esther and the door, did not move.

"Don't be ridiculous, Wong. Please stand aside."

Oz nodded to the Chinaman. "It's the 'after that I don't know,' that troubles me."

Wong stood aside. Esther marched out onto the street.

Oz patted his pockets for matches. "Follow her."

Watching the door close behind Wong, Oz crossed to the hall table. He lifted the listening phone from its candlestick receiver, and cranked. "Central, please get me Mr. Jack West in Macdougal Alley."

Esther had waited for Wong. She smiled. Not at all surprised, he bowed. They traveled the few blocks to Bellevue Hospital in a hackney coach.

There, they found Flora Cooper pacing in the lobby near the entrance, smoking. Visitors and medical personnel went in and out. Two men were poised about ten feet beyond Flora, closer to a pair of swinging doors.

"Ah," Flora said. She pulled Esther to a corner. "Can't trust anyone." She looked pointedly at two men and sniffed. "*Tribune* and *Post.* Johnnies come lately." She lowered her voice. "What do you know?"

"Only that Sophie's been badly hurt. What do you know?"

"She'll live, they say."

"Was it — ?"

"Yes." She offered Esther a cigarette. "It helps you think."

The woman's skin was so white she seemed drained of all blood. Under the sheets, she was nothing but bulk from the heavy bandages. But her eyes were open, staring at Bo Clancy, who held her hand.

"Get the hell away from her," Leo said, as

he and Tonneman came into the room.

"Leo," Sophie said in the weakest of voices. "Don't yell."

"Sophie says he was Eyetalian," Bo told Tonneman.

"Goes with the stiletto."

"Cops." Leo was disgusted. "Anyone can use a stiletto."

"What did he want, Sophie?" Bo asked.

Sophie looked at Leo. "Tell them," Leo said. "I don't want anything to ever hurt you again."

"Delia's locket." Sophie's eyes closed. She was too weak to speak any further.

"Sophie." Bo squeezed her hand, her eyes opened again. "Did you give it to him?"

"I don't have it," Sophie said. "I never had it." Tears ran down her waxen cheeks as she closed her eyes once more.

Bo transferred her hand to Leo. He and Tonneman stepped out of the room.

"Someone wants that locket," Tonneman said, gesturing at Sophie's room. "Very badly."

"And who do you think has it, if not Sophie? Who else did Delia see that day?"

"Esther doesn't have it. She would have told me."

"Did you ask her?"

Dutch tried to remember. "I saw the

photograph she made of Delia. There was no locket."

"She's got you wrapped around her little finger."

"So you keep telling me," Tonneman said.

"I'll bet she knows more than she's saying."

"You're wrong, Bo. I'm going over to talk to her."

"Let's get a cop to watch Sophie's room." Bo headed downstairs to find the telephone.

"I'll wait for you," Tonneman said. At the nurse's station he borrowed the extra straight-backed chair from beside her desk, parked it in front of Sophie's door, and sat.

"Well, lookie here!" Bo's big voice floated up from the staircase.

A moment later, who should appear but Esther Breslau, followed by the Chinaman, Wong. Esther hurried to Dutch, her small face pinched with concern. He stood up at once and offered her his chair.

She sat, resting her parasol against her knee. "How is Sophie?"

"She'll be okay, but she got hurt bad."

"What happened? Do you know?"

"A man with a knife. He was looking for —"

Leo opened the door behind Esther, and Esther stood. "I have something to tell you,"

Leo said.

Dutch moved the chair so Leo could step out. "What?"

Leo looked at Esther. "Excuse me, please."

The two men walked past Wong and far enough away from Esther to talk privately.

"Her name."

"Whose name?" Dutch said.

"Delia's. Her real name was Irene Hall."

Chapter 31

Wednesday, July 19. Early morning.

Farms dotted the countryside on upper Broadway: old wood-shingled farmhouses, all but deserted now. Still, a few tenants remained, with the knowledge that they too would have to leave as the digging for the subway by the Interborough Rapid Transit Company came closer. But the remaining tenants, unsophisticated in their ignorance of the rush to create a modern mass transit system and thus a viable labor force, held onto the hope that the politicians would kill the plans.

One could see cows grazing. Here and there, goats and chickens. The remains of a rural community. On Columbus Avenue, which started at Fifty-ninth Street but was a continuation of Ninth Avenue, the roar of the elevated trains jarred the otherwise bucolic atmosphere.

The hoped-for death blow to the subway

was a pipe dream. In less than a year, the digging would begin.

Baby inhaled the country air. It was heavy with the sweet smell of honeysuckle and wild flowers that grew without inhibition in the area.

Adjusting the brim of his hat to hide from the sun, Baby Burgoyne trailed after the two business partners for whom he worked as private secretary — Harrison Stokes, his brother-in-law, and William Grimes.

Harrison Stokes was, in this thirty-second year of his life, a strikingly attractive man, but his features betrayed a certain pulpy quality that threatened to spread as he aged.

Stokes stood well over six feet and kept his dark blond hair longer than most. He was exceedingly vain about his hair and his deep gold walrus mustache. A man of gigantic ambition, he strode the world as if he owned it. And he planned to.

It hadn't hurt that he'd married — for love of course — Louisa Neldine Burgoyne, the only daughter of an old, socially prominent New York family.

As a graduate of Columbia College, he considered himself a modern man and, while very protective of his wife, had bought her a bicycle, encouraging her to take exercise, even permitting her to wear bloomers. Such concessions to modernity made his life simpler. Cycling and the like kept a woman from idling with her friends, which could breed discussion.

He fervently believed that women talked too much. Especially to each other. Discussion led to radical thinking, as suffrage. What the blazes did they want or need the vote for? Women. Hysterical creatures. He had seen it in his own mother, poor soul. She'd taken to her bed when he was a child and so had died there.

His partner, William Grimes, two years older and only a little more than five feet tall, had thick black hair, save for the spot on top of his head where his scalp shone through. His shrewd, bright blue eyes were well suited to his smooth-shaven face.

Grimes's small stature belied an amazing power. He could outlast any in business, in society, in hard work or frolic. He believed in living life to the fullest, and so he did. It was rumored that he had once killed a man with a knife. Further rumors claimed that he maintained at least three mistresses. And that was only in New York City. His wife and four children remained at the family home upstate.

Although trained as an attorney, Grimes made his money as a speculator. It had been in one such speculation that Harrison Stokes, the hick from Poughkeepsie, had outwitted him, and so won the diminutive lawyer's grudging respect. The suggestion of partnership had come from Grimes, himself, and had been well-received by his competitor. Combined, they had thrived beyond either's wildest dreams.

The land along Broadway from Eightieth Street to One Hundred and Sixth, from Amsterdam Avenue, the continuation of Tenth Avenue above Fifty-ninth Street, to Riverside Drive along the Hudson River made up their investment. They drove up here frequently to survey it, to make sure their tenants knew all hope was lost and they would have to move.

The pure sunlight dazzled Baby's eyes, made his head throb. He and his brother J.N. had been on the town the night before. He'd crawled home alone only hours ago and thus was managing on little sleep and a dreadful hangover. J.N., in worse shape than Baby, was sitting half-in, half-out of Baby's Benz motor car, his head in his hands.

The lowing of cows found a certain communion with Baby's ravaged soul this morning. He looked back at the two automobiles, parked on the other side of the trolley tracks, and his brother, who was upright now, walking toward him.

Horse-drawn carts and carriages passed by, making their way to farther points. He covered his mouth as a yawn became uncontrollable.

Two rows of elm trees on either side of a gracious walkway lined the center divide that separated downtown traffic from uptown traffic on Broadway. The lovely center island continued northward from Seventy-second Street, where town houses lined the side streets and where large buildings were planned for Broadway itself. It was a shame this parkway island and its elms would be lost when the excavations reached this area, but that would take years. And besides, Baby mused, progress was progress. And business was business.

"It's only a matter of time," Harrison Stokes was saying, walking briskly. "Four tracks on one level, running to a junction at Ninety-sixth Street. And veering off Broadway . . ." He walked several more feet. "About here."

"I think we should take McCardle's offer," Grimes said.

"If we wait till the commission gives its approval, we'll do better," Stokes said.

Baby sighed. It was the same old argument. Harrison wanted to wait till the Rapid

Transit Commission awarded the franchise.

They'd been waiting four years since the engineering plan had been adopted, and still no franchise had been awarded. It was being studied, studied, studied. To death, Baby thought. By the time the franchise was awarded, everyone would be old and gray.

"We could be old and gray by that time," Grimes said, voicing what was in Baby's mind. "What are your thoughts, J.N.?"

Baby saw that his brother had come up behind them.

"I think we should take the money and invest it elsewhere. We have ridden this horse well enough. It's time to move on."

"Quite right, J.N." Grimes was gleeful.

"Oh, very well," Stokes said. He and Grimes were investors in the Electric Vehicle Company, which manufactured battery-powered cars, not far from where they were standing. The partners got into their electric automobile, and the two Burgoynes got into Baby's gasoline-operated Benz.

Baby felt resentment boil up inside him. J.N. had an instinct for business. Everyone said so. Business bored Baby. Politics bored Baby. Everything bored Baby. Even women bored him. Well, not all women. He had to admit to a certain interest in the Jewess, Esther Breslau. Except, she was mistress to his cousin, Oz Cook, or so Mama said.

Oz Cook was so old, Baby thought, and she was so young. Mama called her a fortune hunter. Well, Baby would be delighted if Esther Breslau would hunt him for his fortune.

Alas, he had no fortune. His father's mother had been a Neldine, as had Oz Cook's mother. The wealth came from the Neldine side of the family. With Cook having no children, the Burgoyne siblings would have inherited . . . But on Cook's death, should he leave his fortune to the Jewess, Baby counted himself ready to marry her.

"What the hell's the matter with you, Baby?" J.N. grumbled as Baby swerved the automobile, narrowly missing a lorry stopped beside the road.

At Seventy-second Street, Baby nearly plowed into a paperboy running across the road to a customer. He kept going with the paperboy's curses in his ears.

J.N. had an interest in the land. He'd searched the title and drawn up the documents. He would be rich in his own right when the sale went through.

Not Baby. Baby's pockets were empty, his credit stretched. If he could only find the locket, things would be different.

Chapter 32

Wednesday, July 19.

The Sicilian sun was warm and good. The young girl had smooth olive skin and big tits. With moist fingers she peeled the grapes and fed them to him. He savored the tart flesh. Suddenly the grapes were stones. The pain drove him awake.

Tony seized the bottle of grappa on the floor next to his bed and filled his mouth with the coarse brandy, then clutched his jaw in agony. He swallowed, took another drink, guiding it away from the left side of his mouth.

And now this new thing. What was he, Jesus on the cross? His hands, face, and shoulder still stung from the hot water the nigger bitch had baptized him with.

Several more drinks and all his pains subsided, but not the anger. He had to find that damned locket and get the money owed him. For the sake of his honor, the tooth must wait till he'd completed the job, and he'd been paid.

Another drink and he knew that the pain was good. It would goad him on, make him work quickly.

He poured tepid water from pitcher to basin and tried to shave. The only place he could stand the feel of the blade was under his chin. For the rest he'd find some olive oil to soothe him. He would let his beard grow.

The nick on his throat didn't bother him, though it was most unlike him, for he was a perfectionist. He knew that only a little pressure and the artery would feel the blade. Death would come in minutes. And for his suicide, he would burn in hell.

He laughed. "What makes you think you won't burn, anyway?" he asked the image of his father in the mirror. He honed the blade again before he put it away.

Dressed, he brushed his suit with the damp rag and reached for the hand organ leaning on the wall. He hesitated. No. Not today. Today he needed to move fast, unencumbered.

One final swallow of grappa. He was going among the micks. That meant he'd have to subsist on watery beer or tasteless whiskey. He would have to be wary, because he

didn't look like them and he didn't talk like them. They would consider him the enemy.
As they should.

The Harp on Bleecker Street was the fifth mick bar he'd been to. This hole in the wall was near the precinct, where he knew the cops came for the free lunch they got with the drinks. He stood at the end of the bar listening.

Next to him was a mick with breath as foul as the dead goat beard on his ugly face. He was running at the mouth about his friend Mulroony and the pitiful way he died.

The rest clustered round the goat, some actually weeping.

Tony pondered. Buy the goat a drink or wait for him outside and hold Marie to his balls? The goat pushed through the group to relieve himself in the room in the back, then returned and lurched along the bar, drinking the dregs from glasses. He bumped against Tony, who did not move away.

The goat gave him a bleary, pale blue stare. "Tim Noonan's the name. You can call me Wingy."

Tony waited.

"Good to see you again, sir." Wingy groaned. "Ah, the condition of me arm is something piteous today. Truth be told, I could use a drink."

"Tell me about Mulroony, and I'll buy you a beer."

A shrewd glint came into Wingy's clouded eyes. "I'm fair thirsty. A thirst only whiskey can quench."

"Beer."

Wingy sighed. "Beer 'tis, then."

Tony raised a hand.

Pock-faced Jimmy Callahan took Tony's measure. Not many Eyetalians found their way into the Harp. This one's skin was a funny red, but he was dressed clean and neat. But why wasn't he with his own kind? What did he want?

Tony didn't like the scrutiny. "Beer for him, whiskey for me."

"Now is that fair?" Wingy whined. "I ask you, Jimmy, is that fair?"

The drinks were served, the money paid. Jimmy Callahan stood off to the side, watching as he rolled himself a Bull Durham. Jimmy did not trust dagos. He never met one who was worth a fiddler's fart.

Wingy slurped beer, Tony sipped whiskey. "If you tell me slow," Tony said, "I'll finish my whiskey. If you tell me fast, I'll leave it for you."

"What you want to know?" Wingy spoke carefully, biting each word.

"Mulroony."

"Mulroony, the priest, or Mulroony, the cop?"

"The cop."

"Very tragic for his poor ma." Wingy crossed himself. "Hail Mary, Mother of God —"

"The longer I wait, the less you get." Tony took a hearty sip of the whiskey.

Wingy's face screwed up as if he would cry. "You don't want to do that, mister. My friend Aloysius Rafferty, the famous bricklayer and stevedore —"

"Aloysius?"

"Ain't you never heard of St. Aloysius? Well, Aloysius he seen Mulroony tearing after a bunch of young punks right before he found that dead whore in the empty lot a couple of weeks ago."

"Where can I find him?"

"Mulroony, he's in the ground."

"I'm not talking about Mulroony."

Wingy nodded many times. "Oh, you mean Aloysius? His wife runs a rooming house somewhere on the Bowery. He's most mornings on the South Street docks, near Jefferson."

Tony strode out of the saloon, patting Marie sleeping in her sheath strapped to his thigh under his trousers. He rolled the strange name over his tongue, Aloysius Rafferty, Aloysius Rafferty.

CHAPTER 33

Wednesday, July 19. Late afternoon.

As always when Nonna stepped out of her house on Park Avenue at One Hundred and Eighth Street, she stopped to admire her stable across the Park Avenue road, which up here was really not much more than the New York Central Railroad track.

For Nonna, the stable was a work of art. And the obvious aroma her work of art gave off was rich with the smell of horses. Less obvious was that which had no smell: money.

On the second floor was the hayloft. To the side of the loft in an added-on area were the workers' rooms.

The front of the first floor was where she stored the carriages. In the back were fifteen horse stalls. Behind the stalls, a sixty-foot-square manure pit and the outhouses. On the street, coachmen, grooms, horseshoers were all busy. And all of these endeavors and her workers made her richer every day.

Nonna had seen the scrawny little boy helping the horseshoers for several weeks, but had not bothered to talk to him. Today she felt particularly refreshed from her nap. She crossed the road.

"You the new kid, eh?"

The boy removed his cap before the tall, red haired woman. "Si, Nonna."

Nonna Pasquarella cackled. The Pekingese dog in her arms yapped. "Quiet, 'Mazzio." She turned to see who was in attendance today. Her eyes settled on her burly grandson Giorgio, standing first and foremost in front of two of his equally sturdy cousins. "You hear how respectful the little one is with me?"

Giorgio, his face expressionless, nodded.

"What's your name?"

Patsy bent forward, kissing Nonna's hand in the typical Southern Italian expression of respect. "Patsy Hearn, ma'am."

"This is a good boy." Nonna eyed Giorgio for a long moment. She turned back to Patsy. "How come you still here with all these greasy Eyetalians?"

"The food's good."

"Ha!" she said. "An honest boy, too. What do we have you doing?"

"When I'm not helping out around the

stable, I stall for the pickpockets."

"You don't mind robbing from your own kind?"

"I'm my own kind."

"I like this boy. Giorgio, you hear that?"

Giorgio heard all right. He grew hot with anger, but knew better than to reveal it in any way. Nonna liked to toy with her heirs, make them distrustful of one another, keep them unsure. But this runt wasn't even family. "Si, Nonna," Giorgio said, with humility.

"Here." Nonna thrust the Pekingese at Patsy. "I make you in charge of 'Mazzio's walk."

'Mazzio showed his teeth and emitted a nasty growl, which made Giorgio smile. But then the runt whispered in 'Mazzio's ear and what did the Pekingese do, but lick his face.

Nonna smiled benignly. " 'Mazzio is a good judge of people. You come with me now," she told Patsy.

Patsy set 'Mazzio down on the ground and he and the dog followed Nonna.

The fat one with the garlic breath, Pancetta, and the man Benito had pulled him out of the river more than half dead and brought him here to Nonna's world, where there were others like him, orphans and otherwise, who lived on the streets of the City. He fit right in. They were teaching him their ways, and he was grateful.

When he and Nonna had walked out of sight of the stable, Patsy stood with his hands on his hips watching the dog do its business. A strong hand grabbed the back of his neck like a vise and turned him.

The hand brought him tight against Nonna. "So now you tell Nonna why you're in the river. And what is this?" She forced his head up so he was looking at her fearsome face and a clenched fist. She undid the fist and spread her crooked fingers.

Gasping, eyes bulging, Patsy saw his treasure, the gold tooth he'd found next to the dead lady, gleaming in the palm of Nonna's hand.

Chapter 34

Wednesday, July 19. Early evening.

The Bowery wasn't that far from Bleecker. Tony walked to Seventh Street and headed west. When he reached the Bowery, he found more bad luck.

By the variety of signs on walls and in windows there were far too many rooming houses. He would have to sweat to find Rafferty. The object of his search would soon be obvious to all, which might be a good thing and might not, as it would call more attention to himself than he wanted.

Bad enough his tooth hurt. The hot day made his skin sting where the scalding water had hit. Damn that nigger bitch. The saloons beckoned. Which one didn't matter. He opened a door and stepped inside to shouting and laughter. An Irish place, by their lumpy potato heads and the cabbage and pig feet stink.

Irishmen loved to drink and talk and talk

and drink and drink. They were braggarts. He preferred to drink alone, left to his own thoughts.

It was a dark and dank place, the smell of beer and hard-boiled eggs potent. The men sitting around tables or standing at the bar stopped talking to stare at him.

He didn't waste his time asking for grappa. "You have red wine?"

"This is McSorley's. Beer and ale." The tone was unpleasant. "We don't serve wine."

"Or dagos," a customer yelled.

Then, as others repeated the phrase, a firehouse gong behind the bar went off.

Tony felt for Marie. But he didn't bring her out. He flicked his thumbnail on the edge of his top front teeth, spit on the sawdust floor, and left to loud jeers.

He didn't want to deal with another mick saloon. He might have to stick a few bog trotters, then where would he be? He renewed his quest. Two blocks north his luck changed. On the wall, inviting him, was the sign. "MRS. A. RAFFERTY: ROOMS."

He knocked and pushed open the ground-level front door. He was in a tiny vestibule. To his left, a small parlor, to his right, another small room that held a long table and ten chairs. The table was set for dinner. A narrow, tilting staircase led up.

"Yes?" A full-figured woman with a rolling pin in her hand came from around back behind the staircase. Strands of gray hair crept from under her cotton scarf, and she had spots of flour on her doughy face.

"I need a room."

She looked him over. "All full up."

"I hear your husband works on the docks."

"What's it to you?"

"I need a job."

"He ain't home."

"Okay," Tony said, backing out. "Sorry to bother."

"No bother. Goodnight."

"Goodnight."

Tony walked into the alley to the right of the house. At the back he found an open window. An unoccupied bedroom by the looks of it. Good, that's how he'd get in if he had to.

He left the alley and crossed the street to a cigar shop. Either the son of a bitch Rafferty was hiding in the house or he was sitting in a saloon drinking instead of going home.

With one of his twisted cigars between his teeth, Tony stepped out on the street again and fired it up as he crossed the road.

He was a patient man. He would wait. The Bowery was a busy place at night. Carousers and pickpockets. He settled in, his back against the bricks.

Every workman who staggered past him he gave the eye. Two men, sailors, by the bags slung over their shoulders, stopped at the Rafferty house, peered at the sign, and went in. No one came out, not even the two sailors, so the woman had lied. She had rooms. But not for Italians.

The tap of a club on bricks was unmistakable. Now the whistling of some awful Irish tune located the policeman on his rounds, just a block away.

Tony eased into the alley. The abrupt scratching shuffle of claws told him he'd disturbed a pack of rats. He saw the bright eyes staring at him from not ten feet away. Glints of white teeth showed in the dim light. Five or six filthy rats, on their guard and enraged, screamed at him.

He found a broken cobble stone, but didn't throw it, lest the cop hear. The minutes passed with Tony and the rats staring at each other. When he could no longer hear the tapping or the whistling, Tony let fly.

An angry screech. When the stunned rat fell, his mates immediately turned and fed on him. It was to be expected. Such was the world. Tony returned to the walk in front of the Rafferty house.

A long-legged man had his hand on the door.

"Mr. Rafferty?"

"No, I'm O'Neil. What you want with Al?"

"My brother works on the docks with him. I'm delivering three dollars he owes Mr. Rafferty."

"Why don't you come inside? Money is always welcome. I'm sure his missus will give you a taste for the news of it."

"No. If she asks for the money, I'll have to give it to her. Then Rafferty will be mad at my brother."

The man laughed. "Begorra, you've got Alice Rafferty down all right. Don't you worry, I won't tell her."

"Thank you."

Shortly after O'Neil went in, a pudgy man paused in front of the rooming house to straighten his clothing. He was covered with dust. Just the type of husband Mrs. Alice Rafferty would have. Tony could smell the dust and beer on him.

"Mr. Rafferty?"

"Who wants to know?"

"If you're the right Rafferty, I have money for you."

"I'm Al Rafferty." His greedy eyes glinted like the rat's. "What money?" he demanded.

Tony walked into the alley. Rafferty followed, the lamb to slaughter. As soon as they were completely in shadow, Tony hooked his left arm around Rafferty's throat, squeezing and dragging him deeper into the alley.

The stinking mick went and pissed himself. Tony yearned to let Marie chew his guts, but he needed what Rafferty could tell him. He drew Marie through the hole in his right-hand pants pocket, caressing her blade.

Rafferty's eyes bulged.

Arm still around Rafferty's throat, Tony let Marie bite his fat nose. The Irishman flailed his arms. "One sound and Marie will serve you to the devil in slices." Tony took his arm away.

Rafferty fell on his knees, choking and bawling like a babe. "Shit, man, what do you want of me?"

"Information."

"What information?"

"Mulroony, the cop. You saw him chasing boys away from the place he found the dead woman."

"Yeah."

"I want their names."

"Are you crazy?" Rafferty was angry suddenly. "How would I know their names?"

"Tell me how they look."

Tony raged as he listened to the description. These were the lice who had dishonored him. The ones Mulroony chased away from the girl's body were the same little bastards who had pushed him in the gutter on Broome Street last month and stole his penny. By the Madonna, this was luck indeed. He would have the locket and settle a debt with those punks at the same time.

"Okay? Okay?"

Tony could smell the sweat pouring out of Rafferty. "Yes."

Tony gave the Irishman his hand. Rafferty stood swaying, getting himself together. Relief evident in the bounce of his walk, he started out of the alley. Tony touched him lightly on the shoulder. Rafferty started to run. Tony grabbed, whipped Rafferty around.

And let Marie have her way with him.

Chapter 35

Wednesday, July 19. Evening.

It had gotten to be commonplace — Baby remaining in the office well into the night, working on his special duties for Stokes and Grimes. He would wait until the last of the clerks and secretaries left for the evening, then move into his brother-in-law's big office, sit tipped back in Harrison's spacious leather chair, hands behind his head, feet on Harrison's massive mahogany desk.

A lot of time was spent in this position as Baby built his castles in the air.

He lit himself one of Harrison's specially rolled cigars. As the rich fumes filled the air, he planned his marriage to Esther Breslau. The marriage would take place in the elegance of St. Bartholomew's, where the Burgoynes and the Neldines had long worshiped. And if Esther wanted to continue her little Hebrew rituals at home in secret, he would not stand in her way. At least until the children came.

His stomach growled. Baby looked at his watch. It was approaching nine. He would stop at Del's for some supper before going home. The telephone jangled just as he swung his feet to the floor.

Only for a moment did he consider ignoring it. He picked up the instrument. "Harrison and Grimes."

The voice was a gruff echo of the streets. "If you want the locket, bring a C to a Hundred Street and First Avenue. Come alone."

"Forgive my timidity, but I wouldn't dream of venturing up there at this time of night."

This brought a rude noise from Baby's caller. "Yeah, I forgot they call you Baby. All right, Baby. Make it in the daytime. 'Venture' tomorrow morning. Between ten and eleven."

Baby made a telephone call, then locked up the office and crossed Beaver Street to Delmonico's. The original restaurant — there were now others in the City — was in an eight-story building in the Renaissance Revival mode of orange brick, brownstone, and terra cotta.

He passed the familiar four columns of the Pompeii entrance and rode the elevator up to the second-floor dining room, where he was greeted as a loyal patron, which indeed he was. Baby knew how things worked at Del's. Delmonico's kitchen was on the eighth floor. It was connected to the restaurant by pneumatic tubes and hydraulic elevators, servicing the dining rooms on the first and second floors. He had once, while still attending Yale, made an analysis of the business in the hope that Harrison and Grimes would invest in the well-run Swiss establishment.

Much to Baby's disappointment, Harrison and Grimes had not been interested. Their decision was given to Baby in no uncertain terms. Will Grimes was not interested in the restaurant trade. It was Baby's fate to watch on the sidelines as Del's business only got better and better.

There was no profit in looking back. Looking ahead to the future was the secret to success. And right now the future was the rapid transit system that would change the fate of the City and those who lived here.

He sipped champagne while considering the beef steak and the mutton, but in the end he ordered his favorite: corned beef hash, Del's specialty. More champagne. To finish off the meal he had another of Del's specialties: baked Alaska.

The last of the ice cream in its whipped and toasted coating was melting in his mouth when the waiter came over to tell him his guest had arrived.

Battling Jack West made his way through the crowded tables, causing a bit of a ripple as he did, for he was a man of distinctive size.

"Champagne," Baby ordered, as Jack West took the chair opposite him. "Cigar?" He offered West one of Harrison's. Each clipped the tips.

The waiter clicked his heels and lit the gentlemen's smokes, while the wine steward poured champagne into two fluted glasses. The steward left the bottle in the tall ice-filled tub beside the table.

Neither man spoke. Battling Jack watched Baby through the veil of cigar smoke, waiting.

"You'll come with me, then?"

"I will," Jack West said.

"And you understand, you're not to make yourself known unless there's a problem."

"He won't be seeing hide nor hair of me, don't you worry."

"If it's the right locket, I will just hand over the money."

"I wouldn't advise keeping the money on

your person, Mr. Burgoyne."

Baby paused at the mention of his name, then continued. "Where then?"

"I'll hold. If it's the right locket, I can come forward. We don't want you bashed over the head for the money."

A thin line of sweat appeared on Baby's forehead. "You think this may be a trap?"

Jack West shrugged. "The word is out that a particular gold locket is wanted. Up there is like a foreign country, if you get my meaning."

"I'm sure I don't."

The fluted glass was almost lost in Jack West's huge hand. He twirled it once, raised it to his lips, and drained its contents. "Eyetalians, mister. Ain't you never heard of the Black Hand?"

CHAPTER 36

Thursday, July 20. Early morning.

For the first time in his short life Patsy wasn't afraid. The sensation was so alien it made him giddy, almost the way he felt when there was no food in his belly. But this was different. He ate every day. And he slept under a real roof.

Nonna had given him three dollars for his treasure. In itself, the money was a treasure, for Patsy had never had that much altogether. Ever. If them others could see him now . . .

But Patsy wasn't anxious to let his former friends in on his good fortune. For sure, they would spoil it and he'd be back on the streets as quick as that.

And all he had to do to pay for his new life was help Nonna out, go on a few errands, walk her dog. No more stalling for the dips.

This morning's errand was simple. Go to

First Avenue and pick up a package and bring it back to the stable. Easy.

Little Jack stepped down from the wagon and looked around. First Avenue. Farmhouses, shacks, the usual pawnshops and taverns. Italian, mostly. Weber lived in a tenement in Hell's Kitchen, on West Forty-first Street, near the Ninth Avenue El. They had started from there and were working their way toward One Hundred and Tenth Street.

"Ring the bell," Weber ordered, from the driver's seat. He had a thick German accent and spit when he said words with "s" in them. Several of yesterday's newspapers lay on his lap, and he read the *New Yorker Staats Zeitung* as he drove. "I never been late on my route and I don't want to start now. They know when to expect me."

It had cost two bits for the privilege of being Weber's boy for the day, while the peddler's son, Carl Jr., got a dime and the day off.

To be wandering around in Uncle Mico's domain without his blessing was too dangerous, especially for a stranger, especially for a Jew. But Jack always dared to do what he was afraid of. He couldn't live being afraid all the time.

To give credit where it was due, Zio Mico was a fair man. He didn't like anybody. So Jack had worked out a deal with the peddler, who sold his wares in Uncle Mico's neighborhood once a week and paid Mico for the license to peddle and to pass through the country.

"Come on, come on." Weber pulled on the reins and guided his unruffled chestnut to the side of the road, where weeds and boulders shared an empty lot.

Bong, bong, bong, bong. Jack pulled on the chain and the bell sang. Bong, bong, bong, bong.

"That's enough. Get down off here and open up the back." Weber cupped his hands around his mouth and shouted, "Pots and pans, shoes and tools, yard goods, pins and needles, lucifers, kerosene! Come and get it!" Weber jumped down from the wagon and shouted his wares again.

The back of the wagon was set up so that when the gate opened, all the shelves — side by side, up and down — slid out and you could see what the peddler carried. If you didn't see what you wanted, you asked, and Weber was sure to come up with it from inside somewhere.

There was nothing he didn't have. Jack saw people beginning to straggle toward him in the already shimmering heat. Mostly swarthy women in black and children dressed in bright colors, and several dogs that tugged at the children and barked.

Hot. The blue bandanna tied around Jack's neck was soaked. It was really going to be hell come noon. Loosening the bandanna, he waited as Weber greeted the women with the utmost courtesy.

Very quickly Weber sold three bolts of patterned cloth, a hammer, needles and thread, pots with covers, a pair of shoes, and a coffee grinder. After the first group bought their goods and left, it got quiet.

Weber climbed back on the wagon and returned to his reading. He'd finished the *Staats Zeitung* and was now on the *Journal.*

"Is it over?"

Absorbed in his newspaper, Weber said, "Huh? Oh, there'll be more. We just had the early birds."

The horse snorted. Jack came around and rubbed its nose. He was hungry. "You got any apples back there?"

"For the horse."

"Gimme one for the horse and one for me."

"You're costing me dear," Weber said, but he threw down two apples, which Jack caught nimbly.

"What's the Yellow Kid up to?" Jack asked, biting into the sweet flesh of one apple and feeding the other to the nag.

"I don't know, I like the Katzenjammer Kids, myself."

"They're dumb. What's Uncle Mico look like?"

"Is that in the *Journal*?" Weber eyed him over the top of the newspaper.

"No, mister. The Italian that runs this neighborhood."

"I know who you meant. I was just funning. You'd be better off if you didn't know nothing about him."

"So I won't be better off. Tell."

"Big man. Big black beard. He got diamond rings all over his fingers. To cut people when he hits them."

Jack sighed. "You're right, I shouldn't have asked."

Weber pointed with his chin. "Next coming. Old man Rinaldi always gets kerosene. You go take care of him."

Jack went around to the tail, climbed up, and waited for the old coot to make his way to the wagon, while Weber got in the back where he couldn't be seen.

"You ain't the regular guy," Rinaldi wheezed.

Jack nodded towards Weber. "On the truck."

"He give me short measure last time."

Jack could barely understand him. He turned to the side. "Rinaldi says you gave him short measure last time."

"That robber," Weber said. "Tell him —"

"You tell him."

"Oh, shit, he's related to Uncle Mico. Give him another can for free. Hell, give him two."

A half dozen or more buyers showed up over the next while, then it petered out for sure.

Looking up at the sun, Weber began to count his take. "It's over." He climbed onto his seat.

As Jack got ready to close up the tail, he saw a hunched-over woman in black making her way down the road toward them. "Wait," he called. "Here comes one more."

"That's the last, then."

Jack greeted the old woman. "And what can we get for you today, grandmother?"

"It's hot and I'm very tired. Could I ride on back with you for a while?" The heavy coating of white powder on the woman's face did little to cover her poxy scars. Her white hair was barely visible, hidden as it was under the black scarf wound around her head and tied under her gnarled chin.

"So?" Weber called.

"She wants a ride." Without waiting for Weber's response, which came in a growl, Jack motioned the old lady to the back of the wagon. With a grunt he helped her up on the seat. She was heavier than he'd supposed. "Let's go," he shouted.

A mangy black and white dog chased after them, barking, as Weber flicked the reins and turned the wagon. Jack threw an imaginary stick and set the dog running.

"You shouldn't be so nasty," the old lady said in a hoarse, gravelly voice. "It's too hot to make an animal run like that."

Jack, sorry he'd been so charitable, said nothing.

The old woman fanned herself with her hand. "Nice breeze."

Whistling, Jack put his head out the back of the wagon, taking in the countryside. That's when he saw the gentleman, stuck out like a sore thumb, being in the wrong part of town. The gentleman consulted his watch.

"He'd better be careful," Jack said. "Someone is going to slit his throat and steal that from him."

"You think all Italians are cutthroats and thieves?" the old lady asked.

"No, mother. I know you ain't."

She cackled at that. "Don't be so sure."

As they passed the gentleman, raising a cloud of dust, Jack saw what he'd already figured. It was their client, the locket man. Instinctively, in case the client would be surprised and let on that he knew him, Jack looked away.

"What's the matter?" asked the old woman. "You think he's a cop?"

Little Jack jumped off the wagon.

"How far is she going?" Weber called.

"Ask her," Jack replied. "Wait for me on the corner."

"Hell with you, I'm going to One Hundred Tenth Street and Mrs. Kaiser's farm. She makes my dinner every day, and I'm not going to miss it for the likes of you."

The old woman said something in Italian.

Jack didn't care what Weber or the old woman said. While most of his instincts were telling him to go the other way, he was running back to One Hundredth Street.

Chapter 37

Thursday, July 20. Early morning.

No sooner had Patsy came out of a butcher shop where he had delivered Nonna's envelope, when a terrific fight started right on the street in front of him. Four young toughs in derby hats were beating on a fifth man. Fists and what looked awful like a baseball bat flew around so Patsy couldn't see who was getting what, but he could hear the punches landing and the cries of pain. A billfold flew up in the air and landed at Patsy's feet. He reached down and picked it up.

The four in derby hats were very familiar to Little Jack. They were the ones he and Battling Jack had run into outside of Salvatore Galipo's shop in the shadow of the Ninth Avenue El.

And they had the client down and were tearing at his clothes and beating the shit out of him. Little Jack hoped and didn't hope he would get there in time. He needn't have worried.

From his position on the first-floor porch above the client, Battling Jack came flying down like the dark Angel of Death, covering the client and all four assailants with his brawny body.

The Angel of Death now looked like an overgrown boy furiously pawing through his toys, searching for the right one.

Little Jack, who'd pulled a silver dollar from his pocket, sent it hurtling at the bloke with the pigtail. Pigtail didn't know what hit him. Staggering wildly, he held his bleeding forehead with both hands, fell to his knees, then on his face, joining the *schwarz* Indian. Little Jack gave each a swift kick in the face. They'd be no more trouble this day.

The hairless one shook his head. He eyed Battling Jack's stick and spat. Apparently he hadn't learned from their last encounter. "Need a club for me, do you?"

Still holding his stick, Battling Jack punched the grinning tough square in the jaw with a left, putting him out.

Meanwhile, Pigtail and Little Jack were rolling around on the ground. Little Jack had his teeth on Pigtail's left ear. The man stank and tasted like skunk; even so Little Jack held on and bit deeper, though the man had him by the throat. Battling Jack swung his stick and snapped the bugger's arm.

Little Jack bounded to his feet, spitting blood and a bit of ear gristle.

"Are you all right, sir?" Jack West asked the client. "Are you hurt?"

"Just my dignity." Moving his limbs, running his hands over his body, Baby was satisfied nothing was broken. He adjusted his out-of-kilt collar. "And my clothing. I guess this is just another wild goose chase."

"Nothing ventured, nothing gained, as my mother used to say." Jack West picked up his tall topper and dusted it off.

Little Jack, his head down, walked round and round in circles. "You think that dark one was an Indian?"

"How many times do I have to tell you, don't lead with your right?" Jack West grumbled.

"I nailed him, didn't I?"

"Next time you won't be so lucky. What are you doing?"

"Looking for my dollar."

Battling Jack peered past Little's shoulder. A stranger had joined them.

The stranger was almost as big as Battling Jack. His black hair was precisely combed, what you could see under his wide-brimmed hat. His beard was full and so black it seemed touched with blue. The diamond rings covering his fingers glinted in the sun.

"Gentlemen," the bearded man said.

Baby was surprised to find himself half bowing, as if in the presence of royalty. "Sir."

"I am Don Giosuele. I am called Uncle Mico."

"I am Jack West."

"I found it!" Little Jack displayed his silver dollar.

The Don and Battling Jack both frowned.

Little stood very still.

"I know who you are, Don Giosuele," Jack West said. "I apologize for our intrusion. But I assumed that the invitation to my client to do business up here was from you."

Uncle Mico shook his large head. "I know who you are, too, Battling Jack West. There is a charge for coming into my country."

"I'm afraid," said Baby, "they took my billfold."

Standing a few paces away, Pasty saw Little Jack turn in his direction. The billfold. The mug had seen Patsy pick up the billfold. Patsy understood what he had to do. He tossed it to Little Jack, who handed it to the client.

"Will twenty do?" the client asked, checking his wallet to see what remained.

Little Jack motioned for Patsy to skedaddle, which he did.

"Yes." Uncle Mico watched Patsy run off, a benign expression on his face. "But I will ask only ten for ridding me of those vermin."

"We only chased them," Jack West said.

"And we will catch them," Uncle Mico replied.

Later that night the four toughs who had dared to poach on Don Giosuele's domain had their hands chopped off and their tongues slit in the Sicilian tradition, as a lesson to anyone else who might want to dip their fingers into Uncle Mico's pot.

The hands and bodies and a pile of rocks were crammed into three trunks, which two men rowed out into the East River. The trunks were shoved into the salty brine. Four derby hats were added to the inventory in Uncle Mico's basement.

CHAPTER 38

Thursday, July 20. Late morning.

Wingy's greasy tears made tracks down his cheeks. Moaning, he darted through the streets in his ungainly gait, sometimes knocking into pedestrians and once tripping over a small dog.

"Hey, Wingy, somebody steal your drink?" shouted a man whitewashing a brick wall. Wingy was a familiar sight in these parts, always cadging money for the drink.

"Bo Clancy. Bo Clancy. You seen him?"

"Ain't he at the House on Mulberry Street?"

"Where's that? Would you take me there?"

"Are you crazy?"

"Give me a nickel then for a drink."

The painter gave him a penny and went back to his work.

Wingy reeled his way around Greenwich Village, finally settling on a bench in Washington Square Park, where between slobbering and whimpering about needing to find Bo Clancy, he managed to collect eleven pennies from people going by.

The coins clutched tight in his hand, he tottered over to Fifth Avenue and leaned up against George Washington's Arch, snuffling. He had something important to tend to. Looking for someone . . . "Stop your pushing," he cried, opening his eyes. A horse was nuzzling him on the shoulder.

"You shouldn't be here, Wingy."

"Yes, indeed, officer," Wingy told the horse. "But the running has destroyed me fierce today. I was wounded at Gettysburg, you know." He presented his right arm.

"Jesus, Dick Noonan." The huge man on the horse burst out laughing. "You are one for the lying. You weren't even a gleam in your old man's eyes during that war. You hurt your arm in eighty-two, jumping out of a first-floor window when we was running from that mean copper, Ed Patton."

Wingy squinted at horse. "Do I know you?"

"Of course you know me. It's Charlie McNulty you're talking to. But you can't stay here, Wingy. I got to give you the move-along."

"Sure, sure, Charlie. Would you be knowing where Bo is?"

"Bo Clancy? Matter of fact, I just saw him at the Seventh Precinct."

Wingy shook his wobbly head. "Naa. Naa. It's too far. And I don't like cops."

"I'm a cop."

"That's different, you're a horse."

McNulty leaned down and gave Wingy his hand. "Come on up, then. Josie needs a gallop."

"You want me to get on your back?"

"Come on now." After much staggering and stumbling and a full collapse, finally with the employment of his bad right arm, Wingy sat behind the big cop. McNulty gave Josie a nudge with his heels and they were off.

The heavy New York traffic was hardly an obstacle for Josie. No more than ten minutes later they were at Clinton Street.

"Bo Clancy in there?" McNulty called to a cop coming out of the precinct house, while Josie drank noisily from the horse trough out front.

"Yeah. Talking to Ned."

"Thanks. There you go, Dick Noonan."

"Thank you. How'd you do that? Talk and drink at the same time?"

"Just step inside and speak your peace."

"Thank you, kindly," Wingy said, settling himself on the curb. "I'll just wait for him.

I'm grateful for the ride. Next time I'll buy you a bag of oats."

When Bo came out, Wingy was slumped in the gutter near the trough, crying his eyes out.

"Wingy? Is that you?"

"Good day, Bo Clancy. What a coincidence to see you here. You know, I been looking for you all over. But if it's nothing to you, I'll stay right here. The condition of me arm is piteous. Hurt in the war, I was. I'm ruined today by climbing on the back of a giant horse as I looked all the hell over to find you. So it's your fault that I'm dying of the thirst, Mr. Clancy, sir."

"What's this all about, Wingy?"

Wingy cleared his throat. "I could use a drink."

"There's the water."

Wingy moaned.

"Talk."

The pathetic drunk began to slobber again. "Oh, shit, and it's my fault Al Rafferty is dead, sir."

"Al Rafferty? What's it got to do with you?"

"Here, give me a hand up. Mind me bad arm."

Bo half lifted the disheveled derelict, propping him up against the trough. "Tell me about Rafferty."

"I spoke to him during the day yesterday and by night he's dead, and it's my fault."

Bo measured Wingy skeptically. What the hell did a bum like Wingy have to do with the knifing death of Aloysius Rafferty? "You were down on the docks with Rafferty?"

"No, sir. Not Rafferty." He began to bawl. "No, no. Not Rafferty. I done it."

"Jesus, man. Are you saying you killed Rafferty?"

"Are you daft? You should quit the daytime drinking, Mr. Clancy. It's not doing you any good."

"Finish your damn story already and I'll stand you for a real drink."

"He was looking for Rafferty. He gave me his whiskey. I saw no harm in it. Everyone knows where Rafferty lives."

"If you don't get to it, I'm walking away from here," Bo thundered. "Who is it you're talking about?"

Wingy cringed, his hand slipped into the trough. "It was the devil himself, sir, and as I've always suspected, he's Eyetalian."

Chapter 39

Thursday, July 20. Evening.

Wong tapped softly and opened the door to the studio. The room was dark except for the glowing tip of a cigarette, which was immediately extinguished.

"Wong?" Esther reached over and turned on the electric lamp, feeling like a naughty child who'd been caught out. What remained of the cigarette sent up a faint trail of smoke from the ashtray. She'd been sitting in the dark, her stockinged feet up on the footstool, for over an hour, thinking.

"Detective Tonneman." Wong stood aside to allow Dutch to enter, then surreptitiously removed the ashtray and left the room.

Esther caught a trace of a knowing smile on the Chinaman's face. She turned to Dutch, whose expression was not debatable. "Why are you grinning like the Cheshire Cat?"

"I'm with you. Why shouldn't I smile?"

"So this is a social call?"

Flushing, he studied the carpet where her small high-topped black kid boots lay empty. "Well, not exactly."

"Then you're here on official business?"

"I am. But just because I'm a cop doesn't mean I can park my heart downstairs on the rack with my derby."

Charmed, Esther said, "John Tonneman, you are a very sweet man."

"I am." He sat down on the needlepoint footstool and placed his hand on her ankle.

"John, please, no." The words were easy. Moving from under his hand was not. She didn't want to. She reached out and touched his smooth-shaven face. Her hand slid around to the back of his neck; she drew him to her and kissed him.

He held her close, returning her kiss.

Suddenly she pulled away. "No."

"Esther —"

She jumped to her feet and rushed into the dark room. The red light went on as she slammed the door.

"Esther. Please." He stood there like a lump for what seemed like eternity.

On the other side of the door she was waiting for the trembling to stop. When it did, she opened the door.

He took her in his arms.

"We can't do this," she said.

"Sorry." He sat in a chair and watched as she, her back to him, thumbed through several photographs on her work table.

"You have questions to ask me?"

"Yes. I saw Sophie this afternoon."

"How is she?"

"The doctors are confident she'll recover fully. But she's not the Sophie she was. She's frightened by what happened, how easily he got to her, and keeps talking about you. She thinks he'll come for you next."

Esther's eyes slid away from him. "So does Oz. That's why he hired Mr. West."

"I saw him sitting downstairs in your front hall. Impressive sight. Battling Jack and Wong make quite a pair."

"So you see, I'm well protected and there's no need to be concerned."

"I wanted to see you, hold you."

"It's late, John. I have work to do, and a busy day ahead of me."

He stood. "I'll go."

As he passed by her to the hall, she grasped his hand. "Oh, John. I can't bear this."

They'd hardly embraced when she pulled away again and ran up the stairs.

"Damn it to hell." Frustrated, Dutch smacked his hand against the wall, and started down the stairs.

"John."

He stopped and looked upward. "Esther, you are making me crazy."

"I'm not exactly sane myself. Otherwise, I wouldn't be asking you to come with me."

He was sweating. "I think I'd better go."

She gave him a nervous smile. "What must you think of me? Did you think I was inviting you to my room for an assignation?"

Flustered now for new reasons, he all but tottered up the stairs. "Of course not," he lied.

She moved farther up the stairs, so that when he reached her they were both on the fourth-floor landing.

"Take my hand, please."

He shook his head. "I think not."

"Please."

He took her hand and they promenaded along the fourth landing as if they were in the Central Park. All that was missing was the sunshine and her parasol.

"Ask me."

"What?"

"What you've been asking me for the last four years."

"Esther . . ." Where the hell was the old guy? He wasn't deaf. Surely he could hear them on the staircase.

"No, wait." Up the stairs she went again, her hand trailing behind her. He followed. "Stay right there." He remained at the foot of the stairs while she ran up to the fifth-floor landing.

"For Christ's sake, Esther? What's going on?"

"Ask, but not in his name."

"God's sake, then. Stop this nonsense."

"Ask me."

"Will you marry me?"

"Yes." And she ran down the hall.

"What?"

"I said yes, you idiot." She was standing at the door to her rooms, her eyes bright.

He walked very slowly, all the time thinking that this is what he'd been wanting for four years. But now that it was said, how would he deal with Ma?

"What troubles you, my ardent Irishman?"

The door to her flat was open; her arms were open wide. Kissing her, feeling her warmth against him, he thought he would explode.

"Esther." His hands mingled with the thick strands of her hair. "This is wrong."

"I know."

"Miss Esther!" Wong's voice carried up from the third-floor landing. "Come quick. Mr. Oz on the telephone."

"Oh, well." Esther smiled at him, her heart beating wildly. "So much for that. Obviously we weren't meant to be sinners." She brushed past him as she ran down the stairs to take Oz Cook's telephone call.

Dutch was dizzy. He sat on the stairs shaking his head. Was he happy or glad? He couldn't rightly say. Getting to his feet, he wandered through the open door to her rooms, around her sitting room, then into her bedroom, touching things.

He sat in a chair and reached for her white dressing gown, which lay across the bed. He inhaled her scent from her pillow. To his left was a French-style bureau, nearby, a small sink. He crossed to it and wet his face. And wet it again. Straightening, he dried his face with the dainty towel from the hook. Now, with the perfume of her soap in his nostrils, he noticed the partially open bureau drawer.

He folded and returned the towel to its proper place. His hand rested on the edge of the open drawer. Later he would never be able to say if the man who opened the drawer was just a lovesick fool wanting to touch his lady's intimate things, or a cop doing his job.

Dutch fingered the silky lingerie with longing. About to close the drawer, he paused. Among the pale sheer items, he'd caught a dark shadow. His hand went back under the neat pile. What he felt was something foreign. Slowly, he lifted the dainty fragrant undergarments and set them aside.

In clear view now was what had given him pause: a black velvet ribbon. And attached to the ribbon was a gold locket.

CHAPTER 40

Thursday, July 20. Evening.

Baby hurried past the four Pompeii columns. He wasn't late, but at these meetings he didn't want to miss a thing. As the elevator took him to Delmonico's second floor, he thought about Esther Breslau. Once she agreed to marry him, everything else in his life would fall into place.

Damn, J.N. was there before him, buttering up the two most important men in Baby's life: Harrison Stokes, his brother-in-law, and William Grimes.

J.N. was his brother and he loved him. But J.N. was better at this game. Baby told himself, brother or no brother, he had to watch him. The wine steward appeared when J.N. snapped his fingers. When did J.N learn that trick?

The steward poured from a fresh bottle of champagne. Playing host, J.N. offered Baby a glass. Without speaking, Baby accepted the champagne and dutifully listened to Grimes, who was talking as he always did, about real estate, land deals, riches earned through the right kind of speculation.

"Croker sent his man around," Harrison Stokes said, relighting his cigar.

Grimes was angry. "He's too greedy. He's had his cut."

"The Irish can never get enough," Stokes said. "But we can't do it without him, so there it is."

"How much does he want?"

"Another ten percent."

Baby opened his mouth to comment but felt the pressure of J.N.'s boot on his. On consideration, J.N. was right. Richard Croker was the Tammany boss, and probably the most powerful man in New York these days. Baby sipped his champagne and decided to have the beef steak.

Tony had polished his barrel organ until it glowed to his satisfaction. He pushed it along Jefferson until he was at the corner of Broome. This was where it had all started that morning a month before.

He had learned that the four boys he was looking for slept in a crib on Broome Street behind Dinty's Saloon. He had also learned that only a few blocks farther along Jefferson was where Rafferty had worked the docks unloading ships.

When he'd been back of Dinty's, he'd found the place where the boys had been nesting, but no recent sign of them.

Positioning his cart in front of Dinty's, he took a hearty swig from his flask of grappa. The tooth wasn't too bad today, but his unshaven and blistered face now itched constantly. Commanding himself not to scratch, he lit one of his twisted cigars and played "La donna è mobile."

On a stoop next to the saloon a hunched-over, pockmarked woman in black, her head wrapped in a scarf, sat fanning herself with a paper fan that bore the likeness of President McKinley. She smiled her ugly black teeth at Tony and bobbed her head to the music.

It wasn't long before a tub of a man stepped out of the saloon. He focused on Tony. "Who the hell are you?"

"I'm Tony, the organ grinder. Who the hell are you?"

The tub laughed. "Dinty Higgins. This is my tiger you're playing in front of and without so much as a by my leave."

"How much costs a by my leave?"

"A thin dime."

"Too much," Tony replied and started his

organ cart rolling.

The Irishman laughed. "How's about a nickel?"

"How's about the first and last penny I make while I'm here — if I end up with ten cents for myself."

"You don't expect much." Dinty peered up and down Broome Street. "You're right, this is the asshole of the Frog and Toe. From the first dime, you get seven I get three."

"It's a contract." Tony played and sang.

Dinty listened for a moment. "Not bad for an Italian. You know any Irish tunes?"

Tony winked. Without organ accompaniment, he sang in an appalling Irish accent, " 'Well, some may think it a misfortune to be christened Pat or Dan. But to me it is an honor to be born an Irishman.' "

Dinty laughed uproariously.

The hunched-over woman on the stoop frowned and shook her fan at Tony.

"If that don't take the cake," Dinty roared. "A wop singing 'No Irish Need Apply.' "

"And why not?" Tony asked. "I have an Irish godchild. What you call a strapping boy of twelve. You can't miss him, he has orange hair."

Dinty always found reason to laugh, but today he was having a high old time. "Maybe where you come from you can't miss him, but where he come from he's as common as shit in a stable, or drunks at a bar. Got to tend business." Dinty started back inside. He paused. "There is a red-haired lad I let sleep out back with his three friends. I hope he ain't your godchild. The four are closer to death than life." Dinty crossed himself.

Tony did likewise. "No, my godchild works on the dock."

Dinty shook his head. "I ain't seen those boys for a while. Might be dead for all I know." Dinty sighed. "Four mutton-head kids who rush growlers for me for money to eat and have a drink of beer of a night. Lord have mercy on their poor souls." The Irishman crossed himself again and hurried into his saloon.

"Yes." Tony spat into the street. "Lord have mercy. I sure as hell won't."

CHAPTER 41

Thursday, July 20. Evening.

Oz's voice crackled and disintegrated in Esther's ear. She looked at Wong. "I can't hear him." Lifting the speaker close to her lips, she shouted, "Oz? I can't hear you."

Taking the instrument from her hand, Wong disconnected. "He will call again."

Esther was excited. "He's found something. I know it! Where are you going?"

"Your shoes, Miss Esther." Wong was already on the third floor.

The realization came with a breathy giggle. What did she care about her shoes now? It was time for bed. The thought of bed brought a flush to her cheeks and the image of John Tonneman in her rooms. Where was he? He hadn't followed when she came downstairs to answer Oz's call.

She lifted her skirts and ran like a wild child up the stairs, passing an astonished Wong on his way down, her kid boots in his hand. At the entrance to her sitting room, she halted, clutching the doorframe to catch her breath. "John?"

"Esther."

John looked ridiculous sitting in her small sofa, his large body dwarfing it. In his hand, dangling from the velvet ribbon, was Delia's gold locket. Her heart sank.

He watched her with hard blue eyes. "You lied to me."

The sharp ringing of the telephone began again, then stopped.

"I gave my word," she said.

He didn't move; his eyes were cold, his knuckles white with his anger. "I see."

But he didn't, she knew that. "You don't see at all." Who was this stranger, who only minutes before she'd agreed to marry? Her eyes filled but she wouldn't let the tears flow.

"Miss Esther." Wong paused in the doorway. The anguish in the air between Esther and Tonneman was apparent. "Mr. Oz said to tell you he must talk with you before you retire. He's at the Players and will be home shortly."

Tonneman got to his feet, his considerable presence taking up most of the spare space in the small room. "I'll say goodnight then."

"Goodnight," Esther said firmly. She turned away.

"No need to see me out, Wong."

But Wong preceded Tonneman, handed him his hat, and watched with mixed feelings as the detective left.

Rounding the corner of Gramercy Park West, Oz walked briskly, a jaunty swing to his stick. He'd just spent an interesting, enlightening evening at one of his clubs. The Players, on Gramercy Park South, only yards from his home, was an hospitable place for actors, writers, and artists to gather in their own society.

"Well, Detective," Oz said, to a tight-lipped, clearly angry John Tonneman. "A little late to make a social call, don't you think?"

"Don't worry, she's waiting up for you." Tonneman's words and tone were bitter.

Bully, Oz thought, delighted. Manifestly, a major sea change had taken place. Bully.

"I suppose you put her up to it."

"Put her up to what, young man?"

"Never you mind. You won't win." Tonneman headed off toward Third Avenue without looking back.

"My oh my, what an odd lot this new generation of young people are."

Across the street, standing in front of the gate to Gramercy Park, Battling Jack, arms folded, and Jack Meyers, in similar posture, stood watching.

Oz beckoned to Jack West.

The bodyguard trotted across the narrow street. "And a good evening to you, Mr. Cook."

"Why are you outside?"

"The better to do my job, sir. If I was inside, who knows what sort of villains might be outside?"

Oz considered the answer. Finding it sound, he flipped his hand, dismissing West.

"I'll be here if you need me, sir," Battling Jack said. He returned to his post.

Wong was waiting, the front door open. Oz stared at him. The Chinaman's face actually revealed an emotion. What was it? Not dismay. Handing Wong his hat and cane, Oz demanded, "Well, what's the matter with you?"

"Miss Esther is very upset."

"The boor insulted her? I'll call him out. Smile, Wong, I made a joke."

"This is not the time for joking."

"Oh, very well. Where is she?"

"In her rooms."

"Bring me a bottle of Napoleon and two glasses. Don't worry, we'll take her mind off Tonneman. I think she'll enjoy what I've discovered."

■ ■ ■ ■

"Detective Tonneman didn't look any too happy," Jack Meyers said.

"That's not our business," Battling Jack replied, his eyes following a brougham as it made its way around the park streets.

"On the other hand, Mr. Cook seemed in good spirits."

"Enough of your prattle," Jack West growled. "We're here to look out for Miss Esther."

"Yes, sir."

"And you know you don't have to 'sir' me, you snotty bastard."

"All right, Jack, what's bothering you?"

"Anybody ever tell you you're a smart little Jew?"

"You do all the time."

"Go on with you. I can take care of this myself."

"Good. I'm hungry."

"Have it on the run. I want you back on the locket."

"I thought that was over with."

"I think not. Otherwise, our affluent friend wouldn't have called me on the telephone this afternoon and raised the bonus."

"You're just now telling me?"

"I'm the boss."
"Yes, sir."
"Snotty little bastard."

Knocking lightly on her door, Oz called, "Esther." No answer. He put his ear to the door. She was crying. Damn it all, he would have to call the big boor out after all. He tried again. "Esther, I have things to tell you."

"Go away."

"No, my dear, I won't go away. I live here." He rattled the doorknob, like a young swain, he thought, highly amused. The door opened. Esther was sprawled face down on the sofa, crying. Oh, dear, he thought, how awkward. But he carried on. "Come now. It can't be that bad." He sat on the sofa beside her, patting her trembling shoulders. Her sobs began to subside.

"It is," she said.

"I'll call him out."

Lifting her head, she offered a tremulous smile. Her eyes were red and tender.

"Wong didn't think that was funny."

"It's not," she said with a hiccough.

"Would you like to hear what I've discovered?" He handed her his handkerchief.

"Oh, yes."

"Well, our Irene Hall's father was a doctor, an austere man who somehow made an accomplished marriage. Her mother, who died in childbirth, was a Bayard."

"A Bayard? I don't understand."

"The Bayards, my dear, were part of the original Dutch community here. They think of the Neldines and Cooks as utter parvenus."

"Very rich?"

"Oh, my dear."

"Then if Delia was rich, why did she become a prostitute?"

"Yes." He patted her hand. He had distracted her enough from her misery. "That is the mystery for us to solve, and when we do, we'll know why she was murdered. Now do you want to tell me what happened to you this evening?"

Esther sat up and tried to straighten her hair, her dress, all the while hiccoughing. "After your first call, I came back up here and John was sitting right where we are, very, very angry with me. He'd discovered the locket and said I'd lied to him." Esther blotted the tears from her cheeks with Oz's handkerchief.

"And the locket?"

"He has it."

CHAPTER 42

Thursday, July 20. Evening.

Larry Kelly and his brother Ed were falling-down drunk and already mean and belligerent when Lonegan showed them the door.

"This is a decent establishment where a decent working man can have a quiet drink or two," said Lonegan.

Out on the street, the Kellys walked a few blocks looking for trouble.

"See what I see?" Larry Kelly said, poking his brother.

Ed, busy pissing in the gutter, ignored Larry.

Larry swerved down the otherwise empty street toward his prey.

By the time Ed finished his business he saw that Larry was circling a young nigger bitch dressed up fancy like a white woman, big hat and all.

The Kellys swooped in on the nigger bitch, pulling on her shawl, her hat, dancing away, coming back.

"Leave me be," the woman cried.

Larry Kelly doubled over with laughter. "Yeah, yeah, hear that, Ed?"

But the Kellys chose the wrong woman when they went after Velvet Stevens. Velvet's scream was not soft and furry like velvet, no sir. It was as sharp and deadly as the razor she carried under the red velvet garter on her right thigh.

Before she could cut either of her antagonists, the local coloreds were on them, the Kellys screaming like banshees. In fact, every colored and white around for blocks came out of the woodwork to pitch in. But the coloreds way outnumbered the whites, who were escaping, Kellys with them, running south down Eighth Avenue.

Nappy Harris, on his bike, led the chase after the whites, until he almost rode into a wall of white humanity. Nappy's group was turned. They fragmented and escaped through side streets. Nappy himself came face to face with whites hurling cobblestones and swinging club, howling, "Lynch him, kill the nigger."

The organ grinder had been in Gramercy Park again, playing his organ, watching the house where the woman Esther Breslau lived. He'd collected an awesome amount of pennies, but he had not caught sight of the woman. And getting into this house would not be as easy as it had been the other.

Now he walked west and downtown, rolling his hand organ in front of him, stopping every now and then to take nips of grappa from his flask.

Without the boys, without this woman, he'd reached an impasse.

He patted Marie in her sheath as if to assure her she would work again soon. Stopping to relight his cigar, he became aware of many running footsteps, and shouting, close at hand.

From nowhere, a black reeled into him, knocking him into his organ. The colored man, Tony, and the organ all crashed to the ground.

Tony half rose, out came Marie. The movement would have been pleasing to watch were her mission not so urgent. The shiny stiletto found the African's belly. It thrilled Tony to watch her move so elegantly up to the dying fool's breast bone.

"Sweet Jesus," someone screamed.

Tony stepped back from his victim.

"Oh, my God, he's bleeding something awful," a woman wailed. "Did you see that?

He killed Walter."

The mob fell on Tony, kicking him, punching him, tearing at his clothes, his hair, gouging his face.

Tony was unafraid. They were no match for Marie. He kicked people aside, while Marie slashed a path for him. The grappa flask was lost, but Marie was safely in his embrace. He ran downtown to safety, with Mercury's wings on his heels and his organ before him.

Sitting in Richie Dunne's Tavern on Tenth Avenue, Bo was not obviously working, not even asking culls questions. He sipped his whiskey, intent on getting his glow.

Mean Maureen Reagan sat next to him, matching him drink for drink, not saying much, just keeping him company.

"So what do we think about our knifer?"

"Not much."

"Ain't that the truth." Mean Maureen Reagan smiled. Bo didn't really want conversation, just someone to sit with him while he was thinking.

A cobble stone crashed through Richie's front window.

"Jesus, Mary, and Joseph!" Richie and Bo both yelled at the same time. Richie grabbed his bat and the two ran outside in time to see Nappy Harris point his gun and let off two rounds.

The first shot took a nick out of Richie's right ear lobe, which commenced bleeding like a stuck pig. The second blew the glass of whiskey out of Bo's hand, giving him a bloody but basically unharmed hand.

"Son of a bitch," Bo and Richie said. Ready to kill, they went for Nappy, who was standing there with a foolish expression of his face, still holding the smoking gun. If a stampeding mob of shrieking men hadn't come between them and the shooter, the two might have killed him then and there.

Detective Al Pitts, who was riding on the passing Belt Line streetcar, witnessed the mob going for Nappy. He leaped to the street, battled his way through the furious pack, shouting, "Police, stand aside!" When he got to Nappy, who was on the ground being clobbered, he arrested him.

The crowd butted Detective Pitts, trying to recapture Nappy but the detective held his ground. Bo Clancy pushed his way to Pitts's side. Together, they transported the Negro to the West Thirty-seventh Street Station, followed by the howling rabble of angry whites.

A few blocks from the station house the sweating detectives were helped by two roundsmen who beat off infuriated whites with their nightsticks.

By this time crowds of both races were milling dangerously outside the station house, threatening a race riot. Reinforcements were sent for to guard Nappy in the precinct house and keep order in the adjoining neighborhoods. Consequently, twelve coppers, clubs swinging, dispersed the mob.

Only Richie Dunne stood in front of the house, raging. He lumbered like a bull through the club-swinging cops and fell to the pavement, stunned, for his trouble.

Bo ran to his friend's side. "Don't kill him, boys, he's a saloon owner."

The joke calmed the cops.

Bo parked Richie on a bench and asked the desk sergeant for the use of his telephone.

"What have we got here?" the desk sergeant muttered, looking beyond Bo toward the door.

Bo turned. Captain Joe McHugh came into the house, hat under his arm, raking his fingers through his overgrown thatch of red hair. Spotting Bo, he said, "Clancy, just the man I wanted to see. I've got one for your book."

"What do you mean?"

"The Mulroony stabbing you're working

on, and that whore, weren't they both stabbed in the gut, then ripped up to the chest?"

Bo's head dipped in agreement. "Yeah."

"Well, I think your man's going in for dark meat. We just found a colored boy in the gutter on Eighth, near Sixteenth, butchered the same way."

Chapter 43

Thursday, July 20. Night. To Friday, July 21. Early morning.

"Oh, shit," Bo said, as he waited for Central to get him the House on Mulberry Street.

"Sergeant Downey."

"It's Bo, Regis. Have you seen Dutch?"

"Right here, Inspector. Dutch."

"It's me," Bo said. "I'm in Red McHugh's house. They got themself a little black and white brawl. Our knifer's come up with a new wrinkle. Did his knife trick on a nigger. You got anything?"

"Yes," Dutch replied. "Meet me at Bellevue. It looks like the knifer was busy yesterday, too. We've got another one. A guy named Rafferty."

"I know."

Healy's saloon, at Irving Place and Eighteenth Street, was what had been the big front room of a house. The place was as shadowy as a tomb what with only a few of the electric lights lit. The only customers were a white-haired couple in the corner sharing a pitcher of beer.

Bo liked coming to Healy's. He drank free, and this was where, a few years back, he'd beat the crap out of Down-to-the-Ground Conn Clooney when they nailed the bastard.

Dutch and Bo, who had just come from Bellevue where they had observed the remains of the late Aloysius Rafferty, were making some inroads on a bottle of whiskey but were not making much headway on their case. Delia Swann's locket lay on the bar between them. Every so often, one or the other would pick up the heart-shaped locket and peruse it, then put it down on the bar again.

"What we have," Dutch said, "is a dead whore, Delia Swann, a dead cop, Jim Mulroony, a dead colored girl, Daisy Brown, a dead stevedore and bricklayer name of Rafferty, and a disemboweled colored boy, known only as Walter. Each one's been gutted the same way. We also have a half-dead Sophie and a killer who might be branded with a hot-water burn on his face. And we have a locket, with the initials I.B.H., which may or may not be connected."

"Thanks to the generosity of Miss Esther Breslau," Bo said sarcastically.

Dutch refused to rise to the bait. "We have the dead whore's real name: Irene Hall."

"What we've got," Bo said, bitterly, "is five dead bodies and no killer. And what I've got is Commissioner Bernard J. York up my ass about it."

Spots Healy, a lanky fellow with freckles, came down from his quarters upstairs, his pinkies digging away at the wax in his large ears. "No customers?" he said, as if this amazed him.

"Just them," Dutch said, nodding at the old couple.

"And us," Bo added.

"Drinking my profits away, I see," Healy said.

Healy squinted at his pinkie nails, then at the gloom in his establishment. He turned on the rest of the lamps on the wall and those that illuminated the windows, one on either side of the front door.

Bo yanked the high-backed stool, set his foot on the brass rail. "Give us a round. Wipe your hands first."

Healy made a show of rubbing his hands in the bar rag, then served Bo and Dutch each a beer and a whiskey.

Dutch bobbled his glass of whiskey but

caught it before it spilled.

"Steady," Bo commanded. "That's precious stuff."

They drank the whiskey quickly, toasted each other solemnly, and chased the whiskey with some beer.

Bo said, "The kids Mulroony was chasing after. What do they have to do with anything?"

"That's for us to find out."

"Well, not tomorrow." Bo looked at his watch. "Today," he said, winding it. "You start working the name Irene B. Hall. I'm going to try my hand with Mrs. Rafferty."

"After I check out Miss Hall, I'm going back to the *schvitz*."

"Good a place as any."

"So what do we do now?"

"What the fuck do you think we do? We drink."

Chapter 44

Friday, July 21. Morning.

"Irene B. Hall, you got it, Detective?" Dutch wiped the sweat from his face and muttered a curse at the ceiling fan, which did nothing but help turn the pages in the directory.

"Yes, sir." Detective Fogle looked as if he still had soap behind his ears. They were getting them younger and younger it seemed. "You want me to interrogate every Hall and determine the whereabouts of Irene B."

Dutch had come up with fifty-two Halls in the city directory. Sergeant O'Tool, on the desk, had given him a "volunteer" from the duty roster. Which is how he got handed the husky, palefaced lad Willie Fogle, who'd just started on the job that day.

"That's it. Just ask the question and don't offer any information."

"Yes, sir. And I want you to know this is a real honor for me to get to work —"

"Sure, Fogle. Get out your pencil and start copying. And I want a report at the end of your shift every day."

"Yes, sir, Captain Tonneman. Does this mean I have a permanent assignment with you and Inspector Clancy?"

Dutch grinned. "Don't mess it up and maybe."

"Hello, my friend Captain Tonneman." The humped-back leprechaun's Russian accent seemed thicker than usual. Mendy was swirling a stringy mop on the white and blue tiled floor. "Do I owe anybody any money?"

"No, Mendy, nothing like that. You told us Mulroony was the only customer that Sunday night, Monday morning."

The hunchback shrugged, a strange thing to witness. "Only him overnight."

"I'd like to see that room again."

"Why not? Like I've got nothing else to do," he said, dabbing a dust cloth at the orange metal–tiled walls. "Lots of people have been in there since . . ."

As Dutch remembered, the room was just big enough to hold a plain, narrow wooden table and a one-suit whorehouse closet. The table Mulroony had lain on was empty now. In expectation, a fresh sheet was folded neatly.

The floor beneath the table appeared to have been scrubbed, but the streaked and brown stain was still visible.

"If that's all, I've got work."

"Not so fast, please. I would like to talk some more about Jim Mulroony."

Mendy's stubby fingers pulled at his gray beard. Thoughtful, Dutch wondered, or searching for lice. The man's gaze from under his heavy eyelids seemed almost coquettish. "So talk, it's free."

"What did he have to say for himself that night?"

"Nothing. He threw up, soaked his head in a bucket, and went to sleep. Like usual."

Dutch blew out a tired stream of air. "And that's the end of it?"

"The end and the all. Excuse me, please. I got to go see to Mr. Pfiefer. Poor soul got the piles." Mendy shook his head sadly. "I've been telling him for years not to sit on cold stoops. But does he listen? No."

Dutch watched Mendy walking away, shaking his head. Dutch did the same and left the building. "Good morning," he said to the younger, beardless, straight-backed leprechaun. All he received in reply was a grunt. "What's your name?"

"Avram."

"I don't suppose you talked to Officer

Mulroony the night he died?"

Avram shook his head.

Dutch bit the tip of a fresh Garcia Perfecto; he'd been smoking the cigars since Leo had given him one the week before. He lit up; he deserved some pleasure out of the day. When Dutch looked up from his first taste of the Havana leaf, he saw Avram watching him. "Smoke?" He offered the boy a cigar.

From the way Avram beamed, you would have thought Dutch had offered him the moon.

The boy poked a hole in the tip of the cigar with a lucifer and flamed the match stick with a slice of his thumbnail. Dutch marveled how clean and trim Avram's nails were.

They stood smoking on Suffolk Street, not talking.

"So," Avram said.

"So," Dutch replied.

"You ever smoke those twisted cigars?"

"No."

"What do they call them?"

"Guinea stinkers."

"A man in a long brown coat and a dark brown hat. A big mustache."

"What about him?"

"The night Mulroony died I saw such a

man standing on the corner here, smoking a Guinea stinker."

Chapter 45

Friday, July 21. Afternoon.

Bo left McSorley's feeling better for the eye opener he'd just tossed down his gullet. Squinting, he peered through the webs of telephone and telegraph wires at the sun making its way west and started walking.

Two blocks uptown he came to Rafferty's Rooming House.

A big black bow was attached to the front door.

It was a typical block of houses and alleys. Bo was surprised more bodies weren't found in New York alleys than already were. Alleys were perfect places for murder. He stepped into the one to the right of Rafferty's house. Dirt and rubble accumulated in these alleys, and this was no exception. He found what he was looking for in the smear of blood still visible just a couple of feet into the alley and the scuff marks with it.

Charley Ryan, who'd been first on the

scene, had told Bo to look at the directions of the scuff marks. Said it seemed like the poor devil was making a run for it when his killer spun him around and gave him the knife. Charlie said Rafferty's death face had the biggest look of surprise he'd ever seen.

"So would I," Bo said out loud and went up to the house and rang the doorbell.

An ancient priest opened the door. "Thank you for coming. I'm Father Gleason, just step in." From the sound of the man he was just off the boat.

They stood in a dinky entryway, too crowded for the two of them and the small table that held the mass cards. The priest handed Bo a card. He shoved it in his pocket.

"Read it, please."

Bo frowned, then called the frown back. The card said, as expected, "In Loving Memory of ALOYSIUS F. RAFFERTY, July 19, 1899."

"Turn it over, if you please."

While Bo dutifully read the card, the priest whispered the words. "Grieve not, nor speak of me with tears, but laugh and talk of me as though I were beside you."

"Good sentiment," Bo said.

"I thought of it."

"Good for you —"

"I drew the cross, too. You can see stone crosses like that all over Ireland."

Bo was tempted to explain the sin of pride to this mossy old one. Instead he asked, "Can you tell me where Mrs. Rafferty is?"

"In the parlor with the late Mr. Rafferty. Will we see you at St. Francis's? Mr. Rafferty's middle name was Francis, you know."

"I didn't. Excuse me." Bo brushed past the garrulous priest toward the clicking sounds of rosary beads. The parlor was tiny. On the wall opposite the door, under a crucifix, was the bier holding the coffin, the usual kneeling bench in front of it. A half dozen people were lined up waiting for the current kneeling mourner to be done. Apparently Rafferty had lots of friends. Or could it be all the bottles and glasses on the table next to the bier?

Instead of entering the parlor, Bo walked past a narrow staircase leading upstairs and stepped into a dining room where a long table was piled with food. Mostly women in here. He peered downstairs into the kitchen, where more women were preparing food, sharing a few nips and a gossip. He wasn't looking for anything in particular, just having a good cop's look.

He returned to the parlor. Mostly men in here, having a grand old time pouring down

Al Rafferty's whiskey and drinking to his passage. Bo wiped his mouth and started for the bottle he saw on the table to the right of the bier, near a front window.

"How do you do?" said the big woman, enthroned in a large green chair between the bier and the table. "I'm Alice Rafferty. Thank you for coming." Her black scarf slipped from her head. Her gray hair was pinned into a tight bun, held together with amber combs.

"Inspector Clancy, Mrs. Rafferty. I bring you my respects and the respects of our police department," Bo said, formally.

She clutched his arm. "Ach, you're one of our boys. Well, I hope you catch the devil that robbed me of the dearest thing I had in this hard life, my Aloysius."

"We will, Mrs. Rafferty. Was Al fearful of anyone? Did he mention anything to you? You see, I'm looking for a reason why your Al was killed."

"There's not a reason in this world. It's a vale of tears we women live in, you know. My Al never hurt a fly. Everyone was his friend."

Bo had his mind set on a drink before he left. "I'm sure Al's in a better place, in the arms of Jesus."

Alice Rafferty made a sound from the

back of her throat, as if she was preparing to spit. She actually smiled. "If I know my Aloysius, he's done a bunk on Jesus and is off somewheres with his pal Jim Mulroony drinking heavenly whiskey."

Bo had his drink now, a large glass of Irish. He swallowed half. If the sod was Mulroony's mate, maybe that's why he was killed. To the grieving widow, he said, "Did you happen to notice any strangers in the neighborhood?"

"Now that you mention it, an evil-looking Eyetalian was asking for a room just when I was expecting Aloysius home. Of course I wouldn't rent him one."

Bo nodded. "Of course. Describe him."

"What's to describe? Eyetalian. Big black mustache, needed a shave on the rest of his face, but with the redness it would have hurt to put a blade to it."

Bo finished his drink and asked the question he already knew the answer to. "What kind of red? Like he'd been burned with hot water?"

"My thought exactly."

CHAPTER 46

Friday, July 21.

Patsy's job that day was pitching hay from a high loft to the floor below. When he was done he ate his sausage, drank his red wine, and fell asleep.

The sound that woke him made him think a horse had gone mad. It was dark as pitch, but he could tell by the regular snores and steady breathing that none of his mates who slept in the crannied section adjacent to the loft were bothered by the sound. In the murk he edged down the ladder to the first floor and the horse stalls.

The sound hadn't come from any of the horses. Like the men, the beasts snorted in their sleep, but otherwise, all seemed peaceful.

Patsy lifted the kerosene lamp from its hook on one of the upright support beams and turned it up, casting light into all corners of the ground floor.

The din became three separate, distinct sounds. A chugging noise, a humming, and a low roar.

On the ground-floor level, Patsy tracked the noise to an area well hidden behind bales and boxes. He was surprised to see a door. He hadn't noticed it before. Patsy looked around. Except for one man down at the other end of the building shoveling manure, he was the only one there. Though wary of being discovered, he opened the door. Behind it was a gate. He swung the gate open, too, and stepped inside the small chamber. Patsy wasn't very sophisticated, but he recognized an elevator when he saw one. He closed the door and gate. And pushed the lever. Surprised and elated he felt the car move. He grinned at the tortured noises that emanated from the pulleys moving the contraption. Only when the elevator stopped with a bump did he release the lever.

Cautiously he opened the gate and the new door. The heat was terrible, and the smell went from horse shit to coal. And burnt meat.

Walking slowly and deliberately he soon came to the source of all the heat. A large roaring furnace, its doors glowing red. Patsy knew from the dust in his nose that the stuff he was stumbling over was coal. By the light of his lamp he saw a chugging steam engine being powered by the furnace.

The steam engine turned a big flywheel, and cables went from the wheel mounting to the backs of other machinery. More cables led away from them.

Two water pipes jutted from one wall and elbowed their way to the adjacent wall. Three more cables under the pipes led to a wooden board.

To the right, still another cable, leading from a switch box, went up to the ceiling.

This setup had to be what made the elevator work.

Holding his lamp before him, Patsy saw the accumulation of dead mice. Five. It looked like the leavings of a burnt pork roast. From the look and smell of the mice, something had fried the whole mess to a crisp. He didn't know what had killed the mice, but instinctively he recoiled.

Patsy ran back to the elevator and rode it up to the ground floor, the lamp in his hand shaking so he spilled kerosene on the floor. The boy didn't know much about electricity, but he knew it could kill. He'd heard about that fellow who'd been sizzled in Old

Sparky, the electrocution chair, up in Sing-Sing.

And that was much more than he cared to know about it.

Chapter 47

Friday, July 21 to Saturday, July 22. Evening to predawn.

Tony's anger roiled inside him, leaving a bitter taste. The country painting on his beautiful machine was scratched everywhere, and there was an ugly gouge in the farmhouse. The grinder handle was cracked.

He guzzled grappa until he was senseless.

When he awakened, blessed Madonna, the pain in his mouth had stopped, but his head was heavy and his eyesight blurred. Slowly, he mended his clothes and cleaned his cuts. He spent the rest of the day working on the organ.

He turned the handle. Music played. Woman is fickle. True. All except Marie. He stroked the stiletto under his trousers. She was the only female he could depend on.

But, his work was not finished. Nor was his anger. He pulled on his coat and went out into the night.

His destination was No. 5 Gramercy Park.

On the park side, opposite No. 5, Battling Jack West leaned against his Victoria and smoked his cigar. He'd relieved Little Jack an hour earlier. It was well past midnight, and the streets were quiet. At the moment lights dimmed in the Players Club, there came a fierce gust of wind, then lightning, followed by a loud thunder clap. Now it began to rain. Buckets. He turned up his collar and tossed his useless cigar away, patted Sullivan on the rump to soothe the nervous beast.

He was uneasy. Like he'd been waiting for something. He didn't know it would just be rain. He walked to the corner and looked up and down the rain-washed streets. The trees were blowing in the wind. There. What was that? Quick as he thought he'd seen the figure, it was gone. Were his eyes and the rain playing tricks on him?

More than likely what he'd thought was a figure in the bleary light of the street lamp was the moving shadow cast by a tree lush with rain. He shook his head. Conclusions like that could take you down the garden path. He walked up the block a few paces, getting soaked to the skin. Nothing. A cat wailed.

Jack turned away, heard a creak, turned back. His eyes went to the door of the wooden fence leading to the back yard of the house between No. 5 and the corner.

He covered the few feet in one stride, placed his substantial hand on the top of the fence door, and applied pressure. This creak was as soft as a cat's pad on the ground, but it was a tiny brother to the one he'd heard.

The door was latched from the inside, the fence no more than five feet high. Jack peered over it into the quiet yards, one leading to the other, behind the town houses.

He heard nothing except the rain on the leaves and the unhappy mewling of the cat. Finally, he returned to his post.

Tony let out his breath, but waited until he was certain the big brutto bastard had gone. The rain was a fortunate cover of sight and sound. He considered the fifth-floor windows. This was where the woman lived. Getting in would be easy. If she didn't scream, getting out would be the same.

In the darkness a plan formed in his mind. He would enter the house through the basement and bide his time. Esther Breslau had to have the locket. After what he'd done to the whore, the *giudea* would be afraid for her life. Tony patted Marie. His magnificent stiletto sweetheart would taste blood again soon enough.

Inch by inch Tony worked his way up the stairs. From the cellar he worked his silent way into the kitchen, then up a single flight of stairs. On the fifth level he smelled the Chinaman before he saw him. Next he heard the barely perceptible whisper of silk and made out the form of the Chinkie sitting in front of a door.

Tony was certain he could kill the Chinaman, but would the man die silently? If he made a sound the house would be roused and Tony would have to leave without the locket.

He had two choices: go out and work his way up the vines and past the window boxes at the front of the building. To do that he would first have to kill the big one. That would be riskier than the Chinaman.

Or, he could be patient and simply wait.

He spent the night huddled in his wet coat in a closet under the stairs. He heard the activity, the conversation, but couldn't grasp what was happening. Finally, it came to him that the woman and the man were leaving the house for the day.

Cazzo! He should have struck immediately. This country was poison to him. Back home he wouldn't have thought so much; he would have simply acted.

"We'll be home before sundown, Wong," Tony heard the man say.

A door closed. Tony waited, breathing shallowly. Then the outside door opened, and although he didn't hear anything, he knew the Chinaman was back in the house.

He followed the man's progress by the sound of his silk.

The melody stopped. Tony moved his legs to take the stiffness from them.

The rattle of pots and plates came from the kitchen. A span of silence followed. Then an inside door nearby closed. The Chinaman, where was he? Tony waited.

After a long period of quiet, Tony crept from his hiding place and climbed to the *giudea*'s room. If he didn't find the locket there, he would wait for evening when she would return.

Crouching, he put his ear to the bedroom door. He turned the knob slowly and pushed.

Before he could straighten, a powerful blow chopped at his neck, sending him crashing to the floor. He was stunned. Marie. He took her in his hand. Blows to his kidneys and neck shocked him alternately from consciousness to sensibility.

Tony grabbed, caught only the pigtail. Marie slashed. The damn chinkie, bare-ass naked, twisted like a snake.

Marie cut deep. With a hiss, the chinkie raised his foot and kicked. The blow hit Tony under the chin. Waving his hands like a bird in flight, over backward, he flew down the stairs.

He landed on his knees, Marie in one hand, the pigtail in the other. Staggering to his feet, he threw open the front door of the house and fled.

CHAPTER 48

Saturday, July 22. Late morning.

The country roads in northern Westchester County, many of them unpaved, were not always the best. They were particularly unpleasant after a deluge, such as the one that had begun the previous evening.

For that reason and because Oz preferred the creature comforts of the railroad to the discomforting bumps that went with any rural byway, he and Esther traveled by train to Goldens Bridge. This was the closest they could get to the town of Lewisboro, which consisted of six hamlets: Lewisboro, Goldens Bridge, South Salem, Waccabuc, Cross River, and Vista.

The wind had blown fierce hail, then torrents of rain against houses, trees, and intrepid sojourners, almost continuously through the early morning hours, when the storm subsided and the sun emerged at last. And the best news of all was that the heat spell had broken.

In the City of New York, the continuity of power and influence of Episcopalian society, despite its vast wealth and interrelated families, had gradually begun to falter in the face of the new immigrants, who by their very numbers were compelling change. Although he was well connected through the Cooks and the Neldines to this society, the society itself was an anachronism in Oz's blunt estimation. Oz, therefore, was considered an eccentric. Decidedly, again in his estimation, the pot calling the kettle black.

Still, family was family. And it was time he paid a call on his father's elderly cousin, Alexina Cook Brewster, whose fifteen-hundred-acre estate was located near Lewisboro not far from the Connecticut border. Alexina, though well into her eighties, was sharp-witted and knew everyone who had ever settled in the area. And if she didn't know, or hadn't known, these individuals personally, she was acquainted with the families. The truth was she delighted in every bit of gossip that found its way to her. Behind her canny eyes, she was well known to hold a storehouse of historical information, not to mention scandal, about people and events and was considered a legend in the county.

Oz had sent word ahead, and Alexina arranged to have them met at the tiny station in Goldens Bridge, which served the hamlets of Lewisboro proper.

Oz and Esther had been delivered by hackney to the Grand Central Depot on Forty-second Street and Fourth Avenue. A porter collected their baggage, which included the tripod, several cameras, and photographic equipment. The cameras and picture-making paraphernalia were as much a part of the pair as their arms and legs. And this time was singular: Oz intended to make what might be a last portrait of Cousin Alexina.

After boarding, they had only a short wait before the train began to move out of the station and up Park Avenue.

For Esther, who since her arrival from Poland in August of '92, had never been out of the City, the trip was a revelation. Fields and villages, orchards and farms, cows and horses filled her eyes. Her frantic search among the hand baggage and recovery of her small Kodak came with exclamations of "Oh, look!" and "See there!" as she made picture after picture on roll film, engendering Oz's fond smile.

He patted her hand. "Now if you were to accept my proposal of marriage," he said.

"You're a dear man." Impulsively, she kissed his pale cheek, then turned back to the passing view.

On the platform in Goldens Bridge, they were greeted by a boy of about twelve years, clad in rough-hewn farm clothing and clogs. "Mr. Cook, sir, I'm Josiah. Come to collect you for Miz Brewster." He picked up two of the bags with surprising ease and led Esther and Oz to where an immaculate, polished purple brougham and two sturdy matched grays awaited them.

The thick-shouldered, liveried driver sat on the box, staring off into the distance.

"I got 'em, Henry," the boy called.

Henry, startled, tried to stand. "Mr. Oz," he said, putting two fingers to his white braided green hat. The old man's eyes were a faded blue. He tottered and sat down hard. His hands on the reins shook with a palsy.

"Good to see you again, Henry." Oz reached up and shook the driver's hand. "This is Miss Esther Breslau."

"Honored, miss." Henry frowned at Josiah. "Now you be careful with Mr. Oz's gear, you hear me, Josiah? We don't want anything breaking. Mr. Oz makes grand photographs with those contraptions."

Oz opened the carriage door for Esther and helped her up. "As does Miss Breslau."

Henry turned round to look at Esther. "Well, now . . ." But duty first, he cautioned the boy, "Tie everything up good, Josiah."

When Josiah had finished packing the baggage to the carriage, he climbed up on the box beside Henry.

"Thank you, Josiah," Oz said.

"You are most welcome, sir."

Henry beamed. "Josiah is a good lad, Mr. Oz. He's Binnie's son all growed up."

"Binnie is Henry's daughter," Oz informed Esther.

The brougham moved out onto the narrow road, still damp from the rain. Although this road was paved, soon enough they came to a fork and the rest of the route was unpaved and even narrower. Hooves and wheels raised little dust as the brougham maneuvered over the drying mud and ruts filled with small pools of water.

Forests enveloped them; cooler, damper air blew through the woods bearing mixed perfume. The air smelled fresh and sweet. Every so often they passed a long drive leading to a grand and gracious colonial home.

The sign for Brewster Farm was white, with green lettering. It appeared along the side of the road as if part of the wilderness of trees and foliage. The carriage turned into what looked at first like thick woods but was in fact a dirt road, hardly more than a path.

They rode through this passage of woods and into a clearing of spacious lawns and great trees. At the end of the roadway stood a sprawling white house, surrounded by plantings and gardens.

"How beautiful," Esther exclaimed. This time she resisted taking out her camera.

For Oz, not usually a sentimental person, the sight of Brewster Farm brought back lovely memories of his childhood. He and his mother had spent summers here throughout his youth. Cousin Alexina's husband, Robert Brewster, had been a surgeon. Brewster had volunteered for work during the Civil War, contracted malaria, and died. Alexina had never remarried, never had children; Oz, whose early years had been part of her life, was her only heir.

Binnie turned out to be Cousin Alexina's housekeeper, a plump woman who greeted Oz with great warmth and an enveloping embrace, which, to Esther's surprise, Oz returned with enthusiasm. "Come in now," she said, ushering them into the light, airy house.

"Binnie, this is Miss Esther Breslau," Oz

said. "Binnie and I spent our childhood together running through fields of clover, didn't we, Binnie?"

"Well," Binnie said, grinning, "You might say." She gave Esther a thorough inspection. "I'm pleased to meet you, Miss Breslau."

"Esther, please." Oz Cook was full of surprises. Just when she thought she had learned all there was to be learned from him, suddenly there was more.

"You'll have your old room, and we'll put Miss Esther in" — Binnie smiled — "your mother's room."

"Fine, fine. Where's Cousin Alexina?"

"She's in the garden. We have a —"

"Come along, Esther." Oz took Esther's elbow and steered her through the long hall, past the staircase and out the back.

Esther could hear Binnie chuckling. "There's a guest," Binnie called after them.

The back of the house was a veranda with steps leading to the gardens. Wicker tables and chairs with white canvas–covered seats were informally arranged.

Esther saw two women. One, a tiny doll-like creature, was wearing a hat almost as large as she. They were walking in the garden. This individual wearing the hat, wielding her cane more as an accessory than a necessity, had to be Cousin Alexina. The other woman's face was obscured by Alexina's voluminous hat.

"Alexina!" Oz's voice was rich with feeling.

Another surprise, Esther thought.

Alexina turned, saw Oz, and with a wave of her hand, moved forward, giving Esther a clear view of the other woman.

It was Flora Cooper.

CHAPTER 49

Saturday, July 22. Noon.

Alexina Brewster's expression was beatific as she invited the two young women to her table. "I do so love what you young women today are doing with your lives." She'd removed her big hat, revealing a profusion of white hair. "Sit here, my dear, on my left. And Miss Cooper, on my right. I am eager to hear from you both."

Oz was amused. "And I shall dine in the kitchen."

His cousin set stern eyes on him. "Nonsense, Oswald, why would you do that?"

"I thought perhaps this was a ladies' luncheon."

With her fan, she pointed to the chair at the foot of the table. "Sit."

"Ah," Oz sighed to the heavens. "Not in the kitchen, but decidedly below the salt. Ladies, my dear cousin is a suffragist."

Flora grinned. "I wouldn't have thought

otherwise, Mr. Cook."

"I will not live to see the vote for women," Alexina told Esther and Flora, "but you will and you must make the most of it."

"I have no doubt they will," Oz said. "Champagne, I think, don't you, Alexina, to mark the occasion?" He didn't wait for a response, and who knows if he'd have gotten one, for the ladies were absorbed with one another, and he was obviously de trop.

"I so admire your independence, ladies. You travel alone, you work in professions that were for men only not so long ago." To her housekeeper, who was serving the cold potato soup, Alexina said, "Binnie, Miss Cooper is a journalist, and Miss Breslau makes photographs. Isn't it a wonderful new world?"

"It is, Miss Alexina."

A popping cork dramatically presaged Oz's entrance through the kitchen door. He was followed by young Josiah, bearing a bucket of ice in which a bottle of champagne was lodged. Oz himself carried a small tray with four glasses.

Oz displayed the bottle. "Veuve Cliquot. Perfect for the occasion." He filled the fluted glasses. "May I offer a toast? To the company of good women and the grandest of all ladies, Alexina Cook Brewster."

The elderly woman's ivory skin flushed pink right up to the white swell of her hair. She clapped her hands. "Oh, my dears, I am so delighted with this visit. It does get a little dull these days. I seem to have outlived not just my generation, but the next and the next after that."

"We are very happy to be here too, Mrs. Brewster," Esther said, quite captivated by the old lady.

"Mrs. Brewster! Oh, my, no one's called me Mrs. Brewster in over thirty years. You may call me Miss Alexina, my dear, as everyone does. Oswald, you are very quiet."

"Who could possibly get a word in amongst you?"

"Miss Cooper was just starting to explain the purpose of her visit to me, when you and Miss Breslau arrived. My intuition tells me that your visit may have the same purpose."

Josiah set a platter of cold sliced chicken on a bed of greens on the sideboard, then cleared the empty soup cups while Binnie portioned the chicken and greens out on individual plates and placed a plate in front of each person. After the servants both left the room, Alexina looked pointedly at Oz.

"Ah, yes, our purpose." Oz sipped his champagne and nodded at Flora. "Well, the subject may not be quite appropriate for the dinner table."

"Pshaw. My curiosity has whetted my appetite. If you are reluctant, Oswald, perhaps Miss Cooper should begin."

Oz made a flourish with his hand. "By all means."

Flora set down her fork and had a sip of champagne. "Well, okay. We're here to talk about the brutal murder of a lady of the evening, Delia Swann."

"And you've come to me? How curious."

"Actually," Oz said. "The story begins with me. One evening several weeks ago, some gentlemen and I came upon a man beating this young woman, Delia Swann, around the corner from the Waldorf. After we chased away her attacker, she ran off. The next chapter to the story is Esther's; she is working on a photographic study of the demimondes of New York."

Alexina smiled. "I knew from everything I'd heard that I would like you, Esther — if I may call you Esther?"

"I am honored, Miss Alexina. Delia Swann came to me —" Esther stopped, flustered.

"To Gramercy Park," Oz said.

"Yes. To the studio. To pose for me. She left late in the afternoon and no one saw her alive again."

"She was found by some boys in an empty lot down by the East River," Flora said, "half naked, stabbed to death."

Alexina shuddered. "The brutal lives these women live."

"But there's something more here," Flora said. "The copper that chased the boys away from her body was stabbed to death as well. The woman that owns the house Delia Swann worked in is near death, apparently stabbed by this same monster. It seems more than likely that the murderer is looking for something that belonged to this girl. In fact, a gold locket. Therefore, as probably the last person to see Delia Swann alive, Esther is also in danger."

Alexina's hand touched Esther's. "Our Esther?"

Her touch elated Esther. It was a sign of acceptance she longed for, albeit from the wrong family.

At this juncture, Binnie reappeared carrying a bowl of fresh peach ice cream and small plates. She cleared the used dishes from the table.

"Yes, our Esther. Cousin, we believe that the girl Delia Swann had information that someone did not want known, and that it all hinges on who this girl really was."

"So you've come to me because you think

I might know this Delia Swann or her family? Do you know that she came from this area?"

"We believe this to be so."

"Excuse me for saying —" Binnie stood near the doorway holding her tray. "But there was a Swann family lived near Rhinebeck. Harness makers."

"Oh, yes. Now I remember. An old man. Dead years now. Were there children?"

"None that lived."

"Thank you, Binnie," Oz said. "But we've discovered Delia Swann's real name, which is why we're here today."

"And I had heard, Miss Alexina," Flora said, "that you knew all there was to know about anyone who lived in this area, which is why I took it upon myself to come see you." Flora took a quick spoonful of rich peach ice cream, which had begun to melt. "I'm sure you'll know the family, and something in the family history may provide us with the reason she was murdered. Her name was Irene Hall."

A dropped tray, and the clamor of china shattering in the kitchen, by far more dramatic than that of a champagne cork, brought an abrupt halt to the conversation.

Chapter 50

Saturday, July 22. Midday.

Wiping her hands on her apron, Binnie sat herself in one of the side chairs. “When Amos and I were first married, we went to live in Rhinebeck with the old people, Amos’s grandparents, who’d gotten too frail to run their farm. Josiah, get in all the corners now. I’m sorry about the china, Miss Alexina.”

Alexina dismissed the broken china with a desultory wave of her hand. She was deep in thought.

“Go on, Binnie, dear,” Oz said, frowning at the notepad Flora had produced.

“Oh, dear,” Alexina said abruptly, “not the child you and Amos took in.”

Binnie nodded. “I found her near the river, half naked, beaten and bruised, so terrified at first she wouldn’t tell me her name.”

“But the child had been vio—” Alexina

stopped. The women all stared at each other, shocked by the sudden shared knowledge. The truth dawned on Oz as he caught the women's reaction.

"Yes," Binnie said. "Amos's people were very religious. The Halls were a prominent family in Garrison. We had to send her back."

"It was someone in her own family that did that to her?" Oz took a long drink of champagne.

"Irene's mother died in childbirth —"

Alexina tapped the table with her fan. "Ah, it's come back to me. The mother was Irene Bayard."

"Yes, Miss Alexina. Mr. Hall remarried, a widow with two boys. Then Mr. Hall died and the child Irene was left with no blood relatives. It was not long after her father's death that we found her near the river."

"So," Oz said, "she must have run away again after you sent her back."

"She did. But you couldn't have met her recently."

"Why do you say that?"

"Because the second time she ran away, she drowned in the river."

Oz leaped from his chair. "Drowned? Drowned, you say?"

"Poor desperate child," Alexina said.

"Was her body found?" came Flora's sharp question.

"They found some clothing and her shoes is all."

"She didn't drown," Oz said. "Somehow she found her way to the City. She was hardly more than a child, then, with no money, no friends. She had little choice of how to support herself."

"Oh, dear," Alexina said. "The Bayards must be turning over in their graves. She's the last of them, you know, the end of the line."

Flora looked up from her notepad. "Was there an inheritance?"

"The Bayards were old money, as are the Cooks and the Neldines," Alexina said.

"After Irene was thought to be dead, who were her heirs?" Esther asked.

"Why, the second Mrs. Hall and her two boys, I suppose," Alexina said.

Closing her notepad, Flora said, "I shall go to Garrison and see what I can find of these people. Perhaps someone can see me to the train station."

"Of course. Binnie, will you see to the arrangements?"

Flora gathered up her bag, shook everyone's hand and, thanking Miss Alexina, left the room with Binnie.

Alexina sighed. "A nice young woman but she must get herself a new hat." She turned to Oz and Esther. "You will stay the night, won't you, Oswald, Esther?"

"It's my Sabbath," Esther said softly.

"Esther keeps the Hebrew Sabbath. May I smoke?"

"Only if I may join you."

Oz lit a cigarette for Alexina and one for himself. Esther declined.

Alexina had heard all about how unacceptable Esther Breslau was from the Burgoynes. "You are welcome to celebrate the rest of your Sabbath here with me. I had a dear friend, Leah Tonneman — she's been gone many years now — she celebrated her Sabbath here many times."

"Tonneman?" Esther's eyes opened wide.

"Yes. She was one of the first women doctors in the state."

Oz glowered at his cousin and poured what was left of the champagne into his glass. "This is a good time for me to make a photograph, before the light changes."

"Auntie Lee," Esther said.

"Lee. Everyone called her Lee. You're too young to have known her, Esther."

"It is a John Tonneman I know."

"We all know the oaf," Oz growled. "Only too well."

Esther's cheeks burned, and Alexina smiled knowingly. "So, my dears, where do you want to set up your cameras?"

Chapter 51

Saturday, July 22. Afternoon to evening.

"A mustache?" The Salerno-born detective was a short man, at five feet, two inches, perhaps the shortest member on the Force. But he was brawny. "I hear you're looking for a goddam mustache." His scorn was manifest. "Every Italian man in the City has one."

"And about half of the women," Bo said, not bothering to hide his laughter. "You don't have one."

Petrosino growled as he searched the pockets of his dark gray suit. "Where's Dutch?"

"Not like him to be so late." Bo drank down his whiskey and took a swallow of beer.

Almost as if on signal, Dutch burst through the swinging door leading to the private back room of McCourt's saloon on Mulberry Street.

"We've got trouble," Dutch said without preamble. He squinted at Petrosino's beardless, pockmarked face as Petrosino stuck an Italian cigar in his mouth. "Our knifer smokes those."

"What trouble?" Petrosino asked, lighting his cigar.

"Some time last night he broke into Oswald Cook's house at Number Five Gramercy Park. Where Esther Breslau lives. This morning he got as far as Esther's door before the servant, Wong, caught him and fought him off. It was lucky Esther had left earlier."

Bo jumped up. "He's caught?"

Dutch shook his head. "The Chinaman knocked him down the stairs, but the bastard ran out the front door."

Disappointed, Bo sat down again. "Little guy like that takes on a killer?" he said, impressed. "Chinaman get cut?"

"Only his pigtail. The knifer sliced it off."

"Damn," Petrosino said. "To them it's like cutting off their balls. It's the worst shame in the world for a chinkie."

"You're a well of information, you are, Petrosino." Bo raised his voice and called for another round. "What about Irene Hall?" he asked Dutch.

"I've got men working. But to tell the

truth I haven't been thinking too much about Irene Hall. I'm more concerned with the knifer." Dutch turned to Petrosino, "He was seen in front of the baths the time we calculate Mulroony got it."

The Italian cop bobbed his head. "Yes. The word is out in the City. Every cop is on the lookout for your killer." His glance at Bo was disdainful. "Sad to say, with no results. Still, it's a surety he was the one gutted Mulroony and all the others."

"And nearly did Sophie in," Bo added.

"And is a definite threat to Esther." Changing the subject, Dutch said, thoughtfully, "It's been a long time since I've seen you as yourself, Joe."

"Yes." Petrosino was preoccupied with wiping a spec of white powder from his collar.

"Listen, Petrosino," Dutch said, "you must have something to tell us, or you wouldn't have gotten us here."

Taking his own sweet time, Petrosino drained his glass of red wine and, grimacing, knocked some cigar ash to the floor. To Dutch he said, "You remember I thought there was something familiar about these killings of yours. Something I should know. That one stab in the belly and up. I remembered. He's called Antonio."

"Only one name?"

"Only one real name. He goes by another. The Organ Grinder. He roams around, playing one."

Dutch frowned. "An organ grinder. They're all over the place."

"Yes, and every one has a mustache," Bo said. "If he hasn't wised up and shaved it off."

"The one you're looking for will also have a bad burn on his face," Petrosino said. "Perhaps blisters. Maybe he can't even shave. Hard to hide all that."

"And maybe some marks from the riot where he killed the colored guy," Bo added.

McCourt's voice rang loud from the front. "Drinks up."

Dutch stepped out of the room and brought back two mugs of beer in one hand and a glass of whiskey and a glass of red in the other.

Bo took the two beers and the whiskey and slammed the beers on the table. In the time it took Dutch to hand Petrosino his wine, Bo'd tossed off the whiskey in one swallow.

Dutch watched the foam slide off the rims of the mugs onto the scarred, booze-stained wooden table. Now he looked at the Italian, whom he figured for the best poker player in New York. "Butter wouldn't melt in your mouth, Joe. So what's the rest on this organ grinder?"

Petrosino's expression still gave nothing away. "My paisan is going by the name Antonio Cerasani here. He has a room on Prince Street, around the corner from little Saint Pat's."

"Let's go, then." Dutch, on his feet and drinking the last of his beer, started out.

"Wait," Bo called, but he followed Dutch. "Who hired him, Petrosino?"

All three left the tavern, heading for Prince Street. Dutch spoke over his shoulder. "And what about this locket you told me every thief in town is looking for?"

"From what I've picked up," Petrosino said, "Antonio was hired to kill the whore and procure the locket. For some reason he failed with the locket. Until he delivers it to his employer, he won't get the rest of his money. He killed Mulroony because he figured the cop, being first on the scene, took the locket. Mulroony was a friend of Rafferty's, so maybe Mulroony told Rafferty something about the locket. Sophie Mandel is obvious. The others? Just people getting in the Organ Grinder's way."

"Who hired him?" Dutch asked.

"My money's on Nonna."

"That old lady with the stable business?" Bo said.

"You never met an old lady like her. Between her and Uncle Mico, they have their hooks in all kinds of businesses all over the City. That's high class as well as low class. Word is one of her *quality* clients wanted the girl dead. The locket was nothing more than some kind of token. The Organ Grinder is the one who made it serious business."

"Come on, Bo. I don't want him to get another try at Esther."

On Prince Street, Petrosino placed thumb and forefinger between his lips and whistled.

"What the hell was that for?" Dutch asked.

"Lou Fabrizzi, one of my boys, I got him watching the building."

Bo demanded impatiently, "So?"

Petrosino looked up and down Prince Street. "Could be the Organ Grinder is gone."

"Could be," Bo countered, "Lou Fabrizzi is laying somewhere with his guts spilling out."

"You're a funny mick, Clancy." But Petrosino didn't waste any more time. "Cerasani is on the fifth floor. Give me five minutes. I'll go through the building next door and cross over the roof."

Bo agreed. "Sounds good."

The cousins watched Petrosino disappear into the tenement next door, then they entered Tony's building. Bo and Dutch were immediately surrounded by living noise. The stairs tilted, creaked with the heavy stride of the detectives. A baby's cry made them pause on the second floor. The stink of piss and potatoes, sweat and mildew, all blended into the closed-in heat.

When Bo and Dutch reached the fifth-floor landing, Petrosino was poised on the stair leading from the roof, his weapon drawn. "I can't get to his window from up there," Petrosino whispered.

Bo and Dutch drew their Smith and Wesson .32s. At Bo's nod, Dutch smashed his right heel into the door just below the knob. The door burst open. The two plowed in, Bo going left, Dutch going right. They didn't have far to go in the tiny room. Petrosino was right behind them.

Leaning against the left wall was a hand organ. A coat hung on the back of the door.

The three drawers to a small rickety chest were open. And empty. On the table were dirty dishes and an empty grappa bottle.

There was no sign of the Organ Grinder.

Leo patted Sophie's fragile hand. Six days

now, and she was the same, drifting between consciousness and sleep, surviving only on chicken soup and tea. And, he hoped, his prayers.

Eyes closed, head bobbing, Leo chanted, in a barely discernable murmur, his favorite psalm, "By the waters of Babylon, where we lay down and wept when we remembered Zion. We hung up our lyres for our captors required songs of us, and our tormentors demanded mirth. How can we sing the Lord's song in a strange land? If I forget you, Jerusalem, may my right hand wither. May my tongue cleave to the roof of my mouth, if I do not remember you."

Restored somewhat, Leo drew a Garcia Perfecto from his inside pocket. After a downcast look at Sophie, he went out into the hospital hall. He bit the end off the cigar and spat it into the spittoon.

Esther had ended her Sabbath with a strange unease.

They'd returned before sundown to find Jack West in his usual place in front of the house. Battling Jack had helped them from the hackney. "If I may have a few minutes of your time, Mr. Cook," he'd said.

Wong opened the door to greet them. Oddly, he was wearing a dark green fedora.

Oswald Cook's fedora. Because it was pulled low on Wong's forehead, hiding his ears, the soft felt hat had lost its lengthwide crease and its curled brim was limp. "Miss Esther, welcome home." Wong collected the camera equipment and brought them indoors.

Esther had caught the mute exchange between Wong and Oz. Something is wrong, she told herself, as she hurried to her flat, distracted by the image of Wong in that preposterous hat.

Voices in the parlor. She could hear them. She came down the stairs.

A new thought had joined her curiosity about Wong's strange hat. A chilling thought. Something had happened to John Tonneman and they were keeping it from her.

CHAPTER 52

Saturday, July 22. Evening.

Esther, her hand on the door to Oz's study, heard him say,

"We must make certain this can never happen again."

Wong in his foolish hat standing in attendance was the first thing she saw when she stepped into the room. Next, Jack West peering out the window and Oz pacing. They all turned to her, boys suddenly, as if she'd caught them in some kind of mischief.

Her "What can never happen again?" was greeted with silence, and again, the exchange of glances.

It was Jack West who broke the silence. He told Oz, "With due respect, sir, Miss Breslau ought be told for her own good."

"Told what?" Esther became agitated. "Has anything happened to John Tonneman? You must tell me."

Her worry about Tonneman brought Oz

up short. "As far as I know, your John Tonneman has come to no harm." Her relief was palpable. "Here, my dear." He took her arm and helped her sit. "The port, Wong."

"Something terrible has happened?"

"Frightening, but not terrible. There was a break-in last night or early this morning."

Esther paled. "Here?"

Oz touched her shoulder. "Through the cellar window."

She reached up and clasped his hand. "We could have been murdered in our beds."

Jack West nodded somberly. "If not for Mr. Wong. I was at fault, miss. The intruder came over the back fence through the neighboring garden."

With reluctance, Oz told Esther, "We'd already left when Wong confronted the man in the act of opening the door to your rooms."

If Esther had been frightened before, she was doubly so now.

The sharp ring of the doorbell, then the knocker intruded. Wong left the room.

"Did he hurt Wong? Why is Wong wearing your hat?"

"The assassin cut off his pigtail, which is tantamount to depriving him of his manhood and his honor."

"Oh, Oz, what have I done?" She buried

her face in her hands.

"It's young Mr. Burgoyne for Miss Esther," Wong said on his return. "He's in the parlor."

Battling Jack raised an eyebrow, tossed back his port. He hated coincidence, but life was full of coincidence, and everything was connected in one way or the other. It was what the years taught you if you kept your wits about you.

"You should have sent him away," Oz said harshly. "It's the wrong time. It will always be the wrong time."

"He would not leave without seeing Miss Esther."

"I don't want to see him."

"Convey Miss Breslau's regrets, Wong."

"I'd best be taking up my post in front of the house, Mr. Cook," Jack West said. He would make sure to leave without meeting up with young Mr. Burgoyne. "My associate will keep his eyes on the back. The assassin will not get past me again, don't you worry, Miss Breslau."

"Esther!" Baby flung open the door. The sight of Jack West hit him like a bolt of lightening. He stepped back. "Wha— what —"

"Mr. Burgoyne," Battling Jack said smoothly. "I'll be off now, Mr. Cook." Pity.

A more sophisticated man would have given no indication they were in any way acquainted.

But Jack West didn't leave, for the bell and the door knocker began again as if Baby Burgoyne were not only inside, annoying them, but outside as well, unsettling their lives even more.

"This is the wrong time to call, Burgoyne," Oz said. "Esther is not well. Can't you see that?"

"I can see something very strange is going on here." Baby glanced at Jack West.

Jack raised his eyes to heaven. It was time to get out of the detective game. Automobiles! That was the future. He would sell automobiles.

When Wong went to answer the door, they were all talking at once, all except Esther, who huddled in her chair, lost in thought.

The assassin was looking for the locket. What else could it be? She was responsible then for the tragic death of the policeman and for the break-in here, for endangering Oz's life, Wong's life, and her own. If only she had given John Tonneman the locket after Delia's death.

What they had need of was a stalking horse, to tempt the assassin into the open. As the beginning of an idea began to form in her mind, Wong announced, “Inspector Clancy and Captain Tonneman.”

Chapter 53

Saturday, July 22. Evening.

Supper was a strange affair.

As unlikely an assembly of men who'd ever dined at the Cook home were seated the length of the table, Oz at its head, an empty chair at its foot.

Oz, faced with uninvited guests, none of whom offered any sign of leaving, had suggested supper. At that point, Esther had excused herself, promising she'd return. Upstairs she chose a cold cloth for her pounding head instead of the aspirin powder Wong had prepared.

Dutch sat on Oz's right and Bo, his left. An unsettled Lawrence "Baby" Burgoyne sat below the salt, trying not to meet the eyes of Jack West, who was opposite. West was the only one of Oz's guests who'd wanted to leave. Perversely, Oz insisted he stay.

Finally Esther reappeared. The gentlemen

rose. Esther noted that the chair at the foot of the table was waiting for her. Normally she sat at Oz's right. Was it his little game for tonight? Or had some new custom been established. Esther dismissed the notion. As Baby held her chair, she slipped into it.

A welcome breeze gently billowed the sheer curtains of the open windows. Outside, it was quiet. Inside, it was altogether another story.

Baby gulped his wine. "Oz, I demand to know what's going on."

"And by what right do you make this demand?"

"My relationship with Esther gives me the right." Baby repeated his imitation of Grimes and Stokes. "Since you are her guardian it is proper that I broach this with you."

"Relationship!" Dutch got to his feet. "Who is he and what in blazes is he talking about?"

"Stop this at once," Esther commanded. "John, please."

Oz sighed. "Sit down, Tonneman. Burgoyne is my second cousin once removed. There is no relationship between Esther and Burgoyne except in his mind." Oz's lips twitched in a contained, almost nonexistent smile. "Is there, my dear?"

"Absolutely, and you are not my guardian," Esther said. "I am a free, white American woman, not some European chattel."

Chastened, Baby attempted to mend his fences. "Of course, Esther. I beg your forgiveness."

Wong arrived with a tureen of cold potato and leek soup and began ladling it into bowls.

Surveying the room through slitted eyes, Bo said, "This is real nice, but I think it's time we got down to business."

Dutch watched Esther with growing concern. It was something he'd learned about her over the years. She had come to some conclusion and was determined to carry it out.

"In time," Oz declared. "Thus far all we've established is that I am not Esther's guardian. Esther and these gentlemen and I have a busy night ahead of us, Lawrence, please get to the essence. If there is any."

Baby shoved his plate away and poured himself another glass of red wine. "You are forcing my hand, cousin, and I do not thank you for this ungentlemanly behavior. I must know what hold you have over Miss Breslau — Esther?"

Esther was indignant. "Really, this is reprehensible, Mr. Burgoyne. It is none of your concern . . .”

“I am her lover,” Oz said casually, ringing the bell.

“Oz —” Esther couldn’t hold back the flush.

“In a pig’s ass,” Dutch muttered.

“I get it,” Baby said. “You’re pulling my leg.”

“I prefer,” Oz declared, a twinkle in his eye, “to think I have a piquant sense of humor.”

Frowning, Bo drank his wine. He wanted a beer, at least.

As for Esther, she wanted to talk about stalking horses, but restrained herself in Baby Burgoyne’s presence.

Wong cleared the plates, returning quickly with a large platter on which lay a whole steamed fish, head and all, surrounded by a sauce of vegetables.

“Esther,” Baby blurted. “I’m on my way to becoming a rich man. You must marry me.”

“Ha,” Bo said. “Stand in line.”

Dutch pulled out his watch and showed Oz the minutes ticking by.

“I take your point, Detective.” Oz dabbed at his lips delicately. “Lawrence, you forced your way in here to make these impossible suggestions. Good manners and regard for family require a great deal of me, but you've gone well beyond that. I think it's time you took your leave."

Through the open window came the eerie screech of a cat. They were transfixed by the peculiar sound. Esther felt a chill run through her as she watched Dutch and Battling Jack rush to the windows and peer down into the yard behind the house.

At that moment Wong announced a telephone call for Inspector Clancy. Bo excused himself and followed Wong.

"Clancy here."

Petrosino's voice came high and squeaky. His words were terse. "Fabrizzi called in. He followed the Organ Grinder to Gramercy Park."

CHAPTER 54

Saturday, July 22. Evening.

"I'm with Miss Breslau right now."

"Good." Petrosino disconnected.

Bo called the House on Mulberry Street and ordered six patrolmen to report to him immediately. Dutch walked into the hall as Bo returned the telephone to Wong.

"I'm going out back, see what set off that cat. Wong?"

"Be best not to show our hand," Bo said. "The Organ Grinder's somewhere around here, but Fabrizzi's watching him." He didn't notice Wong's dark satisfaction.

"I've got to keep her safe," Dutch muttered. "Wong, I need your assistance." Dutch walked briskly to the front door. Wong, who appeared to be taking his time, arrived there with him. Somewhere along the way, he'd picked up a bull's-eye lantern.

"Get the light," Dutch said, taking the bull's-eye.

Wong extinguished the hall light. He and Dutch exited the house, Dutch heading for the near corner, and Wong, loping silently, moving in the opposite direction to circumnavigate the block.

Wong was only moments late in meeting Tonneman at the wooden fence that opened onto the back yard of the house between No. 5 and the corner. "I saw no . . ." Wong whispered.

On the ground lay the gutted remains of a huge alley cat. In the yard, nothing moved. The only sound came from the lushly leafed trees that rustled in the slight breeze.

"Damn," Dutch said. "Watch yourself, Wong, he might still be close on."

"Not anymore," said a quaking voice from above.

Wong held up the lantern. Little Jack Meyers was roosting on a limb in a large oak tree.

"I think he's in the park," said Little Jack. "You just missed him by a few minutes."

"And when were you going to come in and tell us?"

"When I got my nerve back."

"Well, you better keep it with you at all times from now on." Little Jack stayed where he was, while Dutch and Wong moved back inside where Bo waited, talking to Jack

West. "We think he's in the park," Dutch said. "Your man spotted him," he told West.

"I ordered six patrolmen," Bo said. "We'll go after him when they get here."

Returning to the dining room with Dutch and Wong, Bo shared Petrosino's information, but not Little Jack's. Everyone began speaking at once. Jack West, who stood near the window, sent a worried look to Oz. Baby Burgoyne nodded sagely as he'd seen his mentors Grimes and Stokes do, even though he had no idea what the intelligence was about.

To Bo, Dutch said, "We've got to move Esther to safety."

"All right, coz." Bo tapped his fork on his glass to catch everyone's attention. He considered Baby for several seconds. "How'd you come here tonight, Burgoyne?"

"In my Benz."

"Didn't we run across each other in Cuba last year?"

Baby scrambled to his feet. "I had the honor to be in that country with Colonel Roosevelt."

"Then," Bo said, bringing a blue bandanna with white polka dots from his inside pocket, "as one veteran to another I have a favor to ask."

"What's that?"

"I want you to take Miss Breslau for a drive."

"See here, Clancy," Oz demanded. "Do you mean to enlist this young fool into our cause?"

"A perfect disguise," Bo said. "He has no connection to the case. He's a stranger."

"Bah," Dutch bellowed.

Battling Jack shifted uncomfortably in his position by the window. They deserved to know Mr. Burgoyne's involvement. But the young man was a client. Yet West's concern was with Esther's safety. What was a locket by comparison to a human life, especially Miss Esther's?

"I'll do it," said Battling Jack. "I'm the best automobile operator, and an assassin or a gang of assassins will have to step over my dead body to get to Miss Esther."

Bo shook his head. "I'll wager you've helped put down a few desperados in the Frog and Toe, West. Makes you too well known. That's why Burgoyne is so right for the job. He's unknown. He's a stranger."

"A stranger," Dutch said, frowning, "who will have no idea of what he's doing, and place Esther at great risk. I don't like it."

"Nor I," Oz agreed.

"If anyone's going to take her," Dutch declared, raising his voice, "it will be me."

"I need you here," Bo countered.

Dutch's stubborn expression was more than familiar to Bo. "We both know how hairy this is going to get," Bo said.

"I'll protect her," Baby said with pride. "You have nothing to fear. But what am I protecting her from?"

Oz groaned. He shook his head at Wong, who'd closed the door but remained in the room.

"Gentlemen," Jack West said, "I believe you're placing Miss Breslau's life at risk needlessly —"

Esther clanked her glass with her fork. She'd had about enough of this. No one was asking her opinion. They were all talking as if she wasn't in the room. She scowled at Oz and Dutch. Even Jack West was not safe from her glare. "With all this protection, I don't see why I should leave the house."

"But you must," Oz Cook said.

Dutch nodded.

Bo was silent, studying Esther. Damn this new breed of woman. Now, she had it in her head not to leave, there'd be no budging her. But the Organ Grinder seemed to have nine lives; Bo didn't want to give him the chance of using up one to get Esther. "We need you to lure him out," he said to her.

"No!" exploded from Dutch and Oz.

"Yes," Esther said. "I think it's a capital idea. A stalking horse, am I right, Bo Clancy? I am to be a stalking horse."

Pleased, Bo winked at Dutch.

"You are, Esther."

She turned to Baby. "Mr. Burgoyne, will you do this for me?"

"Gladly." He said to Oz, "If it's for Miss Breslau, I'm ready to serve, sir." The young man saluted, raising his table knife as a sword. " 'We few, we happy few, we band of brothers. For he today that sheds —' "

"Enough," Oz thundered. He didn't care for this scheme at all, but the gleam in Esther's eye and the set of her jaw brooked no debate. And with Baby along, he liked it even less. Still, he'd caught Clancy's wink and felt an iota of respect for him. It was a ruse to get Esther to safety, and it was working.

Baby jumped to his feet, beside himself with joy. He removed a twin to Bo's blue bandanna with white polka dots from his inside pocket, unfolded it, and tied it around his neck.

Bo rolled his eyes at Dutch. Dutch had worn one too. It was the hallmark of a Rough Rider.

"He's a dolt," Dutch muttered.

Oz couldn't have agreed more. To entrust Baby with Esther's life would be disastrous. "Please, Baby. One Theodore Roosevelt is enough."

"Sit down, Mr. Burgoyne," Bo ordered.

Baby obeyed. "Perhaps you'd better explain what this is about."

Jack West was troubled. It would all come out now; Burgoyne would think he had breached confidentiality.

"It's about the murder of a young woman named Delia Swann," Bo said, "the assassin who did it, and the locket she was supposed to be wearing."

"The locket?" Baby turned pale. He looked an accusation at Jack West.

Jack West barely shook his head.

Dutch noticed the exchange. What was that about? "Esther was the last person to see Delia Swann alive, except for the killer. The locket appears to have some kind of value to the killer and the person who hired him."

Bo was grim. "Everyone who came in contact with Delia Swann on her last day of life has been threatened by the assassin, and at least one person has been killed and another brutally stabbed. The killer broke into this house early this morning in an attempt to murder Esther in her bed. It was lucky that Wong stopped him."

His bluster all but obliterated, Baby felt ill. "But Esther, Miss Breslau, couldn't possibly have the locket."

"What do you know of the locket?" Bo demanded.

"Only what you've told me —"

"I'm afraid I did have the locket," Esther said, watching Dutch's face. "I gave my word to keep it safe, which is what I was trying to do."

There it was again, Jack West thought. The matter of coincidence. Search all of New York for a locket for one client, and find it had always been in the hands of the other client: the little lady he was hired to protect.

"Where is the locket now?" Baby was appalled by this staggering news.

Dutch drew his hand from his pocket and let Delia's much-sought-after talisman dangle from its black velvet ribbon. Baby Burgoyne and Jack West were mesmerized as the gold, heart-shaped locket swung back and forth, catching the glow from the electric chandelier that hung high over the table.

"In the hands of the Metropolitan Police, Mr. Burgoyne," Bo said. "Where it belongs."

CHAPTER 55

Saturday, July 22. Evening.

If Flora Cooper had had her way she would have gotten out of the stalled New York Central train, hitched one end of a rope around the engine, the other around herself, and pulled the blasted locomotive into the City. The train hadn't moved in almost an hour. Outside, not one glimmer of light; darkness blanketed everything.

"Cows on the track." Holding a kerosene lantern, the conductor made his way from one dark car to the next, assuring the concerned passengers. "We'll be moving again soon."

"I must get to a telephone," Flora said.

"I'm sorry, miss, but as you can see, we're in the middle of nowhere. But don't you worry, we shouldn't be much more'n an hour late getting into the city."

Flora ground her teeth. She could get off the train, but what would she do and where would she go? Under cover of darkness, she put her feet up on the empty seat next to her and had herself a smoke. Her instinct had been accurate.

The final proof awaited her in the morgue.

Knickerbockers, Esther thought. She held up one of Oz's sporting outfits, which Wong had brought her. And why not? Bloomers was her costume when she rode her bicycle in Central Park, something she hadn't done since Delia's murder.

She shortened the braces with straight pins, and buttoned the Norfolk jacket. Buttoned, no one would see the adjustment. In the mirror she saw a woman in a man's clothing until Wong, slipping into her reflection, set one of Oz's soft caps upon her head. Now each of them wore Oswald Cook headgear. She smiled. At this rate Oz would have none left.

The gray herringbone cap would not stay put; she secured it with a hat pin.

All the men had agreed, which gave Esther pause. How much of a stalking horse would she be if the assassin didn't recognize her? Well, she was on to their game. Having her cover her hair, as if she were back in Europe wearing an awful orange sheitel.

For her own good! Yes, she'd heard that

before, many times. She had dealt with it and she would deal with this. As soon as they were away from the house, she would take off the ridiculous cap. The murderer would spot her and give chase, and they would catch him red-handed.

"What do you think, Wong?"

The Chinaman, his arms folded, did not speak for a moment. "Satisfactory," was his diplomatic response. Unlike the others, he did not underestimate her intelligence. Miss Esther made a very pleasant-looking young man. He was certain she realized this and even the reason behind the disguise: that they were sending her away to protect her, and she had plans of her own. At the moment he was considering how to follow her to keep her safe from her own willfulness. He said, "Miss Esther, I would know you in whatever costume you would wear."

Ready for her great adventure, Esther debated with herself whether to take her camera. Night meant extra equipment. In the end, even though it would probably be pointless, she placed one of the small Detective cameras in her bag. This camera, which had been very useful four years earlier when she'd helped Dutch solve Robert Roman's murder, was disguised as a leather-bound copy of *A Tale of Two Cities.* It held six one-

and-three-quarter-inch by two-and-three-quarter-inch glass plates.

Downstairs they were waiting, all of them, concern on each face. But the concern changed to something akin to amusement when they caught sight of her. Dutch grinned, and Bo gave a guffaw. Baby smiled fondly.

"I'm glad I provide you some amusement, gentlemen," she said in her haughtiest manner.

"Never mind these barbarians, you look absolutely charming, my dear," Oz said. He kissed her forehead.

The grin faded from Dutch's face.

Jack West opened the front door and looked out. Baby's Benz was parked in front of the house. Gramercy Park was quiet as a graveyard. Esther shuddered. She mustn't let thoughts like that poison her mind. After this night, the horror would be over.

"All right, you two," Bo ordered, "get going. Damn it, Burgoyne, don't take her elbow, remember, she's a man."

"No charging up San Juan Hill, Burgoyne," Dutch said, brushing past Baby. He took Esther's hand and brought it to his lips.

"I'll be fine," Esther said, with more courage than she felt.

"Mr. West," Oz said, "watch over her."

"I will, sir, you can depend on me."

On the other side of Gramercy Park, in front of one of the brownstone houses, a hackney waited, it would seem, for someone to come out. The coachman sat slumped and appeared to be snoozing.

Bo made a motion with his thumb, and Baby left the house, ostentatiously checking the street around. Beckoning to Esther, Baby helped her into the Benz and climbed in beside her. Jack West turned the automobile's crank. When the motor came to life, Baby fed the gasoline. Jack West quickly crowded in.

As Baby drew away from the curb, a wagon pulled by a team of four turned the corner and stopped in front No. 5 Gramercy Park in the very spot the Benz had just vacated. Six hefty young men in their blue suits and gray helmets jumped down. Bo and Dutch stepped out of the house with a key to the Park. Bull's-eye lanterns were turned on; the patrolmen placed themselves around the outside of the park, while Bo and Dutch entered.

Only the figure crouched behind telephone pole noticed that the hackney coach from across the way had come to life and was going in the same direction the Benz had taken.

Quickly, eagle-eyed Little Jack raced after the coach. As he'd done many times before, he leaped on the back of the carriage. His feet found bare purchase on the mud guard, his fingers clinging to the woodwork around the shaded rear window.

CHAPTER 56

Saturday, July 22. Evening.

The patrolmen encircling the outside of Gramercy Park held their lanterns high as Bo and Dutch searched for the Organ Grinder.

Strange to say, Dutch felt the night was smiling at him. It was balmy, starlit, and utterly peaceful. He had no sense of menace. Then an image of Esther, gutted like the alley cat, brought him back to reality.

Bo was utterly focused on the task. Get the dago son of a bitch. Catch him or kill him. He'd have himself a drink or two on the villain and go find Flora.

The shout surprised everyone. It came from the wrong direction.

"Stay here and keep your eyes peeled," Dutch yelled to the patrolmen as he and Bo raced to the park gate. Once out of the park it took only seconds to cross the narrow street to the front door of No. 5 Gramercy Park.

The door stood open; Oz Cook waited for them, anguished.

"What?" Bo demanded.

Oz turned to the rear of the house and lifted his arm feebly. Suddenly he was an old man. "The cellar. Wong."

Dutch dashed ahead, leaving Bo to question Oz.

"Wong," Dutch called on the run.

Dutch fairly caromed down the cellar stairs. At the bottom he saw the Chinaman standing over an eviscerated, bloody body.

Wong held up a gold badge and a card. "Detective Louis Fabrizzi."

Esther shivered. She had meant to unpin her hat as soon as they pulled away from the curb, but she was wedged in tight between the two men.

"I thought we'd take a ride on Broadway," Baby said, making a left turn on Twenty-third Street.

"Faster," Jack West snapped.

"I'm sorry, old man, but this is about as fast as the machine will go."

"Blast," Jack yelled. He stretched his thick leg across Esther and stomped Baby's foot, increasing the speed only slightly.

"Hey —" Baby yelled.

"Mr. West —"

"Have you lost your mind?" Baby demanded.

Jack didn't answer either of them. He was trying to get away from the gun aimed at them from the hackney coach, which, having followed them, now had pulled up along side. At last, Baby leaned forward and caught sight of the gun and the man holding it.

Up Broadway they went, Baby weaving as best he could along the road, once in a while stopping short, attempting to spook the chestnut pulling the carriage.

"If I see a good spot, Miss Esther," Jack said at Thirtieth Street, "we'll stop and you jump out and run."

"I'll do no such thing —"

"Turn here, Burgoyne."

They got off Broadway at Thirty-fourth Street but were thwarted in the turnaround by an oncoming drummer's wagon. Baby continued up Fifth Avenue.

"So much for your imported automobiles," Jack muttered. "Can't even outrun a coach."

When they turned east at Forty-second Street, the hackney glanced off the automobile; the chestnut screeched, bucked, went wild. Strong hands reined in the frightened horse. Baby applied his brake to avoid hitting the animal.

A fierce explosion filled the automobile with metallic smoke. Jack West made a rumbling sound and slumped over onto Esther, nearly crushing her. She tried to free herself, but he was dead weight. Something wet and sticky touched her hands.

Dear God, Battling Jack was shot, possibly dead. "Mr. Burgoyne, stop, you must stop. We've been shot." She was screaming.

Baby jerked the steering wheel, the automobile shuddered once and crashed into a trolley car going in the opposite direction. Cries came from the injured on the trolley car. Eyes glazed, staring, Baby crumpled over the steering wheel. People ran to help the passengers on the trolley.

A swarthy man opened the door on Esther's side and roughly yanked Jack West from the car, throwing him to the ground.

"Please, no. Can't you see he's hurt?" Esther struggled to sit up, but before she could their supposed rescuer dragged her out of the Benz. She fell on the ground beside Jack West. He was bleeding profusely from a wound to his chest.

Esther, on her knees, dazed, took his huge hand in hers.

Crowds of people milled around the trolley. Only the swarthy man and another — a ruddy-faced man — who came toward them now out of the crowd, had come to their aid.

Bells pealed as the swarthy man dragged the unconscious Baby Burgoyne from the Benz and threw him into the hackney. "What are you doing?" Esther screamed. "Someone, help us!" She had no weapon to fight with. This couldn't be happening.

Little Jack had tumbled from his precarious perch on the back of the hackney when the horse reared. A few bruises but nothing to worry about. He wasn't concerned about himself, or Miss Esther. Big Jack was down; he had to help him.

Esther tore the hat pin from her cap and jumped to her feet. The cap slipped from her head, exposing her hair. She chased after the swarthy man. As he climbed into the hackney that had sideswiped them, Esther plunged her hat pin into his back.

He barely grunted at the injury; he turned and grabbed her wrist, twisting it until with a cry of pain she dropped the hat pin.

Less than five feet away, Tony recognized Giorgio, Nonna's grandson. Why was he interfering with the *giudea?* He pushed his way to Giorgio and Esther.

Esther felt a whoosh of relief. The real Good Samaritan.

But the ruddy face and burns changed her thinking. No, she thought, it can't be. The man produced an ugly knife.

"Please," Esther said, "I don't have it."

"Look ahere! Halloo!" Little Jack called, as he moved closer to Big Jack, lying so still on the road. "Coppers coming!"

"Get in the cab," Tony ordered, Marie ready in his hand.

"I don't want her," Giorgio said. "He's the one I want."

"Stolto," Tony spat. "She's the one Nonna wants. She knows where the locket is."

Part III

Chapter 57

Saturday, July 22. Evening.

With dread, Little Jack crawled to Battling Jack's bloody body. "Are you living, Mr. West?"

"Yes, you silly little bastard." Jack West groaned and clutched his shoulder. "What are you doing here? Your place is with the client."

"Yes, sir." Little Jack jumped to his feet. Looking for help for Battling Jack, he saw a man get off a bicycle, leave it, and wander to the overturned trolley.

An ambulance pulled up. "Over here," Little Jack called, waving wildly. "Over here."

Flora's return to the City coincided with a mighty traffic jam caused by an accident in the area. Pedestrians milled all around, and no one seemed to know for sure what had happened, yet the entire avenue was lit up like a celebration. She saw hackneys and carriages backed up and flashing lights. No traffic moved on Forty-second Street, except one sulky that sought to escape along the sidewalk. A policeman gave chase.

"What kind of accident?" she asked a Negro porter, who was watching over a trunk and various other pieces of luggage belonging to a very unhappy gentleman, his wife, and two young sons. The latter could hardly contain themselves for the excitement.

"A trolley collided with a hack down the block, miss."

Her reporter's nose twitched. She threaded her way through the crowded streets until she came to two patrolmen who were trying, with little success, to hold back the ogling crowd.

Bo and Dutch stood outside No. 5, smoking and talking over what to do next, now that Esther was safe. Behind the half-open door, Wong waited, listening. He stiffened at the approaching rattle of a bike; he opened the door wide.

Little Jack Meyers wheeled up to No. 5, braking with a squeal of tires. His shout had no breath to it, but Bo and Dutch could make out the words. "Miss Esther, Mr. Burgoyne. The dago knifer. Nonna's, he said, he's taking them to Nonna's."

Oz heard the commotion, saw Bo and Dutch race off. Little Jack was bent over, trying to stretch a cramp from his leg. He intended to get back on his bicycle and go after them.

"Who is Nonna?" Oz demanded of Little Jack.

"Old lady with a stable on a Hundredth and Eighth and Park."

"Why on earth — ?" He looked at Wong.

"She is the queen of crime in New York," Wong said.

"He's going to kill her. I've got to stop him."

Wong nodded. "We've got to stop him."

Leo Stern clamped a Garcia Perfecto firmly between his gold teeth. Though he was dedicated to following the Prophet Micah's advice to do justly, love mercy, and walk humbly with his God, he'd never garnered enough humility to give away his costly black suits, like the one he wore tonight over a fancy white silk shirt. Nor was he willing to set aside any of his fine neckware, as embodied by the dazzling red silk tie now knotted round his neck.

Justice was more on his mind than mercy. Like a giant, he strutted his short, sturdy figure down town; he adjusted his fedora, very much aware of the black yarmulke beneath it.

Tonight he would become an avenging angel. His hand brushed against the .32 double-action Colt revolver with a four-inch, dull-finished barrel in its holster under his coat. The touch of metal moved his thoughts away from love of God to hatred for the man who'd hurt Sophie.

Leo didn't like shiny guns. They caught the light and could get a man killed. It never occurred to him that his abundantly-waxed mustache reflected light from the almost-full moon and the street lamps could do the same.

At Twentieth Street, he turned toward Gramercy Park. Stopping, he pulled a handkerchief from his back pocket and wiped his mouth delicately, as if he'd just eaten a rich man's dinner. He savored this God-given night, this night on which he planned to kill the bastard who hurt his beautiful Sophie.

"You can't go no farther, miss," one of the coppers told Flora.

"*New York Herald.*" She presented her

press card. "Flora Cooper," she added. Immediately, she saw the other cop knew who she was. "If you'll give me your names, I'll be sure to put them in my story." She took her notepad from her bag and extracted the yellow pencil from her hair.

"It's Flora Cooper, don't you know her, Eddie?" the first patrolman said to his partner. "It's okay to let her by. I'm Walter Boyle, miss, and this here's Edwin Parker."

"What happened here?" Her eyes darted around. She saw two ambulances and some people on the ground. Others bending over them.

"A few hurt, none real bad, but the man who was shot —"

"A man was shot?" Here was a story, she thought. The other she was working on could wait till morning. "I'd like to talk to someone in charge."

"That'd be —"

Flora never heard the end of this sentence because she was already on her way to the scene.

The trolley, when she came to it, looked no worse than ordinary wear, except it was tipped over on its side. No one was left inside. There wasn't any sign of the hackney that had supposedly run into it. What she did see was a fancy Benz motor car with its whole side smashed in. Maybe it was the Benz that had run into the trolley.

She moved around to the back of the trolley. A very distressed man in a motorman's uniform was gesturing and talking to a fat man in a derby hat. Detective Mike Flaherty. Bad luck, Flaherty hated her, especially since last time she quoted him, his name was misspelled.

"Best I can tell you, the man in the automobile crashed right into me, but it was the hackney that crowded him. Is he dead?"

Flaherty jerked his head back. "You see the man on the ground?"

"Yes," the conductor said. "But he wasn't the driver. The boy with the mop of hair, he was between the driver and" — he pointed to the man on the ground — "that man. The driver looked real bad, too, all slumped over his wheel."

"Are you sure that man wasn't the driver? No one's seen hide nor hair of the driver," Flaherty said. "Or this boy you're talking about."

"But I saw someone pull them out." The conductor took off his hat and mopped his sweating face with his sleeve.

"Think, man, what happened to the driver and the boy?"

"I don't know."

"Take a second and think."

"All I can remember is that the boy didn't seem to be hurt."

Flora's pencil broke with a loud snap.

"Goddam! Flora Cooper! What the hell are you doing here?" Flaherty grabbed her arm and pulled her off the road to the sidewalk.

She grinned up at him. "Do you have anything to add to what the motorman said, Detective Flaherty?"

"How'd you find out about this so fast?"

"Secret sources," Flora said mischievously. At Flaherty's glower, she said quickly, "I got off the train at the Grand Central Depot and walked into it. What's going on, Flaherty? Who does that car belong to and who got shot?"

Keeping a firm hold of her arm, Flaherty steered her to where a doctor was working on a big man lying in the street. "Come on, so long as you're here, but make sure to spell my name right this time."

Nonna Pasquarella, the tall red-haired woman from Marcianise, stood on the porch of her house on Park Avenue at One Hundred Eighth Street. Before her guests' arrival she'd been admiring how well her electric lights illuminated her empire.

"Mr. Cerasani. So nice of you to pay us a visit." Her eyes flamed at her grandson, Giorgio. He had done the unthinkable. He had brought strangers into her domain, without permission. In his ways he had become too American, too independent. Something would have to be done about him.

"Mr. B., it's good to see you alive and well. I apologize for the circumstances."

Baby shook his head, still groggy, but slowly coming back to himself.

"What is happening here?" Esther cried. "I insist that we be released immediately."

As if Esther wasn't there, Nonna turned her attention to Cerasani. He, at least, being of the old country, had some respect. Perhaps she should send Giorgio to Marcianise, where respect was given proper esteem and treated as a life and death matter.

Tony kept his eyes lowered when he spoke to her. "Nonna, my visit was not my plan." Tony was no fool. He knew that he had breached Nonna's private territory without invitation. For this, she might exact the ultimate payment. "The girl knows where the locket is. I would have that information now, but for an unexpected interruption." He bowed his head to her.

"I want —" Giorgio began.

In the hackney, Esther sat trembling, Baby's head on her shoulder, her handkerchief staunching the bleeding cut on his forehead. She had heard the entire, curious exchange. They spoke in Italian, and she understood the language well enough, having learned it from the Italian girls who'd come to the Henry Street Settlement as she had as a young immigrant. And why, it suddenly occurred to her, had this dreadful woman referred to Baby Burgoyne as if she knew him?

Nonna stared at Giorgio and cut the air with her hand. "*Basta.* What you want is unimportant." She studied Tony before she spoke again. "If what you say is true, Mr. Cerasani, then it shouldn't be long before you have your money."

"And I can leave this evil country."

Nonna smiled. "For me, it is good here." She turned to her grandson. "For my children, and their children, maybe not so." What was she to do with Giorgio? He had violated her agreement with her client. Her client's emissary was not to be ill-used. If she was to get the final payment from him, Giorgio's trophy must live. Her grandson had given her a dilemma. She didn't like dilemmas. "Yes, Giorgio, my pet, what is it you want?"

Giorgio pulled Baby from Esther and threw him on the ground. "I want this one."

"Please, no," Esther cried, jumping down from the hackney and rushing to Baby's side.

Nonna waved an imperious hand at Giorgio. "Take, but you will do nothing with him until we have satisfied our client. Do you understand me?" Her eyes flicked over Esther. What kind of woman with respect for herself wears men's clothing?

Clearly disappointed, Giorgio accepted Nonna's edict. He would deal with his enemy in time. He prodded Baby, then Esther. "Move."

Esther took Baby's arm and helped him up to the porch of Nonna's house, where a small dog quivered, growling at the strangers.

"Good boy, 'Mazzio." Nonna Pasquarella patted Baby on the shoulder to assure him things were better than they seemed. "Come inside," she told Cerasani. "We'll drink *assenzio* and eat." She picked up the snarling Pekinese and stroked its silky coat.

Tony shook his head. "Let us deal with the girl and the locket, then I can take my money and leave."

Nonna's eyes narrowed. "You refuse my

hospitality? Inside. We'll eat, we'll drink. Talk of the old country. Laugh, perhaps. Listen to Gieulietta play the piano."

Tony, who'd been aware of the shadows on either side of the house, could now count them. Men in black, Nonna's protectors.

Three to the left, four to the right. And there would be at least three others. Tony couldn't see them, but he knew they were there.

Tony's first thought was to introduce them all to Marie and have done with it then and there. But his dreams of Sicily were too strong to have him throw away even the smallest of chances. He would play the old hag's game, and if it came to his death he was ready. He would take her with him.

Nonna tilted her head, and one of the men in black appeared and silently ushered Tony, Esther, and Baby into the house.

Giorgio started to follow. "No," Nonna commanded. "Escort them to the kitchen then go outside." She knew Giorgio would only torment his enemy, and that was not needed just now.

"Gieulietta," Nonna shouted. "Out of your bed. I need you to play sweet music."

The plain girl, fully dressed, in a gray muslin dress, appeared on the staircase.

"Good," Nonna said. "Gieulietta will play

while we eat and drink. Her music always calms, eases digestion, and helps take the webs from the mind. We need that tonight." She arched her neck and called, "Patsy."

The small Irish youth in black trousers, a clean white shirt, and wearing a black cravat, appeared.

"Son of a whore," Tony exclaimed. The little Irish could have had the locket. Did Nonna have it from him and was playing Tony for a fool? Or perhaps she didn't even know.

"*Assenzio* for my guest and me. Put our other guests in the kitchen with Raffaella."

"Si, Nonna." Patsy bobbed his head.

"I take grappa," Tony said.

Nonna smiled. "Indulge an old lady. Have some *assenzio* with me."

Tony hated the green, stinking absinthe. To him it was bitter licorice piss. But now was not the time to thwart the old woman. The only thing that could save him was the *giudea* bitch and the locket. The question now was, who had it? Nonna, the *giudea,* or the Irish?

Chapter 58

Saturday, July 22. Evening. Night.

"Faster!" Dutch yelled at Sergeant Fletcher, knowing full well that the team of horses was going as fast as it could.

With Bo directing the rangy sergeant, they skirted the traffic jam Little Jack had warned them about going up First Avenue. Bo knew it would take them through Uncle Mico territory. He also knew that Uncle Mico paid well to keep the police out of his country and would not be happy about the intrusion.

But if Petrosino was right, and he always was about the dagos, Uncle Mico might not be displeased if the cops were going after his arch rival, the old grandmother known as Nonna.

Counting Dutch, himself, Fletcher, and four coppers, Bo had only seven to go up against Nonna and her gang. Good thing he'd left O'Meara in Gramercy Park to call the House to send a riot squad to Nonna's stable.

Be strong, Esther told herself as they were herded down a dark and narrow passageway past the narrow staircase. She made an effort to block out her fear, for it would confuse her thinking. At this moment, she saw no way to save either herself or Baby, whose hand was oppressive on her shoulder; he was too weak, too ill, to do either of them any good. But God had been good to her. She prayed for a miracle.

In the kitchen, which was a large box that hugged the rear of the house, an old woman stood over a succession of steaming pots, stirring one after the other. In spite of the heat, the old woman wore a black wool dress and her head was wrapped in a black scarf.

Similarly dressed and seated at the rectangular table in the middle of the kitchen was another old woman. It was difficult to tell who was the older, though the one at the table was hunchbacked and had a dense layer of white powder on her face to cover her pockmarks. This one sliced one of a dozen or more fat loaves of bread into thick pieces.

The pockmarked woman muttered in Italian, her voice raspy, like coal going down a chute. What she said sent shivers along Esther's spine. "Here come more lambs for the slaughter." Her cackle was echoed by the one at the pots.

"Sit, and don't move," Giorgio ordered Esther and Baby, pointing to a bench opposite the old woman slicing bread. He held out his hand to the old lady. "Give me, mother."

Cackling, the pockmarked woman spread a garlic-smelling mixture on a slice and handed it to him. "Maybe your friends outside would like."

Eating the garlicky bread voraciously, Giorgio ignored her suggestion. Sharing did not enter his thoughts.

The knife, Esther thought. If I can get hold of the knife.

The pockmarked woman nodded her head with such vigor that for a moment Esther thought it was in agreement with her thoughts. Esther watched the woman as she prepared the rest of the loaf with the garlic spread. "I take to your friends. You have another piece." The old lady gathered up the slices, got up awkwardly, and went out the back door.

Where was the knife? It was gone. Had Giorgio picked it up? "You can't keep us here," Esther told him. "The police will come." Baby swayed beside her, leaned against her, eyes shut.

Giorgio laughed. "You hear that, Raffaella? She says the police will come."

"And give up all that money?" Raffaella considered such a notion extremely funny.

"Don't think of running for it."

Esther tried to keep her face blank. Giorgio had terrible, crazy eyes, and they frightened her more than his words.

"We have men everywhere," he said. "You won't get past the door." Giorgio left the kitchen and went stomping down the long hallway.

Baby opened his eyes and sat up. The wound to his head had crusted, and he seemed more aware of his surroundings. All he could think was that whatever was happening was his fault.

In a short time, the old bread lady returned and sat down again. She resumed her bread-slicing chores. So, Esther thought, she must have taken the knife outside with her. Again, as if she read Esther's mind, the old lady looked at her hard, and said in broken English, "It's not good to make Nonna angry. What you think, Raffaella?"

"I think you very funny, Lina." Raffaella

stirred a pot viciously with her wooden spoon.

Witches, Esther thought. Two witches. She felt Baby tense beside her. He caught her hand under the table. His eyes were on the knife slowly slicing the bread. Was he going to try for it? She stared at the knife, then at the hand holding it. The old lady's fingers were stained with blood.

Chapter 59

Sunday, July 23. Just after midnight.

A bell. Flora, bleary-eyed, lifted her head and at first didn't know where she was.

"What a ninny you are, Flora Cooper." She was in the *Herald* morgue, and lord, she'd fallen asleep over the pile of newspapers she'd been reading. Stiff as a corpse, she rubbed the back of her neck.

The clock had chimed midnight, waking her. She'd been exhausted by the long day upstate, and then coming on the accident near the Grand Central Depot. She'd written the story and filed it.

Flora was troubled. The shooting of Jack West didn't make any sense. She would go over to Bellevue in a few hours and talk to West again. Maybe he'd be more willing to talk to her than he was last night. Next, over to Mulberry Street to see if she could pry something out of Bo Clancy.

Yes. She got up and stretched. She'd done

a good job covering the story. Lucky Flora Cooper. Always at the right place at the right time. She sat down again hard.

What was it she'd thought of before falling asleep? She backtracked in her mind, trying to jog her memory. After leaving Alexina Brewster's estate, she had traveled up to Rhinebeck in order to trace the Hall family and Delia Swann's parentage. And she'd been successful.

That's what she'd been thinking about. But she'd been so tired she couldn't keep her eyes open. She had put her head down for a minute and —

"Oh, my God!" Delia's — Irene's mother was heir to the Bayard fortune. Whoever controlled that fortune —

Excited, she pawed through the stack of old *Herald*s once more. There was the article, staring her in the face. Now she had no doubt of it. She'd found Delia Swann's killer.

"Shut up," Bo ordered as the wagon approached One Hundredth Street. "Find a spot around a Hundred Third," he told Fletcher.

Fletcher reined in the frothing animals just south of a Hundred and Fourth.

"What's the plan?" Dutch asked.

"Attack," Bo replied.
"Yes, sir, Colonel Roosevelt, sir."
"I wish he was here."
"Amen," Fletcher said.
The other cops mumbled agreement.
Silently, they edged up to One Hundred Seventh. "Halt," Bo ordered, raising his hand. "We could wait for reinforcements," he whispered to Dutch.
"While Esther's getting her throat cut? Or worse?"
"If we were a larger force I'd deploy half around back."
"But we're not." Dutch was bristling with impatience.
"Then it's Teddy's way. My order stands. Attack."

Little Jack, following the rear lights of Oswald Cook's Porsche, was frustrated. He could pedal faster than that automobile was going, but he had no lights. So, all he could do was follow in the Porsche's wake.

Esther. If she died, Oz believed he would have no reason to live. The moon spread a thin veil of light, cold in spite of the summer night. He shivered. The face in the not-quite-full moon seemed to be mocking him.
Cursing the machine, Oz shouted at Wong

to push the Porsche faster. Wong complied, but speed did not go with control, and they were sometimes on the road and sometimes off.

Suddenly, in the diffused glow of their battery-powered headlamps, a figure loomed up in front of them.

Wong's decision whether to stop, swerve, or simply barrel through was made for him by the gunshot that pinged the automobile.

It was still dark when Flora, having bathed and changed clothes at her furnished room on West Twenty-fifth Street, arrived at the press shack across from 300 Mulberry Street.

There was no one around. This was strange in itself. Usually one or two reporters slept the night, afraid they'd miss a reportable event.

Across the street, police headquarters was in a frenzy of activity, with patrol wagons loading up, everyone carrying rifles.

"What's going on, Kreuger?" she called up to one of the drivers as he was about to pull out.

"A dago riot, upper Park Avenue. Best get out of my way, Flora."

Frustrated, she watched the wagons pull away. Damn. Where would she find a hack at this hour? Well, she would try . . . maybe in front of one of the blind tigers or a whorehouse. She had to see for herself what was happening. Besides, she needed one more bit of corroboration on Delia Swann's murderer, and she couldn't get that until dawn. Flora heaved an omnipotent sigh and smiled; she had time to kill.

"Get the wine from the cellar, Lina."

The old lady called Lina put her hands flat on the table and pushed herself up. As she tied her scarf tighter around her throat, she lowered her right eyelid briefly. Esther watched closely as Lina lumbered to the end of the room where an open door probably led to a cellar. Something was very strange about that old lady.

Baby pressed her hand again. Had he noticed it, too?

Raffaella uncovered a mound of dough from a big wooden bowl. After first spreading flour on the surface of the rectangular table, she slapped the mound of dough onto it, creating a small explosion of flour dust that flew in the prisoners' faces. Esther put her hand over her mouth, coughing. Baby sneezed.

Lina reappeared carrying a crate. "Where you want, Raffaella?"

Raffaella didn't look up. She pounded the mound of dough several times with her rolling pin. More flour escaped. "You back, Lina? Good. Put it down. Give me a hand here."

"Anything you want," Lina said. Setting the crate down, Lina came up behind Raffaella, placed her hands on Raffaella's neck, and whispered, *"Scusi."*

"What's the mat — ?" Before Raffaella could utter another sound, Lina squeezed.

CHAPTER 60

Sunday, July 23. Just after midnight.

"What the hell?" Nonna took a broom leaning against the side of the house and smashed out the electric porch lights. She ran bent-over toward the stable, where the horses were whinnying and kicking at their stalls. She yelled, "Idiots! Turn out those fucking lights." Immediately most of the lights went out.

Tony stayed directly behind her. She moved pretty good for an old hag. "Looks like you got trouble."

"I don't get trouble," Nonna snapped. "I give trouble."

At the first sound of gunfire, Giorgio decided that his well-being was more important to him than Nonna's. Revenge could wait. He ran for the stable. He knew where Nonna would go with the money.

■ ■ ■ ■

"Get that blasted machine off the road, you fools," Sergeant Fletcher ordered. Bo had posted Fletcher as rear guard while he and Dutch led the other police officers into Nonna's domain.

Oz got out of the Porsche. "I demand —"

Gunshots sparkled the night view, ending all conversation as Wong dove from the automobile and pushed Oz into a ditch. Fletcher, also flat on the ground, tried to find where the gunfire was coming from.

One group of flashes seemed to originate from a higher point than others. The next time a shot came from there, Fletcher returned fire and was rewarded with a cry and the sound of a body falling through branches and leaves.

The gunfire up the road continued.

Fletcher called to Oz. "Don't go no farther, and move that goddam contraption off the road, by orders of Inspector Clancy." That said, the sergeant was off and running in a half-crouch toward the compound.

"Keep down, sir," Wong whispered to Oz. He jumped back into the automobile, drove it off the road, and shut down the engine. It was then they heard the sound of hoofbeats on the road behind them.

Oz stood up, peering down Park Avenue, where he could see a faint bouncing light as it came closer and closer.

Wong got into the ditch beside Oz. "Please, sir," he said, "stay down. We have no idea if this new arrival is friend or foe."

Reining his borrowed gray gelding to a halt beside Oz's automobile, the new arrival said, "Well, what do we have here?" The man had to be a considerable horseman, controlling his animal with only one hand while the other gripped a kerosene lamp. To be sure, he was strangely dressed for a man out riding. Around his shoulders was a tallith, the Jewish prayer shawl.

The newcomer held his lamp high. When he located Oz and Wong in the ditch near the Porsche, he said, "Good evening, Mr. Cook. Wong. Out for a bit of a ride?"

Oz stood and dusted himself off. "Just so, Mr. Stern. And you?"

Leo Stern took a moment to reassure his mount. His smile in the spectral light of the swaying lamp was frightening. "There's a little unfinished business I have to attend to on Sophie's behalf."

"Hurry," Lina said, her movements showing no sign of age or infirmity. She opened the back door and pushed Esther and Baby out. The smell of death was everywhere now. Two men in black suits were propped up against the side of the house, hats pulled down over their faces. Esther gagged, hugging herself in the darkness. Baby's hand touched her elbow, and she was grateful for the warmth.

Screaming horses broke from the stable. Panicked, they thundered out to the road and galloped up Park Avenue.

"Run!" Baby shouted, shoving Lina.

Baby was astonished to find himself in an iron grip. The old woman scanned the street. Esther had disappeared. And so had the terrified herd of horses.

"Shit," Lina muttered hoarsely. She propelled Baby across the dimly lit street to a side door of the stable, where the smell of horse manure was intense. If Lina was aware of Patsy following them, she didn't comment.

As for Patsy, himself, he had no doubt about his self-interest. His instinct told him to wait and watch and choose the winning side.

"You fool," Lina told Baby. "You've probably gotten that girl killed. I'm going to find her. Get inside here and wait until I come back for you." Without another word she was gone.

Oz and Wong returned to the Porsche, but Wong didn't start the engine.

"Well?" Oz said.

"There's nothing to do but wait," the Chinaman replied.

"We'll take Esther home, Wong, don't you worrry." Oz spoke to comfort Wong, but he was filled with dread. Considering the gunfire, he wasn't sure if anyone would come out alive.

Wong swung himself out of the Porsche.

"Where are you going?"

"I must leave you now."

Out of nowhere, a riderless gray horse galloped through Nonna's country, drawing gunfire from every direction, sending anyone out in the open for cover. Colt drawn, Leo watched the gray race away.

"Look where you're shooting, idiots," a woman screamed. "Nonna commands no shooting without fucking target."

Her remarks were answered by further gunshots. A few lights flickered and went out. The result was only partial darkness.

"Cerasani," the same voice yelled. "Are you with me?"

There was no response.

Leo had never seen Anthony Cerasani, never heard his voice. He wasn't even sure of his name. But some atavistic instinct told him this was the man he'd come looking for. He moved in the direction from whence the woman's voice had come.

All of a sudden the lights from the stable building came on again, catching a man and a woman with flaming red hair in raw light. Their backs were to him, but Leo knew the woman, spitting off a string of curses, to be Nonna.

"Turn and face me, you dago bastard," Leo shouted.

The man was unshaven, yet his blistered face told Leo all he needed to know. This was the bastard who had hurt his Sophie.

Leo raised his gun and fired. The man went down. Nonna ran.

Gunfire came from various directions as if returning Leo's fire. Leo paid no attention. Deliberately, he walked to the fallen body, his free hand holding his prayer shawl in place.

Cerasani rose like a spectre, wielding his dagger. Leo hit him across the face with his pistol. Again the man went down, still clutching the damnable knife.

"Animal," Leo muttered, kicking the man

in the ribs.

The man slashed Leo's boot with his knife. Leo staggered. Someone, not Leo, kicked the man in the head. The blow dazed Tony.

His sight blurred. He thought he saw a Chinaman standing over him, smiling. Then the Chinaman faded away, and like in a dream Tony watched the Jew in the white shawl steal Marie from his hand. Tony wasn't concerned, for he knew his Marie would not betray him.

"Sicilian bastard." The dagger went into Tony's stomach, then tore up to his breast bone.

"Marie!" How could she forsake him? With that amazed thought, the man known as the Organ Grinder died.

Leo fished in his pocket for a Garcia Perfecto. He offered it to Wong, who demurred. "No matter," Leo said, serenely. "It's done." Leo stuck the cigar in his mouth as he walked off, undaunted by the bullets cutting the air around him.

Wong crouched over the body of the Organ Grinder and methodically searched his clothing. When he found what he was looking for, he uttered a faint sound, tucked the object into his shirt, and blended into the shadows near the stable.

■ ■ ■ ■

"Pancetta," Nonna called when she got to the stable. To hell with the Organ Grinder. She had Pancetta, a more reliable slave.

"I'm with you, Nonna." The pig woman handed Nonna Pasquarella two guns, then lifted two bulging suitcases in each hand, and kicked a third forward with her foot. Thus the two women made their way past various coaches and broughams to the extreme corner of the ground floor and to Nonna's secret elevator, concealed behind a pile of bales and boxes.

Pancetta went around to the side of the elevator, opened a large metal cabinet installed in the wall, and spat a curse. "The switches are in place."

Nonna jerked at the elevator door. It didn't budge. "Some treacherous *bastardo* is already down there." Nonna thought for a moment. "We'll deal with this when we have to."

Pancetta fetched the valises, and the women moved past the switch cabinet to a second door, also well-hidden. This door led to a flight of stairs to the basement. When they opened the door, the chugging and droning from the power source punished their ears. The way before them was lit by a succession of electric lights.

"Go first," Nonna ordered. Should Pancetta fall with the suitcases, Nonna was not about to be squashed under her.

The basement of the stable presented a completely different world. Constructed atop ancient boulders, much of the ground was impenetrable. Impenetrable or not, Nonna took no chances. Many years earlier, she'd had an escape tunnel built leading from behind the furnace in the basement of the stable all the way to Lexington Avenue. Her corkscrew out, she called it, because to get around the hard rock the tunnel, by necessity, was dug with more twists and turns than a corkscrew. This was good; it made the way harder. She had sent those who had dug the tunnel back to the old country to ensure her secret. Before now, she had never had to use it.

Although it was like a steam bath in the basement, Nonna didn't notice. Pancetta, on the other hand, dripped oily sweat, exuding her strong odor, which stood alone from that of horse shit and coal dust.

From his hiding place behind the huge coal bins, Giorgio waited. Nonna would come with the money. It was the only way out —

through the tunnel to Lexington Avenue. He had plans. Nonna was old, she had lived her life. It was now his turn.

The noise of the furnace and the steam engine made all other sound impossible. A shadow on the wall made him start. She was here. He was ready for her. He stepped out from behind the furnace with the shovel.

A fierce blow knocked the shovel from his hand. “What the hell are you doing here?” Giorgio screamed.

Baby smiled. “I imagine I came to say goodbye.”

Giorgio’s knife came out, slashing at Baby’s chest.

Baby stepped back, stumbled over cables that inhabited the floor like so many snakes. The blade cut a slice in Baby’s coat and vest. In the pause that followed, Giorgio held his knife in his right hand, low, seemingly ready to castrate, then tossed the weapon to his left hand and stabbed at Baby’s chest.

Baby, brought back sharply to San Juan Hill and a Spanish bayonet, sidestepped the blow and slammed Giorgio in the ear.

“Cazzo.” Giorgio’s howl was lost in the din.

Chapter 61

Monday, July 24. Just after Midnight.

Checking over his shoulder, Little Jack saw a trail of new lights behind him, coming up Park Avenue. In spite of all his instincts screaming at him to turn the bicycle and peddle toward them instead of forward, he'd taken what Battling Jack said to heart, that he must look after the client. And that's what he intended to do.

He paid scant attention to the Porsche in the ditch and concentrated on following the bent-over silhouette of the police officer heading toward Nonna's country.

"Stop!" Oz stepped out of the ditch to the road, but the bicycle tore past him. Little Jack, that was the fellow's name. Damn it all, everyone was getting into it except him. And with Esther's life in the balance, he had more at stake than any of them. Oz returned to the comparative comfort of the automobile and pounded the steering wheel in frustration.

When he let up on the wheel, the pounding persisted, but louder, like rumbling thunder. Turning, he saw horses and wagons coming up the road fast. They went right by without a second look. There were four in all. He noted with relief that they were carrying police.

From a block away, Esther had watched Lina push Baby into the stable and leave. Suddenly, gunfire exploded from all around.

What had she done? She should never have listened to him. Now he'd be killed, and it was her fault. But Lina had left too quickly, and she hadn't entered the stable at all.

Esther held to the shadows as she made her way back to the stable, praying no bullet would come her way. Entering through the side door Lina had pushed Baby through, she saw at once she'd made a mistake. There was no sign of Baby, and two of Nonna's men had taken over the stable and were shooting at those outside from the cover of various wagons and carriages, since the horses' wild escape had shattered the doors.

Esther dropped to the ground. Too late, they had seen her. She scurried back to the side door.

"Get that bitch," one said.

A shot rang out. As she lay still on the straw-covered floor, her hand closed on a wooden handle.

"Got her," a voice said triumphantly.

"Make sure," another voice said.

She heard feet crunching through the straw. The smell of straw and manure mixed with the gunsmoke. It was an ugly combination. And it might be the last scent of her life. She gave the wooden handle a gentle tug. It was a tool of some sort. If she could get a good grip on it —

The man stood over her and prodded her with his boot. "She's dead, all right, but I'll put one more in her to be sure."

Esther called on all her strength and swung the tool. But having no leverage from where she lay on the ground, she missed her target.

Still, the man made a gurgling noise. The gunshot seemed to come immediately after, but of course, it had come first. Her enemy clutched his throat; he took a step and dropped in front of the metal door.

The other man cursed, but kept firing, now with two guns. The noise would make her deaf. In her nostrils, the smell of hell.

■ ■ ■ ■

Little Jack had just seen a woman, Miss Breslau it looked like, go into the stable by a side door. After an curious moment of silence, shooting came from all directions. No place was safe. What would Battling Jack do at a time like this? Protect the client.

Little Jack hunched over the handlebars and kept pumping, the wheels hardly skimming the ground. Ahead of him he saw dark figures running and a big barn with wide open doors. A flash of gunfire came from the barn. They were shooting at him.

Wildly, he looked about for escape. A horse trough. If he could get behind it . . . But his wheels weren't turning. He was sliding. Horse shit, probably. "Horse shit," he yelled as he skidded into the barn.

"Madonna!" a man shouted.

The bicycle hit something human, knocking the man to the barn floor; things flew in the air; the bicycle bucked. Jack slammed into the ground. A woman screamed.

Dutch felt he would go mad. In front of the farmhouse they found four of Nonna's men, dead. Out back they found two more propped up against the house, also dead.

But these two had had their throats cut. Inside, a terrified girl and a crazed old woman, who was so confused she kept muttering gibberish.

"Lina tried to kill her," the girl Gieulietta said.

"And who is this Lina?" Dutch asked.

"An old lady."

It was senseless, all of it. But he'd learned one thing that was good. After attacking the old lady, this Lina had then disappeared with the two prisoners: Esther and Burgoyne. Alive.

"Jack Meyers."

Little Jack shook his head, sat up. Where was he? He smelled gunpowder and horse shit. And blood.

"Are you shot?" the voice came again. A woman's voice. He knew the voice and thanked God for it.

"Miss Esther, you're alive."

"Barely," she whispered. "Quickly, you must help me find Mr. Burgoyne."

"Where is he? Is he hurt?" The client, Jack thought. The client.

"I don't know. I saw him come in here, but I can't find him. It's my fault he's got into this, and he's been trying to protect me." She put the gun she'd taken from the dead man in Jack's hand. "We may need this."

"Don't you worry, Miss Esther, I'll find him." The weapon felt right in his palm, like it was meant to be there. "You stay here. Inspector Clancy and Captain Tonneman are here already." Gleaning a bull's-eye lantern from the floor, he called, "Inspector Clancy, Captain, don't shoot. It's Jack Meyers talking. I'm here in the barn with Miss Esther!"

But they'd forgotten the man Little Jack had run down.

The noise was like a cannon blast.

This time Esther charged with the tool, like a knight of old. She caught the shooter in the arm with the pitchfork. The man screamed. Little Jack shot him in the head. The man stopped screaming and fell to the floor.

Little Jack was so unnerved by killing a man he dropped his gun. Picking up his pistol he wiped it under his armpit. "Good weapon," he said about the pitchfork, pulling it free. He handed it back to Esther.

She shook her head in revulsion.

"Take it," Little Jack insisted. "You're good with it. Or do you want the gun?"

CHAPTER 62

Monday, July 24. Just after midnight.

Patsy, from his hiding place in the loft, had seen everything unfold below him. Nonna and Pancetta had carried valises to the end of the barn and disappeared into the nook he knew hid the elevator to the basement. What was in the valises? Why would they go to the basement? Swinging like a monkey from beam to beam to the rear of the stable, Patsy came down on a pillow of hay and slipped out the side door.

Surrounded by the mind-deadening noise of the steam engine and the howling furnace, Nonna and Pancetta hurried across the coal- and cable-strewn floor, past the red-hot doors of the furnace.

Nonna was pleased to see that the hidden opening had not been touched. Pancetta dropped the heavy valises and watched as Nonna pressed herself against the stone wall. With a bear-like growl, a section of the wall shuddered, then swung open.

The feeble electric lights that lit the tunnel all the way to the shack on One Hundred and Tenth Street near Lexington Avenue were a welcome sight. In a few minutes they would be safely in the tunnel. They would escape through the manhole hidden in the shack, no one the wiser.

Outside, the shooting had stopped. An eerie quiet settled over Nonna's compound. The electric lights came back on, and armed police swarmed the area combing for last holdouts. The score was three wounded coppers, eight of Nonna's men dead, four captured. Some might have gotten clean away. There was no way to tell.

Tonneman turned a slow circle. Not a sign of Esther or Burgoyne. The night was warm and the air heavy with moisture, dung, and death. A chill passed over him. Nonna had taken them, God only knew where. How had she managed to get them out of the stable in full view of everyone?

His revolver at the ready, Tonneman walked through the huge stable one more time.

Moments after Nonna and Pancetta entered

the tunnel and pushed the stone opening closed, Esther and Little Jack made their way down the steps to the basement under the stable.

The intensity of sound made Esther dizzy. At the foot of the steps, she raised her hand. She peeked behind the staircase and gasped. Little Jack stopped moving at once. "What?" he whispered, his voice scarcely audible.

Esther shook her head. Baby Burgoyne, blood streaming from various wounds on his face, stood with clenched fists over an equally bloody Giorgio.

She took a step forward. Baby's attention strayed toward her. A mistake.

Giorgio came up with hands clasped together and hit Baby between the legs. Baby doubled over. Giorgio seized Baby by the throat. The two men sank to the ground.

Gasping for air, Baby saw shards of light, then darkness. *I'm sorry, I'm sorry, Esther,* was his last conscious thought.

"No!" Esther raised her weapon, but she couldn't use it. Tears made paths in the grime on her cheeks.

Little Jack stepped around Esther and fired. The gun, its barrel jammed with dirt, blew up in Jack's hand, knocking him on his back. Giorgio howled with laughter, easing up on Baby's throat.

Esther knew that Baby was a dead man if she didn't act. She raised the pitchfork high in both hands and ran at Giorgio.

Lina had watched Esther and Little Jack descend the stairs, but she waited in her hiding place. Citizens, she thought in disgust. They didn't understand anything.

Once Esther and Jack had gone in the opposite direction, Lina was ready. She stepped out from her concealment. In the noise the old woman was unaware that someone else stood on the stairs behind her.

"Where are you going, Mother?" Dutch Tonneman screamed in her ear, his Smith and Wesson jammed in her back.

"Fuck," Lina said.

Dutch looked closely at the garish, white-powdered face; Lina motioned to him to follow.

Giorgio pulled the pitchfork from his shoulder; he staggered to his feet and poised the pitchfork over Baby. Baby crossed his arms defensively above his face and tried to roll away.

Esther's scream pierced all other noise in the basement.

Dutch charged past the bales toward Esther's voice, fully aware that Lina would escape. He saw Giorgio about to stab Baby with the pitchfork.

Tonneman's shot caught Giorgio in the side, flinging him back, but not before the pitchfork went through Baby's left arm, pinning him to the floor.

Tonneman and Esther ran forward. He pulled the pitchfork from Baby's arm. A gout of blood rose in the air. Esther removed the blue Rough Rider bandanna from around Baby's neck and attempted to stanch the wound.

Breaking the handle of the pitchfork over his knee and using a piece of his shirt, Dutch made an ungainly but effective tourniquet.

"Locket," Baby babbled over and over. "Didn't know . . . sorry . . . my fault . . . my fault."

Pancetta, struggling to follow Nonna in the winding tunnel, set her two valises down side by side. Sparks spattered from the electric cable running along the rocky ground.

Pancetta moved the suitcases away from the sizzling wire, crossed herself against the devils that dwelt down here, and sat on the cases. "Ey, Nonna, wait for me." The air was cool, at least cooler than near the furnace. Still, she felt she was choking, buried alive. She pivoted and looked back at the stone door they'd come through. At least they were safe now.

Abruptly, she was on the ground.

"Get up, bitch." Nonna had come back and kicked the suitcases out from under Pancetta. "This is not a holiday." She picked up the valises. "What do I need you for?"

In shock, Pancetta watched Nonna disappear into the dark tunnel with the suitcases packed with money. She got to her feet and pulled out her gun. Nonna didn't need her? Well, she didn't need Nonna.

"Halt!"

Where had that come from? Ahead somewhere. Pancetta smiled a little pig smile. Nonna had walked into a trap.

Cautiously, Pancetta followed the path Nonna had taken.

Bo's Smith and Wesson bucked in his hand.

Pancetta grunted and returned fire.

Giorgio's eyes were open and staring.

Esther forced herself not to look at Giorgio so she could properly secure Baby's bandage. While she and Little Jack helped Baby to his feet, she prayed Baby's wound would not start bleeding again.

Baby tottered, half up, half down, mouth open, gasping.

Dutch leaned over Giorgio. His fingers could detect no pulse.

"Is he dead?" Esther asked, knowing the answer.

"Yes."

Death, Esther thought. She'd seen more than enough of it. Yet as she looked down at the body of the man who had kidnapped her, she had a disquieting reflection: what an extraordinary photograph she could make.

Dutch's most fervent wish was to take Esther in his arms and carry her to safety, but there was no time. Standing, he saw that Little Jack was nursing a raw and swollen hand. "What happened to you?"

"Gun blew up."

"Can you get Burgoyne up the stairs?"

Little Jack nodded.

"I saw an elevator," Esther said. "Back near the stairs." She pointed left. "I believe . . ."

A bullet flew by so close Bo could feel the heat. It glanced off a boulder, raising chunks of rock. He heard scuffling sounds and peered out. No one. It was as if the ground had swallowed the woman. It had to be

Nonna, but he wasn't sure. Nonna was said to be tall and thin; this one was short and fat. This damn tunnel had too many different passageways, many of them dead ends. He should have waited for Nonna in the shack.

"Stay here." Dutch took the bull's-eye lamp from Jack. Quickly, he scouted the basement area. To the left was the way out. Stairs, perhaps elevator. No one there. To the right, past the furnace, also seemed deserted. Where had Lina gone?

He was about to head back to Esther and the others when he noticed something odd about the stone wall. Part of it was ajar.

He ran back to the others, handed the lamp to Jack.

"Esther." He took her hand and kissed it, then signaled to Little Jack. "Take them out of here."

Esther held tight to Tonneman's hand. "Aren't you coming with us?"

"There are things I need to attend to."

"I'll take care of Miss Esther, don't you worry, Captain," Little Jack said, half carrying Baby. The bull's-eye swung from his free right hand, making eerie shadows. As he proceeded with his rescue mission, Little Jack Meyers savored the moments, looking forward to the glorious tale of his deeds he would have to tell Battling Jack West when he visited him later in Bellevue.

Tonneman ran back to the door in the wall and passed through.

The electric lights continued here, but someone had broken many of them. Those remaining barely lit the tunnel. Dutch moved along quickly, his .32 at the ready. The machine noises faded, making the crunching sounds as he walked over broken glass as loud as a claxon. At least it sounded that way to him.

"Go to the devil." A woman's voice, followed by a gunshot echoed off the tunnel walls.

"Out of my way." That was Bo.

Flickering threads of light sparked the ground. Dutch ran toward his partner's voice.

CHAPTER 63

Monday, July 24. Just after midnight.

There were more shadows than illumination.

One of the shadows moved. Bo Clancy fired.

A muffled cry.

Sparks ahead on the ground. A form. Clad in a black dress. Nonna! An airy spike of fire licked out from one of the sparks and kissed the cloth of her dress. The cloth flashed with incandescence, then settled into a calm ember.

Suddenly, a glaring arc of light billowed.

Lina spied a muted bloom of light ahead as the tunnel veered right and downhill. She followed the strange beacon, which led to a small spark, a tiny flame. At once, Lina saw her enemy, lying on the ground waiting. But something was wrong. The body of the woman glowed with an odd light. She nudged the body with her shoe. The whole tunnel filled with a peculiar radiance.

"Shit." Bo's voice again.

"Bo!" Dutch called.

"Run!" Bo answered.

"Are you —"

"Shut up. Turn around and run like hell."

The explosion rocked the ground beneath Dutch's feet, and the walls on either side of him cracked and began to crumble.

Behind Dutch, crunching glass and gaining, was a heavy footfall he recognized. "Is that you, partner?" he yelled panting.

"Don't talk, dunce," Bo said.

As they reached the opening in the wall, a ball of fire seemed to swallow up the far end of the tunnel. The two detectives stumbled out of the stone door and into the basement of the stable.

"What happened?" Dutch shouted as they raced for the stairs. "Nonna was sneaking off with bags of money."

"Most likely it's all ash now."

"I think I hit her, then the whole place burst into flames, like hellfire for sure."

"Too much Catholic school," Bo called as they finally emerged into the night air.

Esther, Wong, Baby, and Little Jack were gathered on the porch of the farmhouse.

Police patrolled the area.

Dutch found Esther, or perhaps it was she who found him. They came together in front of the farmhouse and held onto each other for dear life.

The ground heaved beneath them, and for an instant Dutch thought God was approving. Or was He disapproving? Tonneman grabbed Esther and shouted, "Run!"

This explosion, when it came, broke ground like a mighty earthquake. Flames engulfed the stable, shot so high in the air they were later said to have been seen in Philadelphia.

When the explosion occurred, the person known as Lina was moving slowly away from the shack on Lexington Avenue. Thoughtfully, she watched a horse and cart disappear into the darkness of upper Park Avenue. She rubbed her white-powdered face, now smudged with soot, and tugged at the dirty white wig. She wrapped the black scarf tighter around her head.

Lifting his old lady skirts, Joe Petrosino started back to Mulberry Bend.

Chapter 64

Monday, July 24. Morning.

Flora Cooper twiddled her thumbs as she waited downstairs at Del's. She'd sent a note up to Richard Croker, boss of the City's all-powerful Democratic organization, Tammany Hall.

Tammany was an octopus, its tentacles into every enterprise from trolleys and omnibuses to the police to real estate. It was rich and fat and corrupt, as were its leaders.

Croker, an Irish immigrant, had been a machine tool worker and the head of the Fourth Avenue Tunnel Gang. He had used this as a platform to work his way into Democratic politics — Tammany — and had become a man of considerable wealth. Theodore Roosevelt himself had butted heads with Tammany and had come away bloody.

Everyone knew that Boss Croker, surrounded by cronies, ate breakfast in a private room at Del's every morning but Sunday. It was also a place for favors granted to supplicants. And where debts were incurred.

Flora was no supplicant. She had come only for confirmation of something she already knew. And she was willing to make a deal to get it. She stood absolutely still as the messenger boy returned and whispered to the doorman.

The doorman gave her a nod. "He says you're to come right up, miss. Just follow the boy."

Croker, a white linen napkin tucked into his collar, sat at a round table over-laden with oysters, griddle cakes, eggs, and sausages. Pitchers of ale were being passed around. He stood when she came in and motioned for his four cronies to do the same.

"Boys, the little lady from the *Herald* and me're going to have a heart to heart, so grab your hats and skedaddle."

After the cronies filed out, Croker took his chair and downed an oyster. "You'll join me for breakfast, of course, Miss Flora. What're you drinking? Coffee? Ale?"

"Coffee will be fine." Flora pulled out a chair and sat, feeling suddenly a little light-headed. The sight and smell of all that food made her realize she'd had little to eat since dining in the country at the Brewster estate on Saturday.

A waiter arrived and set a place for her, then returned with a pot of coffee and a bowl of sweet rolls. Flora took a sweet roll and cut it into quarters, eating one immediately. The waiter poured the coffee and left.

"Now then, Miss Flora, what can I do for you?"

She wiped the sugar from her fingers and sipped her coffee. "Actually, I've come to tell you a story."

"A story? Sure and I'm a sucker for a good story." Croker had a wary look behind his heartiness.

"But it's a sad story."

"Ah, then it's an Irish tale you're telling." He slurped down the last of a dozen oysters and began digging into a gigantic stack of griddle cakes. "Go on now, go on."

"Once upon a time there was a little girl who lived upstate in a nice country house with her father. Her mother had died and left her a wondrous inheritance that would pass to her after she came of age. Her father remarried a widow with two sons, then the father died, and the young girl ran away from her home but was returned to her stepmother's care. The second time she ran away, her clothing was found on the banks of the Hudson."

"Drowned, did she?"

"So it was believed."

"This is a very sad tale indeed," Croker declared, dipping chunks of bread into the remainder of syrup on his plate.

"As there were no other claimants to the young girl's inheritance —"

"The stepmother claimed it for herself and her sons."

"Aw heck," Flora said, "you know the story." She took another swallow of coffee and finished off the sweet roll. It would do her for the while. She found a cigarette in her bag.

"It's an old story, my dear." Croker lit his cigar, then Flora's cigarette. "Sad to say, sometimes terrible things happen in this world."

"But the girl didn't drown, it seems."

"Ah, I thought you said there wasn't a happy ending?"

Flora tilted her head back and blew a perfect smoke ring. "I did say that, didn't I? Yes, well, the young girl *it seems* was afraid for her life. She made her way to the City, took another name, and became a prostitute."

"I see what you mean. Did she know an inheritance waited for her?"

"Only vaguely, I believe."

"She had no protector."

"No."

"Well, go on, go on."

"One night, at the Waldorf-Astoria, who should the young woman run into but her stepbrother, the very person who had threatened her life."

"Indeed. He must have been as shocked to see her as she was to see him."

"Yes. Especially as he was using her inheritance to bankroll an enormous deal that would make him richer than — well, what do you think happened to the poor young woman, without a protector?"

"You tell me."

"I think you know, Mr. Croker. She was murdered."

"Yes, a very sad story," Croker said, touching the napkin to the corner of his eyes. "But what does all this have to do with Richard Croker?"

"According to my sources, Mr. Croker, you do business with this murderer."

"Little lady, I do business with all sorts. Unfortunately some of them are scoundrels.

And some scoundrels commit murder."

"I must tell you, sir, that I have written this story and left it with my editor. I don't think, considering what is happening with Tammany right now, your connection to a murder would be received well by the public."

Croker smiled. "And what makes you think I give a damn?" For the first time his temper pushed through; he tore his napkin from his neck and threw it on the table. "If you were a man, I'd break your back."

"And if my editor didn't have my story, you'd throw me in the Hudson."

Croker reflected for a moment. He'd gotten his. No skin off his nose if the deal went sour. "What're you after, missy? Come right out with it."

Not flinching, Flora said, "If you verify the information about the land deal, I'll be happy to remove any mention of you and Tammany from my article. What do you say?" She got to her feet and held out her hand.

Boss Croker stood, too. He looked down at the small woman and the small hand in front of him with something like respect. "Well, little lady, if I don't know a good horse trade when I hear it, I'm a damned fool."

CHAPTER 65

Monday, July 24. Late morning.

It was business as usual in the office of Stokes and Grimes. Present were William Grimes, Harrison Stokes, and J. N. Burgoyne. Grimes was furious.

"Where the hell is Baby?" Grimes growled. "His job is to open the office in the morning. The mail was piled up outside the door. What are we paying him for? I have a good mind to fire him —"

"Oh, do, by all means."

The three turned. A ghastly-looking Baby Burgoyne stood facing them. He wore no topcoat. His head and left arm were wrapped in bandages, his face a design of bruises, abrasions, and lacerations.

"Jesus," J.N. blurted. "You look worse than after we took the Hill."

"Get out of the line of fire, J.N." Baby brought a pistol from behind his back and leveled it at his employers.

"Have you lost your mind, man?" Stokes, his brother-in-law, said quietly. He rose and came toward Baby.

"Yes, and regained it. Not another step, Harrison."

J.N. shook his head. "Brother, this won't do."

The pistol in Baby's hand swayed, as did Baby. Grimes leaped to his feet.

"No!" Baby yelled. His hand was steady again.

From the open window facing the street came the furious sound of many horses and wagons, then running footsteps. Closer and closer.

The door burst open. Baby shifted position, his back now against the wall. Suddenly the room was full of police. Hovering near the door, notebook in hand, was Flora Cooper.

"Drop that gun, Burgoyne," Dutch shouted. "What the hell do you think you're doing?"

"I'm killing a murderer."

Bo reached over and whacked Baby's wrist. The gun fell to the floor.

"Well, thank you, gentlemen," Grimes said. "You arrived in the nick of time to save us from this madman."

"We got here in the nick of time to arrest

you for murder, Grimes," Bo said.

"What?" Stokes's face was red with shock. "Grimes, what is this?"

"Ridiculous. Pay no attention," his partner replied. Grimes sat back at his desk and lit a cigar. "These dumb cops don't know what they're talking about. J.N. get me Boss Croker on the telephone."

J.N. lifted the receiver and asked the operator for Tammany Hall.

"What does the name Irene Bayard Hall mean to you?" Dutch asked Grimes.

"Poor crazy thing. My stepsister. She drowned herself in the Hudson years ago."

"Liar!" Flora Cooper's voice came from the doorway. "She didn't drown. You treated her cruelly enough for her to run away, then you declared she was dead and stole her inheritance."

"How dare you?"

Grimes's protest didn't even slow Flora down. "The land owned by the Bayards made a nice speculation, didn't it? You were going to turn it into millions of dollars. It was a sad day for Irene Hall, who was going by the name of Delia Swann, when you found she was still alive and could claim her birthright."

His flush bleached out pasty as Stokes

listened to Flora's story. "William, is this true?"

"Mr. Grimes calling Mr. Croker," J.N. said, eying Grimes for the first time with apprehension. J.N. showed no emotion as he listened to the person on the other end of the line. At last he said, "Thank you very much. I will tell him."

"What is it?" Grimes reached for the telephone.

J.N. evaded Grimes's hand. Very deliberately he hung the earpiece on the hook, disconnected the line. "I was informed that Mr. Croker says he has no business with you."

"Huzzah," Flora said.

Chapter 66

Saturday, August 19. Late afternoon.

"John Tonneman, Father Duff says you haven't been round to see him like he asked." Meg had confronted her son just as he was on his way to Mulberry Street.

Dutch had groaned inwardly. "But I have a time or two, Ma. He wasn't there."

"A time or two. What a thing to say. Go see him on your way home tonight."

She wouldn't stop treating him like he was ten years old, and here he was near thirty-three and getting no younger.

"Ma, if the two of you have some nice Catholic girl to match me up with, forget it," he'd said. "It's Esther Breslau I'll be marrying, or it's no one."

And then she went and got that hurt look on her face, and he couldn't stand it. What was he going to do?

It turned out to be a slow day on the job, which was good, as the City was preparing for the celebration honoring Admiral Dewey, home from his victory — destroying the Spanish fleet — in the Philippines.

Sweat was dripping off him when he got to St. Agnes. The flowers someone had put at the feet of the Madonna were limp from the heat. Even St. Agnes herself looked wilted.

"I know how you feel," Dutch told St. Agnes.

He entered the church, genuflected, blessed himself with holy water. The scent of incense was strong, hanging like a divine cloud from the vaulted ceiling. Inhaling the fragrance, he stared at the cross above the altar with Catholic eyes. No denying, it was wonderful to be a Catholic. And terrible. Terrible because it kept him from Esther.

Ah, who was he kidding? It was Meg and Esther both keeping him from her.

Halfheartedly, he looked around for Father Duff. The old geezer was probably asleep in the confessional. Passing the confessional, Dutch heard the low hum of voices. Okay, he would wait. He walked around the church, stopping to slip a dollar into the poor box.

As old Mrs. Mulligan skittered past him he heard, "Dutch, is that you?"

There was no mistaking that voice. He

turned to see Father Duff standing outside the confessional.

Father Duff didn't carry himself as straight and tall as when he was a soldier fighting for the North, but he still had the chest of a bull. His black priest gown fit his large body like a tent, but did not hide his old man's belly. He wore a black eyepatch over his empty left eye socket. Folds of skin descended from his neck.

The old priest was fingering his rosary; his keg-like chest heaved with each breath. "Good to see you, boy. Come sit with me a minute. Unless of course, you want to go in there."

Duff grinned at him. They were evenmatched in height.

"Not today, Father. Ma's been telling me you want to see me."

The priest straightened his bent shoulders. They fell back into place as he extended a ham-like hand. "I've missed you, boy."

"I've been busy."

"You should come by more often. I'm not talking as your priest, I'm talking as your friend, as an old friend of your family." Duff sat on the back pew and motioned for Dutch to sit beside him. "I've missed you. God misses you."

"I have my reasons."

The priest fussed with his eyepatch. A Rebel's blade had taken his eye in '62 at Antietam. Now he scratched at the folds of his neck. Finally he said, "Before I became a priest I was a stonecutter."

"I know."

"I was in love with a wonderful, beautiful girl. She was a Jew."

Shocked, Dutch said, "Is that why you didn't marry her?"

"No, I would have married her, given up everything to marry her. My beautiful Hanna was killed by a madman with a knife."

The hairs stood up on the back of Dutch's neck. Then and now the world was filled with deadly lunatics. "Would you have become a Jew?"

"I planned to. I loved her deeply, with all my heart. But then she died. And I found salvation in Holy Mother Church."

"What happened to you has nothing to do with what's happening to me."

Duff nodded. "Your father was a Presbyterian."

"Bad enough," Dutch said with a grin.

Duff went on. "Though he came from Jewish stock, that's only blood. You and your sisters are Catholic, through and through."

"And?"

"You're doomed if you marry outside the faith."

Dutch stood. "The way you would have been had you married your beautiful girl."

"Yes . . . yes." The second yes came with a groan of pain. "But I am not talking to you as Patrick Duff, I am talking to you as your priest. If you marry that girl you'll burn for all eternity."

"No, Father." Dutch reached out and touched the old man's hand. Very gently, he said, "If I don't marry her, I'll burn for all eternity."

CHAPTER 67

Saturday, September 30.

Oswald Cook stood on the roof of Alexina Cook Brewster's New York town house. The building overlooked Madison Square and was a wonderful place to enjoy the unseasonable warmth of the fall day.

Oz crossed to the midpoint at the railing of the roof, to his favorite camera, a Scovill, and ran his hands over it. Esther planned to use a Kodak and roll film. Oz didn't think much of those toys.

He moved the tripod somewhat to the left and focused on the arch. It was a too-bright day. He'd have to take that into consideration when he made his pictures.

Stanie White had sent him a junior architect to design a platform just for the occasion. Oz, for all his sophistication, was thrilled at the prospect of viewing Admiral Dewey's triumphant parade down Fifth Avenue to and through the resplendent victory arch that had gone up in Madison Square at Twenty-third Street.

All of New York had followed in the newspapers the day-by-day reports of the return of Admiral Dewey and his ship, the *Olympia,* after he destroyed the Spanish fleet in Manila Bay on the first of May and freed the Philippines.

Oz made a final inspection of the platform. Columns supported a large green and white striped awning that would be unfurled to protect his guests from the sun, but not if it got in the way of his making photos. The area was scattered with white cast iron garden furniture and potted plants, delivered the day before.

"Splendid," Oz exclaimed, his slender fingers dusting ash from the new blue suit Lord & Taylor had made for him. He put a lucifer to a fresh Virginia Bright.

Whistling the tune to "When Chloe Sings Her Song," the coon song Lillian Russell was performing in the new Weber and Fields show, *Whirl-i-gig,* Oz peered over the rooftops to look at the arch and the tall columns lining the route. He would be escorting Esther to the performance this evening. "Splendid."

He sat on one of the chairs and inhaled the soothing smoke. His hands toyed with the opera glasses on the table beside him.

Nine weeks had passed since John Tonneman had delivered Esther and Wong to him as the darkness faded into dawn. Tonneman's tenderness with Esther and hers with him had distressed Oz greatly.

Wong had turned the automobile around and followed the patrol wagons while Esther had fallen asleep in Oz's arms.

With Delia Swann's murderer dead and the man who ordered it in jail, Esther was safe. All should have been well and life should have continued on its proper course as if none of the horror had happened.

But there had been a change, and Oz was very aware of it. Although nothing had been said between them, he knew Esther had come to realize the frailty of life, something young people rarely confront. And with that realization, she had turned to a more visceral relationship, ergo, John Tonneman.

If true, and he was certain it was, there was little he could do about it. She was her own woman. He would make the best of it. What Tonneman would never appreciate was the intellectual bond that would always exist between Oz and Esther.

Oz lifted the opera glasses to his eyes. The bleachers were ready, the white arch glistened in the early morning sunlight.

■ ■ ■ ■

He awoke to Wong's tap on his shoulder. In the chair on the other side of the table was his cousin, Alexina. An enormous hat with green ostrich feathers was perched on her white hair.

"How are you today, Oswald?"

"I am very well. And you, cousin?"

She smiled at him. "Tolerable, considering my years. These celebrations can be exhausting. I might try one of those, my dear." She pointed to his cigarettes.

"You are an amazing woman, Alexina." Oz lit a second cigarette and handed it to her.

"I am indeed, Oswald."

Oz glanced at the patient Wong. "Yes?"

"Mr. Tonneman is here."

"Splendid," Oz muttered, getting to his feet.

"And Mrs. Tonneman."

Oz raised his eyebrow.

Wong raised his eyebrow. "His mother."

"Splendid." Oz smiled. This would be amusing.

"And Inspector Clancy and Miss Cooper."

"Delightful," Oz said, finally bored with "splendid." "Inform Miss Esther that our guests have arrived."

"I was an actress, you know," Meg Tonneman said, sipping champagne, careful not to look at Esther, who stood near Dutch. "With Edwin Booth. But that was before John's dear father swept me off my feet." Meg pretended not to notice that her only son scarcely left the side of the woman who terrified her, the woman who would take John away from her.

"Is that so?"

"Oz." There was a warning in Esther's voice that made him grin at her.

"How charming," Alexina declared. "I never knew Edwin. John Wilkes, yes, Edwin no."

"Alexina!" Oz exclaimed in mock dismay.

Oz's cousin fluttered a lace-fringed hand at him and turned her attention to Meg. "Mrs. Tonneman, might you be related to Miss Leah Tonneman, a physician?"

"Auntie Lee," Dutch said. "I remember her."

"My husband's family were the odd ones, truly. I don't hold with a woman taking on man's work," Meg said. "She was a Hebrew, you know."

Dutch was mortified. "Ma, you forget that I —"

Meg shook her finger at her son. "Don't you say it, John Tonneman."

"Leah Tonneman was a dear friend of mine," Alexina said severely. "Not a day goes by that I don't think of her and miss her sweet presence." She raised her fluted glass. "I propose a toast to her memory."

"To Leah Tonneman, may her line live on," Oz said, as the ensemble lifted their glasses.

"To be sure," Meg said. "Where was I? Oh, yes, my last performance was with the Booths, all three, in *Julius Caesar* on the day after Thanksgiving."

Oz turned to Dutch. "Well, I had no idea, Mr. Tonneman. Perhaps you and Mrs. Tonneman would like to join Esther and me this evening at Lillian Russell's new show."

"And I am not invited?" Alexina asked.

"Of course."

"Thank you, my dear, but no thank you. I shall be asleep in my bed, quite content."

"Oh, yes, we would love to join you, Mr. Cook." Meg fluttered her eyes flirtatiously at Oz. "You must call me Meg, and I shall call you Oz."

Esther made a photograph, ostensibly of the arch. What she had was a charming shot of John framed by the arch.

The sound of a marching band and shouting ended conversation. Confetti and ribbon streamers began to pour down from buildings all around. Roses tossed by admirers filled the air.

A bag of equipment and three slotted boxes containing glass plates rested on the roof floor, off to the right. Taking a plate from the box, Oz murmured, "First plate,"

He ducked under the hood. He squeezed the bulb and made the photograph.

"Second plate," Oz said, going through the same motions and making another photograph.

As his guests watched the festivities, Oz and Esther made photograph after photograph of the honorees and the thirty-five thousand marchers advancing down Fifth Avenue to Twenty-third Street.

In Madison Square, the seventy-foot white triumphal arch stood waiting; its presence and the victory it celebrated virtually declared America's new position as a world leader.

Cantering grandly at the front of the parade was Governor Roosevelt, dressed in tails, seated on a huge horse. The awe-inspiring hero of San Juan Hill, dramatic in black and gray and flashing his top hat, rode like a god. His majestic appearance quite dwarfed the presence of all the others in the procession, including Admiral Dewey himself.

Bo and Dutch rose to their feet at the sight of their colonel, shouting, "Hooray!"

Admiral George Dewey, President William McKinley, and Senator Mark Hanna rumbled behind Roosevelt in mere carriages.

Crowds of people stood along the way. The viewers on Alexina's rooftop heard the music. People sang Paul Dresser's song "Come Home Dewey (We Won't Do a Thing to You)." The crowds on the street pushed to see and cheer the heroes, leaving only a narrow lane for marching soldiers.

Dutch beckoned to Esther, and when she came to his side he took her hand and pulled her close. They stood side by side with Flora and Bo, each couple with arms round one another's waists.

Bo didn't believe what he saw. He touched Flora's dark golden hair. "For Christ's sake," he whispered, removing the pencil.

"Oh, hush."

Now he contemplated her left ear. He'd never noticed how much it resembled a shell. He leaned toward it. Bo Fingal Clancy was a great talker, but you couldn't tell that by the way he was acting on that roof that day. "I want to ask," he mumbled. He didn't go on.

"What?" Ignoring the others on the roof, Flora stared Bo full in the face. "For a police inspector you look awful afraid," she answered softly.

"That I am."

"I'll save you, then. If you understand I have my career and I don't cook, my answer is yes."

"You don't even know what I'm asking."

"Yes, I do, you great fool. Yes, I will marry you."

Bo crossed himself. "You're scary."

"Bet your ass."

"What?" Dutch asked his cousin.

"Mind your business," Bo replied, grinning broadly, his face beet red.

"They are the young ones; the world is theirs," Oz told Meg Tonneman. "It is our duty to move out of the way."

But Meg's eyes were on the parade. "Oh, how much finer it would be if there were Irish bagpipes."

And lo, along came the bagpipes piping their Gaelic tunes.

Meg beamed.

Oz made a picture of the pipers, then examined the exposed plates, in their light-tight holders. He was tired.

Leaving Tonneman's side, Esther handed Oz her small roll camera and took over on the large one.

Dutch watched her with something like jealousy, but not. Esther and Oz were like Dutch and Bo. Partners, anticipating each other's needs. It made sense. If that was the way it was, so be it.

Esther made several pictures with the Scovill, then seemed to lose interest. A very odd occurrence, Oz thought. But Esther's focus was on John Tonneman, no camera dividing them.

About to signal Wong to take the equipment away, Oz paused. No. Who knew what interesting pictures might present themselves? After a while he thought it might be nice to make a photograph of Alexina with Esther. Definitely one of Esther. But not with Tonneman.

Inspiration struck. Of course. A photograph that had to be made. He found the longer cable, attached it to the Scovill.

"Come, everyone," he said, "let me make a photograph of us all to commemorate this occasion. You, too, Wong."

They gathered, the young generation standing behind the seated Alexina, Meg, and the empty chair where Oz would sit. Wong sat cross-legged on the floor in front of Esther. "Ready?" Oz asked, after he had focused the lens. He sat down in the empty chair and adjusted the cable, the bulb in his right hand.

Esther looked up at John Tonneman. The Jewish New Year had passed. The new century would soon be here. A century of automobiles and subway trains and so many exciting and unimaginable things.

And women would get the vote.

Oh, what a wonderful world awaited them.

Oz made the picture.

A Footnote

As the twentieth century drew closer, the 1890s bristled with change. During April of 1894, in what previously had been a shoe store, the first kinescope parlor opened at 1155 Broadway. Above the entrance portal was a dragon with electric globe eyes. Inside, against two walls, were ten Edison machines with peepholes. The fee to see was a mere twenty-five cents. Twenty-five cents was also what a working man earned an hour. The Edison machines offered five presentations, the longest lasting sixteen seconds.

In 1894, the first print paper sensitive enough for enlargement became available, and the art of photography took another giant step into the future.

On Saturday, December 28, 1895, the *New York Times* reported that the newly formed East River Bridge Commission had announced plans for a new bridge connecting New York and Brooklyn: the bridge would face Grand Street between Willet and Sheriff Streets along Delancey Street on the New York side. On the Brooklyn side, it would be at the junction of Broadway and Bedford Avenue between South Fifth and South Sixth Streets.

The Spanish American War began with the sinking of the battleship *Maine* in Havana Harbor in 1898, and ended with Admiral George Dewey's defeat of the Spanish fleet in Manila Bay in 1899.

Theodore Roosevelt was commissioned a lieutenant colonel and raised a regiment that quickly came to be known as Roosevelt's Rough Riders. Twenty-three thousand men — lawmen, lawbreakers, college boys, cowboys, aristocrats, even Indians — volunteered to fight alongside Roosevelt, who eventually picked one thousand to join him.

William Randolph Hearst sent Frederic Remington to Cuba to illustrate America's war with Spain for the *Morning Journal,* the newspaper Hearst bought to compete with Joseph Pulitzer's *New York World.* A journalist named Jim Creelman worked for Pulitzer. Hearst stole him to write for the *Journal.* Creelman is the man who claimed that on the eve of the Spanish American

War, Hearst cabled Frederic Remington: "You furnish the pictures and I'll furnish the war."

With much fanfare, the five New York boroughs were unified in order to create a bigger and better city in 1898. Greater New York was ready to greet the new century.

Automobiles had started claiming the space that had belonged to the horse, but there was resistance. The horse was cheaper and more reliable. The first Packard car body delivered to the manufacturer had a whipstock on the dashboard. Being towed by a horse was often an essential part of motoring.

The Automobile Club of America was formed in New York City on June 7, 1899, by a group of visionaries (or some might say dilettantes) in the Waldorf-Astoria Hotel. This same month, automobiles were banned from Central Park because they frightened the horses.

Although the City was electrified by overhead cables, most houses were heated by wood and coal and illuminated by candle and lantern and gas. Indoor plumbing was a rarity among the poor and middle class. You had to pump a handle to get water to fill your basin or your tin bathtub. Nature's call was answered outside in the outhouse.

Food was preserved in an ice chest, and ice was delivered by horse and cart. The air was fragrant with incinerated fuel and human and animal excrement.

Omnibuses, carts, coaches, and hackneys all relied on the horse. Trolleys guided by overhead electric connections moved on tracks around the City. They were finally abandoned after World War II, for various unsubstantiated reasons. The City is now planning to bring the Forty-second Street trolley back.

Arguably, the City's first major leap into the twentieth century was the Rapid Transit Commission's plan for the building of the New York subway system that was finally approved in 1899. Digging began on March 26, 1900, and the method was "cut and cover." (Dig the hole, do the work, cover up the hole.)

Because there were few steam shovels and bulldozers at the time, the City had to rely on a work force, at its peak, of seventy-seven hundred laborers, mostly Irish and Italian.

The rapid transit system opened opportunities for land development, and therefore speculation, in upper Manhattan and the Bronx. Working people could live in "rural" areas and come to work in lower Manhattan with ease.

Technological advancement with elevators and steel allowed for taller and taller buildings.

New immigrants, as potential voters, had to be taught how to live in a democracy. There was a vacuum here that the Tammany Society, the Democratic party machine, led at the time of our book by Richard "Boss" Croker, eagerly filled. Every member of the executive committee of the Tammany Society held some appointed or elected office in the City or was a "favored" contractor: that is, one who received a city contract without competitive bidding. Corruption and influence peddling were rampant.

In the late 1890s, the state legislature (Republican Theodore Roosevelt was governor) sent the Mazet Committee to the City to drive out the corruption. It was generally felt by the public that the investigation was partisan and that its work was inefficient. However, it produced considerable detail showing the existence of gross maladministration and a ramified system of corruption. The disclosures that drew the greatest public attention were those relating to Boss Croker's relations to city government.

Croker maintained that the Tammany Society was entitled, that that's what the people voted Tammany's ticket for. "We are giving the people pure organization government," he said. He declined to answer questions tending to show that he profited by a silent partnership in many companies that benefited directly or indirectly by his power. Where his money came from he said was his "private affair."

Richard Croker had been born in Blackrock, near Dublin, in 1841. He was fifty-seven years old at the time of this book. He would die in Ireland at the age of eighty-one, a very wealthy man.

Advances in medicine came with the acceptance, albeit reluctant, of the germ theory of disease. Bellevue Hospital had begun its life in 1736, as a six-bed infirmary of the Public Work House and Home of Correction at the bottom of Broadway where City Hall would eventually be. Toward the end of the eighteenth century, the City bought a building on five acres at Twenty-sixth Street and First Avenue. An almshouse was established in 1816. It was called the Bellevue Establishment. The hospital became Bellevue Hospital in 1825, when it was used primarily for epidemic victims. By the end of the nineteenth century, Bellevue was a major hospital complex in the City of New York.

The first Gouverneur Hospital opened in 1885, in what had been a public market building in the middle of Gouverneur Slip, which was a fairly wide tract of land. It was three floors high and not equipped with an operating room. Market wagons habitually impeded ambulances.

Gouverneur Hospital was severely damaged by fire in 1895.

In 1897, the City began to build a new five-story hospital that faced Water Street and away from the East River. The style was Renaissance, the facade redbrick. Gouverneur Hospital moved to 227 Madison Street in 1972.

The New York detective Joe Petrosino, who appears in this book, was a real person. He was born in Salerno in 1860. Petrosino joined the New York Police Department in 1883, made detective in '95. He was perhaps the shortest member of the force at five feet, two inches.

Petrosino covered the area of Mulberry Bend, which drew most of the criminal element in the City. He spoke many southern Italian dialects and used many disguises: bootblack, coachman, sometimes a hobo, or a laborer, a priest, a starving peasant just off the boat. Possibly even as an old woman. He knew every saloon in Little Italy.

The detective fought the Black Hand all of his professional life. While investigating Italian connections to organized crime in America, he was shot to death in Palermo, March 12, 1909.

On April 12, 1909, Joe Petrosino's funeral cortege traveled from old St. Patrick's Church on Mott Street to Calvary Cemetery in Queens, accompanied by a band playing Verdi's "Requiem March," and one thousand policemen. Two hundred thousand people thronged the funeral route.

To New York City's Irish Catholics, old St. Pat's was their church. The Fighting 69th, in the Irish Brigade, the regiment manned by young volunteers from the Lower East Side, marched past its huge doors in 1861, on their way to fight in the Civil War. The priests were Irishmen. That would gradually change as the Italians made the neighborhood theirs.

At the time of our book, there was no single organization called the Black Hand. It was made up of many competing groups, all with their origins in Southern Italy.

In 1895, Don Giosuele, known as Zio Mico (Uncle Mico), conceived the Black Hand in his small saloon on First Avenue, between 109th and 110th Streets.

Our Nonna was also a real person. She

was a tall, red-haired woman from Marcianise, near Naples, by the name of Pasquarella. Pasquarella was the grandmother of organized crime in New York. She owned a horse stable on upper Park Avenue that filled an entire block between 108th and 109th Streets. This was her legitimate business. In reality, she commanded a legion of cutthroats, gunmen, knife men, burglars, safe crackers, and pickpockets. Her rules were simple: loyalty and silence.

She resented the arrival of competition in the person of Uncle Mico into what she considered her domain.

Admiral Dewey's victory over Spain in Manila Bay and his voyage home shared newspaper headlines with the Dreyfus Case in France.

Dewey's arrival in New York Harbor came on September 28, 1899. He cruised up the Hudson on the 29th, amidst a welcome that used more ammunition than had been needed to destroy the Spanish fleet.

For a victory parade to honor Admiral Dewey on the 30th of September, a seventy-foot-tall arch of triumph, constructed of wood and painted white, was erected on Fifth Avenue and Madison Square. It was modeled on that of Titus of Rome and was intended to symbolize America as the new world power. But amidst the confetti and showers of ribbons and roses, the bursting of champagne corks, and all the dignitaries, including President McKinley, it was not Admiral Dewey who received all the attention and the roar of the crowd. It was the impressive figure of a man who rode in the procession on a huge charger, like an emperor himself: Governor Theodore Roosevelt.

The beginning of a new century, the twentieth, was greeted with a genuine spirit of optimism, somewhat mixed with anxiety. Utopia was not at hand, but certainly things would be better than they had been.

A.M.
M.M.
New York, 2008

ABOUT THE AUTHOR

Maan Meyers is the pseudonym of husband-and-wife writing team Martin and Annette Meyers. Annette Meyers is the author of eight Smith and Wetzon mysteries, two Olivia Brown mysteries, and the stand-alone novel *Repentances.* Martin Meyers is the author of five books in the Patrick Hardy series. Together they have written numerous short stories and novels in what has come to be called The Dutchman Historical Mysteries: *The Dutchman, The Kingsbridge Plot, The High Constable, The Dutchman's Dilemma, The House on Mulberry Street, The Lucifer Contract,* and the seventh, *The Organ Grinder.* They live in New York City.

The employees of Thorndike Press hope you have enjoyed this Large Print book. All our Thorndike, Wheeler, and Kennebec Large Print titles are designed for easy reading, and all our books are made to last. Other Thorndike Press Large Print books are available at your library, through selected bookstores, or directly from us.

For information about titles, please call:
(800) 223-1244

or visit our Web site at:
http://gale.cengage.com/thorndike

To share your comments, please write:

Publisher
Thorndike Press
295 Kennedy Memorial Drive
Waterville, ME 04901